Dark One

Sydnie Beaupré

FORGOTTEN PLACES
PUBLISHING

Other Titles by Forgotten Places Publishing

Luke Coles and the Flower of Chiloe
by Josh Walker
Luke Coles and the Forest Assassin
by Josh Walker
Monster Attack
an anthology compiled by Samie Sands
Unleash the Undead
an anthology compiled by Samie Sands
Forgotten Places
an anthology compiled by Josh Walker
Heir of Merlin: Serene's Awakening
by Q.S. Khan

DEDICATION

For Mummy, thank you for standing by me since I can't do the math, but neither can you so we're a great pair.
Daddy, you taught me to love writing- thank you.
Grandma, you showed me that knowledge is my best friend, and you always stood by me no matter what.
All of my family who I cannot fit onto this small page but who have showed me what true love is; I love you so, so much and thank you for being there for me. And *yes* Liam, you count as family, you wonderful, smart man.

For all of my friends (of which I have many); I love you. You all have supported me to the end, even when I went a little bit crazy. But you're crazy too, so that's okay.

And finally, for me; because I have overcome so much in my short life, and I can finally see that it was all worth it. All of it has lead up to this.

One for sorrow,
two for joy,
three for a girl,
four for a boy,
five for silver,
six for gold,
seven for a secret,
never to be told,
eight for a wish,
nine for a kiss,
ten for a time
of joyous bliss.

Celtic counting poem

Prologue

I sit on the windowsill watching her sleep for as long as I can, taking in every last second. Her brown hair is spread out on the pillow like a Japanese fan and the moonlight catches her skin just right so that her face is captivatingly bathed in it. I don't often watch her sleep, but as of late I've sensed danger, and this is the only way to ensure her safety. I can't watch her twenty-four hours a day; I have pretences to upkeep. I keep tabs on her every once in a while-and have a friend doing the same.

It would be so much easier if I wasn't one of the Fallen – I'd be invisible to all humans.

I sigh to myself and stand. My wings unfurl, causing a hot whoosh of air to stir the branches of the tree behind me-and a sad smile dances its way across my lips as I watch her sleep, surely dreaming.

I can't help but fleetingly wonder if she has ever been in love with somebody and if that's who she's dreaming of now. I can hear people's thoughts if I am close enough to them, but I've never been close enough to her to even get a glimpse into her mind. I only ever watch her from afar, not close enough to know anything about her other than what she shows the world – the way she rambles or bites her lip when she gets nervous, or how she squints her eyes and crinkles her nose when she's thinking.

I know nothing of her inner thoughts even though it is my duty to protect her and keep her safe at all times. If I don't – I don't even want to know what could happen to her.

But I was the one who volunteered for this job, and it is I who must make no mistakes. If I do, she'll surely pay tenfold and I will lose the only thing that has any real meaning to me. Nobody wanted to take her on but I simply needed to because as soon as I saw her I felt a pull that I'd only ever felt once; it was the pull of the purest soul on earth, the reason I had Fallen in the first place so many years ago. I was destined to stay on earth until I did something worthy of returning back to Heaven.

In the instant that she was born she was also chosen to be the bringer of the Great Battle as her soul was the purest, but she was born very ill and her parents made some foolish mistakes due to selfishness and greed. As a result, she was cursed by a lesser Goddess to walk the earth with no soul mate or Guardian.

She would have no help in bringing the Battle. She would surely die alone and evil would prevail.

Though I was no longer welcome in Heaven and not considered important enough to hear about news such as this first hand, even I knew everything had changed in the world when she was born. Every Angel, Demon, and everything in between on Earth, Hell and Heaven, knew something had changed when she was born.

In all of my existence, I never wanted to protect something so fiercely and to this day I don't regret my decision. And so seventeen years ago, I begged to be her Guardian, because this would be my only chance to keep her safe. I didn't care that I shouldn't interfere with a curse set upon by a lesser Goddess. I needed to protect her and she couldn't fulfil her purpose alone.

Because nobody would accept her and because God is fair, here I am. But working against a curse has its drawbacks.

One

In the early morning light, I can just make out my dog's face. His tongue is lolling to the side of his mouth and his right paw is over his eyes. Pug doesn't like to be awoken by light and my thick red curtains are usually drawn so he's a little annoyed this morning because I must have forgotten to close the blinds. The fact that my room is painted light beige doesn't help; it just makes the room feel like it's filled with more light. I smile at him and reach out to stroke his head. He is the ugliest yet surprisingly adorable dog in the world and people always laugh when I tell them my pug is named Pug.

I try to remember the dream I'd been having before the light woke me up but all I can remember is that it had something to do with being trapped in a hall full of mirrors.

I get up to take my shower but decide that since I had a shower last night, my hair's fine. It's just school anyway, it's not like it's a beauty contest because if it were, I would probably not win. My long, plain brown hair could pass for pretty I suppose, if I did the right stuff to it. It has natural highlights in it during the summer, but towards the winter, it tends to kind of even out in colour.

I yawn and think to myself, *Whatever, I had a rough night anyway.*

I couldn't shake the feeling of being watched all night, which has been a regular occurrence all of my life, but as of late it's been a lot worse. I awoke to the sound of light tapping at my window and it was probably the branches of the willow tree outside my bedroom, but I'm not above being paranoid.

My hands reach up to my head and lazily tie an elastic band around my hair in a low ponytail. I walk to my wardrobe which is littered with picture frames, body spray bottles, and various other things. I open the second drawer and stare at its contents for so long that I'm sure I look like I believe it holds the meaning of life. I'm so damn tired I really ought to just stay home to catch up on my sleep, but that would upset Cara, my best friend and to be honest I'm not the type of kid to miss school. Cara's the complete opposite of me from head to toe, and you'd think that would stop us from being friends but honestly, I think it's the reason we like each other so much.

My hair just doesn't know whether to be straight or curly- it doesn't even seem to want to be *wavy*, and she's got chin length red curls that shine like the sun is forever in her presence. I've managed to get by with meagre B cup breasts while Cara's got double D's. Her whole body curves pleasantly in all the right places and mine just barely has an hourglass shape. Though I'm slender, I don't have that much definition. Sometimes I joke that I'm built like a wooden board, all straight lines and no curves, but Cara gets mad when I put myself down like that.

The only thing I have going for me are my eyes, though they're a little too big for my face or so I've been told by many people in town. They're a darkish shade of green with black flecks spattered all about with a vibrant orange around the irises.

Some days they appear browner and other days they appear a lighter green, but the orange never disappears. Cara's eyes are always a lovely sky blue, never changing except through emotion.

When I'm done dressing myself in my somewhat unflattering purple and green school uniform, I walk to the kitchen with Pug by my side and pop some toast in the toaster for myself, and put down a fresh bowl of water for him. He can't eat in the morning because that would mean two meals a day and Pug's a little on the chubby side of things. The vet said that he's got to be on a strict diet. I guess I over feed him a little but I swear it's out of love.

As I butter my toast my phone rings making me drop the knife on my big toe, getting butter all over the place. I sigh and answer, knowing full well that it's Cara by the ring-tone.

"Hey, yeah, I'm just getting ready. You made me drop butter all over the floor and my foot. Don't ask."

"But Babe, I thought we agreed that you wouldn't be so clumsy! I'm gonna be there in like, five minutes so you'd better make breakfast to go." She says over the sound of cars. She's driving and talking on the phone again. Cara knows if she gets caught she'll get a major fine, but she keeps doing it anyway and I keep trying to get her not to.

"Okay, well get off the phone. I'm trying to eat and you're trying to drive. See you in five. The door's unlocked, as always." I say.

Cara walks right in five minutes later.

By then I've eaten my toast, much to her dismay because it seems that she hasn't eaten. We sit down and laugh for a bit while I prepare her something quick to eat and soon we're out the door.

Two

"You drive like a maniac!" I say as we pull into the parking lot of our school, Serene Falls High. We live in the town of Serene Falls, Maine, though there are no waterfalls all that close to us so I don't know why it's called that.

Cara has lived here since she was born, but I moved here with my parents when I was about one years old – they were living in Ireland when they my mother became pregnant with me. It's not too small in the sense that we don't have our own mall, theater and stuff, which is pretty rare for towns up here to have – okay, more like a miniscule strip mall that includes a food court (four small chain restaurants), and an old movie house that plays movies that have been out for months and that have been donated by us locals – but it's also not exactly on any maps either *unless* they're local because we're so out of the way.

The only tourists we get are people lost on their way to somewhere more important than here. I don't mind, because tourist activity could get really annoying, but it's nice now and again to see people stopping through. We often get tourists from Canada since we're not too far from the border.

To get to us you have to get pretty far from the nearest highway. And we've got a pie place owned by the oldest resident, Millie Theodore, which will knock the socks off of any pie connoisseur.

"Why thank you," Cara replies, "I've been just dying to hear you compliment me all day."

I don't question her sarcasm; I always say something about her atrocious driving skills and she always says something sarcastic in return. It's our morning shtick.

I've been asked repeatedly by people at school why I don't just drive myself to school but in all honesty my old Volkswagen Rabbit is on its last legs and I'm trying to prolong its life.

Cara's got a shiny gently used Mercedes convertible, a beautiful mandarin coloured car that drives slightly better than my own but looks so much better, so it's not a far stretch to see why I don't drive myself once you take a look at both our cars.

We make our way to the main entrance of our school and part ways when we get inside because our lockers are at opposite ends of the school. We begged to share a locker but the school doesn't allow it. I honestly don't see why, it's not like I'm going to steal any of her things, and vice versa.

As I walk to my locker I get the familiar feeling of being watched. When I reach my locker, my thoughts are interrupted though as I notice that it's slightly ajar. *Not again!* I think to myself.

I open it and find that though it's been opened, it appears that nothing has been taken just like every other time it's been broken into. My locker has been broken into about seven times so far since the beginning of the school year.

I don't understand why somebody would open a locker and not plan to steal anything. It's just plain strange. Which is just like my life: strange. I'm a magnet for the weird, though I have no idea why. I guess that's why I have that feeling of being watched all of the time.

I take out the books that I need for first period and smile politely as I pass Damien in the hall. He looks at me with those deep, prodding dark brown eyes and my heart speeds up a little, and my palms begin to sweat. I don't really know what to think of him but he's Cara's friend so I generally have to deal with him since he hangs around us a lot.

He appears to be a nice guy, and seems eager to be my friend, but he gives me this strange feeling in my gut. At first, I thought it was some type of crush or something, because he is *very* good looking- and okay, at first, it could have been a small crush. But when he talks to me, he's got this…look in his eyes that I can't quite pin. Almost as if I were a puzzle he can't quite figure out.

Damien moved to Serene Falls this year from Canada and on his first day he already fit in with the popular crowd. His skin is a very light brown; almost tan in colour. He's rather good looking, I admit.

His girlfriend Victoria, whose skin is around the same colour as his, though maybe a little lighter, runs up to him. When she notices him looking at me she scowls in a rather unflattering way that makes her face look all wrinkly and awkward. She too is very good looking, and she actually could pass for someone younger than her years, probably fourteen. When she speaks, she always has the hint of an accent, and I've often wondered if perhaps she has Egyptian heritage. Of course I'd never ask her, because I'm sure she'd find some way to make it seem as if I were being rude. We don't interact much but she appears to intensely dislike me.

Victoria's black hair is cut in a fashionable bob, and her eyes are a beautiful blue, though not as blue as Cara's. She's kind of the queen bee around school and yet she's been here for the same amount of time as Damien.

They both fit in so fast though it didn't help that they were already dating when they both started here, having apparently met the summer before, and here I am with only one real friend having been here all of my life.

It probably doesn't help that I don't do the whole hunting thing, since kids around here are kind of big on it – especially in turkey season.

"Did you hear me?" Cara waves her hand in front of my face. "Hello, earth to Khiara!"

"What?" I say, completely embarrassed that I didn't notice her presence sooner.

Cara shakes her head at me and smiles, "I said, don't forget the party tonight! Everybody from school's gonna be there and you have to bring the chips and drinks. You promised *and* volunteered to bring refreshments so there is no backing out or forgetting now."

I just nod my head. When it comes to Cara, nodding your head and saying "mmhmm" to everything she says doesn't offend her, it just makes her think you're listening.

Cara's into parties and I'm not, they're way too loud for me honestly. Whenever we go out, I'm the designated driver because she just ends up getting so smashed that she doesn't remember where she lives. It sounds like a sad existence, but it's mine and I'm okay with it. Somebody has to keep this girl together and it's not the many idiot boyfriends and false friendships she's had over the years;

it's me. We take care of each other no matter what – that's just how it is.

It's what friends do, even if you want to punch them in the face at times. Most of the time, your fist will end up turning into open arms, and the punch a hug.

We reach the door of our English class and exchange glances. Mine is filled with contentment and hers distaste. I roll my eyes at her and we walk to our seats, which happen to be right next to each other and the reason why we both hardly get any work done. She's always yammering on about something while I'm trying to do my work and I'm always trying to tell her to kindly shut the hell up. For some reason though I always get peace when I read. When I'm reading, it's like the whole world disappears around me; even Cara. I pray we get to read in today's class.

As the rest of the class files in I notice that the feeling of being watched is at an all-new level of high. I'm really uncomfortable or maybe it's just that I'm a little bit hungry because I guess I didn't eat enough this morning. My stomach is beginning to twist and my head feels strange.

That's when I notice Damien watching me from the back row of the class.

Definitely not hunger, but why is this feeling coming from him? Maybe I'm tired…

For some reason, his usual cool composure is replaced with a hard stare. I catch his eyes just for a second and he turns away like he's seen something that's disgusted him. *What was that all about?* I mean, he usually gives me the creeps, but the feeling I got when he was looking at me was, well, not good.

When everybody is seated, our teacher Miss Jane walks in holding her usual clipboard to take attendance, and starts as soon as she reaches her desk.

"Lesley O'Connor"

"Here."

Cara passes me a note. I unfold it and roll my eyes at its contents.

Take a look at Damien! He's so in to you! I bet he's going 2 dump that witch Vicky and go 4 you my girlie!

"Amanda Jones"

"Here."

I write back, *Yeah that's never going to happen. He was giving me mad dirty looks before; you should've seen him! Plus, you know he makes me feel kind of gross, I can't explain it, but the feeling he just gave me made me feel more than icky. No matter how hot he is, I just don't like him like that.*

"Khiara Banning"

I pass the note to Cara who's giving me a really funny look that I don't know how to interpret. She's gesturing wildly and I'm sure that she'll get in trouble when Miss Jane walks right up to my desk, grabs the note and crumples it.

"Miss Banning, if you want to talk to Miss Williams so much, maybe you two should do it in detention after school. Would you like that?"

I shake my head and give her the best puppy dog face I'm able to muster up.

"Then I guess you'd better think before you do such things," she scolds but I can see her smiling under her rough exterior. I'm her favourite student and she just doesn't like me falling behind. She walks back to the front of the room to finish up attendance.

I look at Cara who's giggling hysterically and doing a pretty bad job at hiding it, and I just smile at her. As always, we've made it through without so much as a scratch. We always do whenever a teacher catches us passing notes; or sleeping in Cara's case. It's just so funny that my face can have that effect on authority figures.

Miss Jane passes around the day's assignment. We have to read the first two chapters of *Flowers for Algernon* by Daniel Keyes (a book which the local church has been trying to ban for years, but always gets overridden).

I finish half the book by the end of the period while almost everybody else besides a select few is having trouble understanding it. I love this book and vow to finish it next period.

By the time lunch rolls around, I am starving. Cara and I go to our usual table where we sit with Damien, Victoria, Janie (who pretty much hates my guts but seems to love Cara), and Janie's boyfriend Chris. I notice that from across the table Damien is giving me the same look as before in English class.

I'm completely unnerved by this and try to avoid his gaze, but to my dismay he gets up and walks around the table and sits down right next to me.

"Hey. Sorry about Victoria this morning. She's just not in a good mood today," he says.

"I'm *so* sure that's the case. She's like that every day, Damien. But that's beside the point. What's up with the looks *you've* been giving me lately? It's like I stabbed you with my pencil or something." The instant it's out I regret saying it because he looks like I just slapped him in the face. Christ, when did I become such an ass?

"What?" He asks me, brows furrowing in apparent confusion.

"It's nothing. Never mind. It's just that…" I pause and awkwardly bite my lower lip, unsure if I should just spit it out.

"You were staring at me in English class. You looked angry, and I was getting worried that maybe I did something to upset you," I say, though I have no idea what I could have done because when I'm not avoiding him, I'm rather polite to him.

Damien smiles at me and mock punches my arm. "You couldn't piss me off even if you tried. You know that don't you?" He's smiling at me like he really means it and I feel super bad that I could've hurt his feelings, but at the same time, a voice inside of my head is screaming. It says, *He's lying to you!*

Pushing the voice out of the way, I smile back at him apologetically and say, "I'm sorry Damien. I've been feeling off lately. Maybe it's lack of sleep. I don't know. I usually feel off anyway, but it's been worse lately, you know?"

He seems to understand, and shrugs as if to say, *what are you gonna do?*

He reaches over and grabs my hand, squeezing it lightly. Victoria notices and shoots him a look of annoyance from across the table though.

He waves her off with a small smile, and something passes between the two, something unspoken. My heart pounds wildly in my chest and I notice that the light squeeze has turned into something much more firm – almost painful, and he's looking at me with that strange look from earlier.

I get chills on the back of my neck leading down to my spine in two seconds flat. *Okay, so I wasn't imagining the weirdness.* There is definite weirdness coming from him.

"You're very hard to figure out, Khiara." He says, letting go of my hand, but something flashes behind his eyes and my heart gives this little flip-flop into my throat in a very not-so-good way.

Victoria seems pleased that he's let go of my hand and she turns away from us as if it never bothered her in the first place. But the look in her eyes as we make eye contact for a split second says otherwise.

She's pissed.

So I look at him. Take a real good look at him.

I'm not sure what I'm trying to see, but I'm not sure I like it. I nod my head at him to acknowledge the conversation as being over as he walks back to the other side of the table and sits down next to Victoria, who looks ready to burst into flames.

"*Don't* touch her," she hisses at him so quietly I almost miss it. He frowns, seeming genuinely confused. Damien says something under his breath in a musical language I've never heard, but makes my heart stir in a way I can't explain.

Victoria instantly pales but tries to hide it, placing her hand on his arm lovingly, replying in that same language.

It doesn't fool him though and he shakes her off.

Something hits me in the head but I ignore it as I keep staring at Victoria, who begins yelling at Damien. I don't know why it's affected her so much, it's not like we made out or anything. I turn to find that the thing that hit me was celery from Cara. I throw it back at her with a small smile.

"What was that for?" I ask.

Damien storms off, Victoria trailing after him in a hurry.

She laughs it off and everybody at the table follows suit, but my eyes linger on Victoria's retreating form.

To get my attention back on her, Cara swats at me with her hand playfully like a kitten. "We were just talking about the party. Did you know about a hundred people are coming? Maybe more! That's amazing isn't it Kiki?"

There are only about six hundred people in our town and most of them are adults. How is that even possible?

"Yeah. I guess, though I bet most aren't even from here. *Caroline.*" She's called me Kiki since we were kids, and I hate it. In retaliation, I call her Caroline.

"The name is Cara, look at my birth certificate." She says to me, her eyebrows drawn together in fake anger. She hands me one of her cookies and mouths *I love you Kiki,* giving me a little wink and making an obscene gesture with both hands to get me to smile.

I laugh and she goes back to talking with Janie, who's prattling on about some fashion show they watch.

After the lunch bell rings I stop by my locker to get all of my things for music and accidentally bump into a girl from a lower grade as I turn to walk to my class, knocking all of her things to the floor.

She's got long blonde hair and a cute spattering of freckles on her nose and cheeks. Her eyes are a beautiful green and her skin is the same peaches and cream colour as Cara's. Her glasses are small, square and practical, but the frames are a shade of beautiful gold.

"I am so sorry!" I say as I bend down to help her pick up her things.

"It's okay! Really. I'm used to it by now. I'm always in the way of other people. I'm not good at anything but falling down and bumping into people," she says.

I'm shocked at this statement; she shouldn't feel this way, hell she's gorgeous, and seems really nice. But I too know what that feels like. I was called Klutzilla until seventh grade because I tripped over my shoes in the hall one too many times.

I sigh and hand her some pencil crayons that fell out of her pencil case as she gathers up her papers. "Don't feel like that. Believe me, I know how it feels to be called annoying things and it is *not* fun. But don't worry, you'll get over it and people will get over making fun of you once they get to know you."

I reach out my hand, "I'm Khiara Banning."

She stares at me for a second before extending her own hand. "I-I'm Lisa Foster. You're in grade eleven right? I'm only in grade seven;. I just started here not long ago."

My school is a middle school/high school combo. The younger kids get the lower levels of the building while we get the higher levels. We don't share a lunch.

"Well Lisa, it's nice to meet you. And if you get into any trouble you can talk to me okay? Come and find me sometime." I say as I hand her the last of her things and pick up my own.

She nods her head and beams, "Thank you. Really, I appreciate this so much! You're the first person to be nice to me in the whole school!"

I smile at her and for the first time today, I'm not worried about feeling watched or creeped out by somebody. I'm just happy that I've managed to make somebody's day.

Three

I'm looking into a really old mirror. It's all cracked and the sides are rusty. I stand in darkness, not sure where I am and not liking it. I'm afraid of the dark, I always have been.

I keep staring into the mirror, unsure of what force holds my gaze. I certainly don't want to look at myself right now; I'm a mess of tangled, bloodied hair, cuts and scrapes. Just as I'm raising my hand to touch the mirror, a man who looks a lot like somebody I know but whose name I can't recall appears, holding out his hand.

"The Dark is calling," *he whispers.* "We will win the war."

And I'm jolted awake by the school bell.

"Ugh!" I groan.

I must've fallen asleep in French. This is how it goes every time I'm in this class. I just can't stay awake because Madame Belle, her real name Miss Amanda Florence-Belle, just can't speak the language well enough to hold my attention. I think she's actually Russian, or something.

My father was born in France so I speak French fluently. *Proper* French, that is, not the stuff that they teach in school.

I pick up my things and slowly walk out into the hallway towards my locker. Thank god I get to go home. I think I'm just going to go to bed when I get there.

As I trudge through the hallway, I get the sense that I'm being followed. I turn around and see Lisa, the girl from before, standing behind me with a sheepish look on her cute freckled face.

"I'm sorry to bother you Khiara, it's just…I was wondering…I'm having trouble in French and I see that you just came out of the advanced French classroom and I was wondering if you could tutor me sometime. It doesn't have to be soon." She says.

I nod my head and reply, "Oh yeah, sure. No problem. Listen, I have to go now. My friend is waiting for me outside so I'll talk to you later okay?"

She smiles and runs off, happily skipping to her locker, but she turns around halfway there and yells a series of numbers at me, which I realize a little too late is her cell number. I'll try to remember it later, or I'll catch up with her and ask for it again.

Once I get outside, I head straight for Cara's car. Much to my chagrin though, she's talking with some random boy in the front seat when I get there. I knock on the window of the shiny orange convertible and they both jump ten feet in the air as if being awakened from some sort of spell.

Normally Cara is kind of promiscuous. I mean, she's a big flirt and when she dances at parties she gets a little too close and personal with whoever she's dancing with, but she never *usually* acts on anything, though I have to admit she has in the past.

Awkwardly, I slide into the front seat as Mystery Boy slides out. He has a look of shame on his face and I can tell he's extremely embarrassed. He's kind of cute with his giant thick-rimmed black glasses and a mess of red curls on his head.

"Hey, dude. There is no use being embarrassed. Be proud. Being caught with me is an honour, really," says Cara, reapplying her lipstick in the driver's side mirror as if she were making out with him instead of just talking.

As Mystery Boy runs off, I say, "Cara, you *ass*. He looks so sweet and he's got to be a member of the freaking chess club or something." It sounds mean and presumptuous on my part, but pocket protectors, thick glasses, and the innocence of Bambi don't lie.

"His name's Paul Virtue. He is indeed in the chess club, the captain of it in fact and he's in grade *twelve*. Sorry okay? I got bored waiting for you. He was cute though wasn't he? He tried to say no to me, but I'm just so irresistible. He made for a good companion while waiting for you. We talked about math."

"You were *only* talking right? Nothing else? Cara this isn't like you…well it is, but not this far. You looked like you were going to eat his soul or something…"

Cara turns to me and rolls her eyes but nods her head. "Let's get you home so you can rest up before the party. It's not like I was doing anything wrong, we were just chilling, talking about the wonders of trig since he's in my class, and okay, *maaaybe* I turned the charm factor on a bit high, but I needed to know if I was on the right track on my homework."

Sometimes, I wonder why I'm friends with her at all;, we're so God damned different.

As soon as I get home I head straight for bed. I don't bother looking for my parents. They're never home unless it's absolutely necessary, sometimes making me feel like I'm really not important enough to them, which I know is ridiculous but can't help feeling sometimes. They're always at work or out at the latest party they know they can't afford. It's not really bad though, it just leaves me to take care of Pug and entertain myself.

Pug is curled up on my bed, waiting for me and wagging his little curly tail like crazy. I'm glad we can't communicate with words. If you could talk to your pet like you would with a friend, the bond would be less strong I think. I depend on him for comfort and company and he depends on me to just make sure he's alright; we don't have to talk. He's not a social little dog and he hates most people.

I can see why though, he was beaten and left for dead by his last owners when he was just a newborn puppy. I found him and took him in a couple of years ago.

"Hey, buddy!" I say, patting his head and lightly pulling his tail.

He sniffs my hand to see if I've got a treat for him, which I usually do. When he sees that I don't, he whimpers, stands up on his hind legs, and begins to lick my face until I get up to get him one.

"Okay, okay! I'll get you a treat, Fatty."

Pug barks appreciatively as I get up to get him a biscuit.

~*~

My head hurts so much. The pain is almost unbearable. I reach out my arms into the darkness that surrounds me and I know that though I can't see anything or anybody, I am not alone. Not by a long shot. I hear a male scream and I begin to run as fast as I can towards him.

The closer I get, the more it sounds like he's screaming my name. Who is this person? What do they want?

"Help me Khiara!" he yells.

"Who are you? How do you know my name?" I scream, fear taking over every emotion that I possess. The voice that I just heard, I know it…

"Please! Hurry, before it's too late! They want you but I won't let them have you. Please, find me! Hurry!" His voice is hoarse from yelling so loud.

"Okay! Keep yelling so I can find you," I say.

I do not get an answer. Instead, I find myself falling down, deep into the darkness. And there is no way out.

"Khiara get your ass up now!"

Somebody is shaking me. But it doesn't matter. I am encased in the darkness.

"We're gonna be late! Can you wake up already? God, I knew you'd do this to me."

"Ugh, my head. I had the most messed up dream in the history of life," I groan as I finally wake up.

"Good. You're up. You've been screaming for like, fifteen minutes, it was disturbing. Anyway, you got the stuff for the party?"

I nod my head yes. "I got it all beforehand yesterday."

Slowly, I get up and walk to my closet to get a party appropriate dress. I open up the doors of my large closet and stare into it, not sure what to choose. Cara walks over and pulls out a red dress. It's made out of a satiny red fabric with black mesh over it, ripped in just the right places. I didn't even know I had this dress! It's beautiful.

"Wow, when did you get this?" Cara asks me, her eyebrows drawn together in thought.

"I honestly have no idea," I reply. "Maybe my parents bought it for me for, I don't know, being a good daughter or something."

Wherever I got this dress, it's perfect and goes with the black nail polish I've already got on. I'll have to ask my parents later so that I can thank them. Sure enough, as I move towards the bed, a note from my parents falls out, telling me they love me.

I strip out of my clothes and pull the dress over my head. I struggle to pull my arms through, so Cara, giggling all the while, helps me get it on. When I turn around to face my mirror I can hardly believe that the person in the reflection is me. I gasp and just stare.

The dress fits me like a glove. It accentuates the small curves of my body, making them look rather sexy;, a word I've never associated with myself before. Usually that title goes to Cara. It falls just above my knees which surprises me because I thought it was much longer. The rips in the mesh form a pattern all the way down the dress and it's just *so* beautiful. My hair doesn't even need to be brushed from the mess of tangles it's in. It looks like I put it that way on purpose.

I grab some hairspray and spray it onto my hair.

"Wow..." is all Cara manages to say.

"I know. It's eerie, right? I am *so* glad my parents bought this for me," I say.

All of a sudden there's a huge crack of thunder and it begins to pour outside. My window bursts open and everything in that vicinity gets soaked.

"Aww crap!" I yell, "This so can't be happening! I'll take care of it when I get back home, you know change the sheets and stuff."

As always, Cara remains calm, giggles and says, "Yeah. Let's get going." She sticks a nametag on me that says, *Hello, my name is: Khiara.*

"Are you really doing the nametag thing?" I say. Cara nods, "It helps people get to know each other better."

When we get to Cara's huge house the party is in full bloom. I can't believe she left her own party just to come get me. That's what friends are for I suppose. Cara lives in a house similar to my own, a rather large, white colonial style dwelling complete with a wraparound porch. We bonded over this when we first met in daycare at the tender ages of four and five. Cara is a couple of months older than me and likes to hold it over my head sometimes.

There are people dancing in the large living room and so many making out on the five luxurious couches that occupy the middle of the room. There are guys in the kitchen drinking bottles of beer while the girls drink little pre-mixed fruity drinks. I'm the one with the chips and drinks, though drinks seem to have been taken care of. A giant bowl full of red liquid sits on a coffee table, Cara's famous punch I presume.

"Chips and soda!" Cara calls out. At hearing this, many people flock towards us and grab for the bags I've brought.

Having decided that I may as well have fun, I walk away from Cara, pass through the throngs of people milling about and out into the backyard where more people are dancing to the throbbing beat of a heavy techno song under a canvass that covers the large patio. I look over to my left and there in a crowd of people, is Damien talking to Victoria. Not my favourite people, but they're about the only people I know besides Cara at this party.

I begin to walk toward them when somebody catches my eye and smiles at me. He's got curly black hair and *beautiful* blue eyes. He has on a pair of ripped jeans and a Beatles t-shirt. Nobody is talking to him at all and I get the feeling that it isn't because he's not dressed appropriately (it's kind of a come dressed like a fancy-pants party, as Cara would say.)

He's emanating this strange vibe that I can't quite put my finger on, but I feel the sudden urge to speak to him.

I walk over to him – he's standing by the stairs that lead to the yard and where the patio ends – a little awkwardly and say, "Hey, do you go to school with us?" I don't really think that he does; he looks a little older, college or even university age but you can never be so sure these days. His nametag tells me his name is Cael. I assume it's pronounced like the vegetable, kale.

He shakes his head. "No, I don't go to school. I've never gone to school in my life, to be honest." He's got a slight Irish accent that makes the sides of my lips turn up ever so slightly into a smile. *They're after my lucky charms,* and all that. But still, never gone to school? What a strange thing. Maybe he was home schooled. He looks to be about nineteen years old, give or take.

"Were you home schooled?" I ask.

"Kind of. History and current affairs were always my least favourite subjects to learn about. Until recently that is. Now both are *very* important to me," he replies quite fervently.

"Okaaay…" I say, dragging out the word, unsure of how to reply.

He blushes and ducks his head, "Yeah, sorry I sounded strange there, I realize. It's just, I really enjoy those subjects." His voice goes up at the end like a question, and I get the distinct impression that he's trying to cover up something.

I mentally smack myself for sounding like such an ass, though. He's probably really shy. "Hey, I mean, I kind of get it. I love English, a lot. I'm Khiara Banning by the way, Cara's my best friend." I extend my hand towards him.

He shakes my hand, his grip strong and his hand warm. "Cael." I was right about the pronunciation. *Point to team Khiara!*

"So, how do you know Cara?" I ask, smiling at him.

"I don't," he says, "I came here with a friend, but she seems to have left me to my own devices."

I frown, "Ugh, I know the feeling of being ditched at a party you totally don't want to be at. I actually didn't really want to come tonight, but hey, if I didn't come we wouldn't be talking to each other right?"

He nods his head, "Aye."

Strange as he may be, I feel a pull towards him that I've never felt with anybody else. I feel safe with him and I've only known the guy for like, ten minutes. I admit that this feels almost sparkly vampire-esque but I'm ignoring that in favour of the real world. I decide that after looking him over, he *could* be dangerous; I very much got that vibe from him.

Though he's wearing a baggy shirt, judging by the toned muscles of his arms I'd say he's probably rather strong. But I don't at all feel threatened by him.

He's different, and I like different.

All of a sudden, the lights go out interrupting the moment. We're still holding hands and I'm not letting go. It's way too dark and I'm not comfortable with that *at all.* And okay, I kind of admit, I like the feel of his hand in mine and I don't want to have to think about what that means.

In second grade, I was just getting over my fear of the dark when it was reinforced all the more by the fact that I was kidnapped. I can't remember the details of how it happened or what led up to it, but I remember waking up, being engulfed by darkness and being tied to a chair, crying and crying until finally the police came for me. They said it was just some kids from out of town looking to cause trouble, but for a while my parents were hyper vigilant about keeping me safe.

"I've got a problem with the dark…" I say very quietly.

"So do I." He squeezes my hand, but I have a feeling he doesn't mean it the same as I do. "I think you should go inside now."

"Can you come?" I ask, not wanting to go by myself.

"No. I think it's better if I stay here," he says. And then, almost to himself he says, "It's safer that way."

This confuses me. "What do you mean it's safer?" I ask letting go of his hand.

He smiles a sad smile that makes my heart break for him without knowing why. "I'm not even supposed to be talking to you."

"What do you mean?"

He just shakes his head. I guess it's because he's not from our school or something.

"I wasn't even invited by the main hostess. I really shouldn't be here. I just wanted to see…" He pauses, as if he's putting himself in check, "I just don't really go to many parties and haven't really ever been to a High School party before." It sounds like a weak excuse, but the way he says it makes me feel…something.

I smile at him and reach out my hand and unexpectedly cup his cheek. I don't know why I'm doing this to a guy I just met, but whatever it is that he's making me feel, I like it.

Call it insta-like or whatever, but there's a pull I'm having a hard time ignoring.

"Well," I say, "you're at one now and you might as well enjoy it I think."

He smiles in appreciation, nods his head once, and I'm surprised when he takes my hand and just holds it there on his cheek.

"Thank you," he says softly, before letting it go.

Four

He came with me inside after all.

We're sitting on Cara's guestroom bed, which surprisingly, nobody is... *using*. We just talk about everyday life as we sip on some punch that tastes suspiciously like sangria that we got from the kitchen. We ripped off the stupid name tags as soon as we sat down, happy to stay antisocial.

Cael works at a bookstore somewhere in one of the bigger cities an hour away and I feel bad that I don't remember the name of the place. He lives alone and likes video games, especially if they have anything to do with zombies, and he – and I have to promise not to laugh before he says this – sometimes likes to knit.

Most of the night passes that way, us talking and getting to know each other. Suddenly I'm curious as to why he never mentioned his last name, since he kind of made it seem like he has none.

"Cael, you never told me your last name and kind of made it seem like...well...like you don't actually have one." I say, wanting to have my mouth stapled shut for all of eternity as I realise that he probably just goes by his first name for a reason.

He smirks, a little twitch of his mouth. "It's not like that. It's-" he pauses.

"Complicated?" I supply.

Cael nods his head. "It's kind of like I've been disowned in a way and I've distanced myself from that life. Maybe I'll tell you my last name sometime. But not yet."

"I didn't mean to pry..."

He looks up at me, surprised. "No, you don't have to be sorry. Honestly, I don't mind telling these things to you, you're a good listener. I trust you."

My heart skips a beat. He trusts me? We've really only just met but I feel like I can trust him too. I've never felt this way before and it's intriguing. There is one thing though that I can't put my finger on. Maybe it's because he's new, or because he's cute and Irish, or it could even be because there's this strange pull I feel towards him. But whatever it is, it doesn't feel *wrong*.

"Cael, do you wanna maybe, get outta here and catch a bite?" I ask suddenly having grown a pair of extra-large male parts.

"Yeah, I do, really. But would be better if we just…" He looks around, then strangely up at the ceiling like it'll give him some kind of strength and then says, "I do. Cool, thanks."

"You're sure?" I ask, not wanting to pressure him. He nods his head and smiles at me, making me blush. He has dimples on both cheeks.

I grab him by the wrist playfully, lead him out the room and go downstairs to find Cara though as usual she finds us first.

"Hey! Are you having fun, my main man?" she asks me. God she's so drunk, tomorrow is not going to be a good day. She'll be calling me puking her guts out for sure, asking me to help wash her hair.

"Yeah Cara, I am. Listen, my friend Cael and I are going to go get something to eat, and then I'm going to go home, okay?" Speaking to Cara when she's drunk is like speaking to a five-year-old.

"Okay. Who is this guy anyway? Do I even know him?" she asks.

"Nope. He just showed up with someone here. You should really pay attention who comes into your house, you know," I reply, rolling my eyes.

"How old're you?" she slurs, pointing at him. Cael smiles, "Nineteen."

Cara seems to accept this and puts her arms around me saying, "I love you babe. You're the only friend I've got to rrreally rely on, you know? You jus' don't care about everything *everybody else* does. That's why I like you, you're so coooool, babe. So…cool…so…" She pauses. "I'm thirsty!" and she walks away to the kitchen to get another beer, probably having forgotten that she was even talking to me.

Once we reach the front door, I do a double take as Damien shoots Cael the dirtiest of looks from across the room. *Who peed in his cornflakes?* I wonder. Obviously they have a past together, and I want to know what exactly transpired between them.

When we get outside I remember that I didn't drive myself here. *Damn! I should've known there was a hitch in my plan.* I'm not good with plans I guess.

Cael studies my face. "Hey, what's wrong?"

I blush, "I forgot that Cara drove me here. I hardly ever use my car anymore; I just always catch a ride with her. My car is kind of a piece of junk."

He reaches into his pocket and produces a set of keys, "Lucky that I've got a car then, eh?"

I smile and hug him impulsively. God, I'm usually not like this. I should get myself under control before I do something stupid.

As we pull apart something strange happens. Not *"Ohmigod this guy is so cute! My heart, it fails me!"* strange, because I am not the gushing type. It's more of a feeling that all of a sudden, I'm alone, more alone that I've *ever* felt. It's like something's been torn right out of me and it *hurts.* Cael doubles over in pain as if he feels it too and panic fills me.

"Cael, what's happening?" I ask completely confused.

His face is pale, his eyes are glassy, and his black hair is matted to his head from a sudden burst of sweat. He's trembling fiercely and I fleetingly wonder if I look the same because I feel like utter crap.

"Khiara, I- I need to sit down. I just feel dizzy is all. I'll be okay in a bit," he says, trying to assure me that he's fine by brushing it off. But I won't let him brush this –whatever it is– off.

"Cael, you should go home. I'll drive you if you can't drive." I say, eager to get him home, because obviously we've both got the flu or somebody has spiked our drinks, or something *normal.* The way he's looking at me is making me nervous, though. *This is normal, this is normal.* I chant it like a mantra in my head.

"I'll be fine. I don't get sick easily," I lie to make him feel a little better. In fact, my immune system isn't the best out there. "My immune system is great, it's like there are these little people inside of me fighting to keep me healthy all year round yelling, '*Don't let her get sick,*' and I *never* do."

This is why I don't often lie. I suck at it.

He smiles like he knows I'm lying but appreciates it all the same. "Thanks, yeah. I should get home. It's probably the flu. You said you'd drive me, but you're sure you'll be okay? You seem to be feeling sick yourself."

I nod my head but think better as a wave of nausea washes over me. "I'll call a cab."

Five

We sit in silence for a while as the cab drives around town, trying to find Valour Street, building number 667. I giggle to myself, knowing what Cara would say if she were here with us, *"667, the neighbour of the beast!"*

"What's with the giggle?" asks Cael, who seems to be feeling a little better- I still feel dizzy, but I push it aside.

I reply honestly, "Cara. She'd say something silly about the apartment you live in; you know 667, the neighbour of the beast."

He thinks about this for a second and then, "I guess it's fitting," he says almost inaudibly.

I shake this off as I've been able to do with his strangeness before, and the cab pulls to a stop in front of his house. It's a large duplex, the first reading 665 and the one above, his, 667. I undo my seatbelt and get out of the car to go around to his side. Cael beats me to it, as he opens the door and walks out.

"You don't have to," he yawns loudly, "come in. It's kind of a mess and I'm sure you want to get home, too."

I shake my head, "No. I want to make sure you get to bed; I don't trust you. I'm sure you'll go right to whatever instrument you play and play it all night or something equally as distracting."

"How did you know I play an instrument?" he asks as we walk up the steps to his door.

"Just a guess that I hoped I'd get right. You have musician's hands."

He smiles, looks down at his hands and says, "Aye, you're right."

When he opens the door he looks over at me and gestures towards it dramatically. I don't understand what he's getting at. *Is he asking me to come in?* I bite my lip to keep myself from smiling.

"Well, since you're here, you might as well come in..." he says awkwardly, covering up for the strange flailing arm display he just put on.

I walk in and to my surprise it's not a bit messy. "You said it was messy," I say, laughing as I take in the crisp black furniture, the wood floor, and the plasma screen TV.

He shakes his head, "It's a mess. I've never had it this messy before! Don't you see the clothes on the floor?" All I see is a pair of socks and a couple of shirts on the floor and one coffee mug on the table.

"Oh, so you're like *that*," I tease.

He shoots me a mock look of false hatred, which just makes me laugh even more. What is it with this guy that brings out such impulsiveness in me? I'm laughing like I've never laughed before in my life or like I'll never laugh again and I just met him.

He leads me to his couch so I can sit down and says "make yourself at home." It's funny how we're acting as if we've known each other forever, while at the same time we can't forget that we just met.

Cael disappears in what I assume to be his bathroom and comes out a minute later wearing red tartan PJ bottoms and a white shirt.

"I'm dressed for bed," he says to me as if I'll kill him if he's not, and I just might've if he weren't ready for bed. He needs sleep if he's sick and so do I.

"I'll be going to bed now Miss Khiara Banning. Would you like to accompany me to my room to make sure I don't somehow get distracted while lying in bed with my eyes closed, presumably snoring as soon as my head hits the pillow?" he announces.

I hop up regretting it when my head pounds and slap him on the arm. "Yes."

As I follow him into his room, I notice that there's a poster of Beethoven on his door. I smile. I love classical music. When we get inside the room, he plops himself onto his bed and lets out a huge yawn while stretching his arms. I look around his room and gasp as I take everything in.

The walls are painted black. He's got a violin, a piano, and a guitar sitting in the corner farthest from his bed, a simple double, which is placed on the wall at the back of the room. The bed has an elaborate red and blue patchwork quilt that looks like it was sewn hundreds of years ago. The pillows are all the same colour as the quilt. Almost every inch of the wall by the headboard is covered with symbols and text in many different languages. I recognize a few but don't know enough to know what the words mean.

"Cael, this is beautiful!" I exclaim.

He just shivers and yawns in response. I almost forgot that he wasn't feeling well and that I should get him into bed. I pull the covers back and help him in. I feel his forehead and note that he's got a bit of a temperature. I feel pretty much the same, but he seems to have worsened.

"Take your shirt off," I say. "It'll help with the fever. I'm sure you're only wearing it because I'm here anyway."

He obeys.

"You're wearing boxers, right?" I ask him.

Cael nods, rolls his eyes and takes off his pants, sensing what I was about to say. "It's better to sleep light if you have a fever," I explain.

I help him under the covers and pull them over his shivering body. I turn on the fan that's on his bedside table, feel his forehead again, and sigh. He's burning up. Fleetingly I wonder if I am as well, but that can wait.

"Your room is really something. The wall, right there," I point to the text and symbols, "what is all of that?"

He smiles as his eyes droop, "It's what I get to take with me. I've traveled to many places and I always learn some of the language of the land. I guess you want to know what it all means?" I nod my head. "It's all the same sentence. It says, 'I will never regret.' I've yet to write it in English for some reason, which is kind of funny considering." I smile as I notice it written in French, my dad's native tongue, just over the headboard on the left side.

I think about it. *I will never regret.* What does he mean, he'll never regret? What will he never regret? I find myself asking him out loud and am met with another yawn. I shouldn't bug him too much, he's pretty sick, and we hardly know each other. I think we've gotten to know each other pretty well though, in the last couple of hours. It's been so natural. I mean, hell, I just put the guy to bed like I'd do for *Cara.*

Awkwardly, I brush some hair that's fallen over his eyes, "I'll be going now. Feel better Cael, and hopefully this isn't goodbye. You seem like a cool guy."

He's already passed out and snoring lightly. I smile and grab a paper pad and pen from his bedside table to write my number so he can call me, if ever he wants to hang out for real. I decide to write a note:

Cael, thanks for being so cool about everything. You're really something; you're very different from anybody I've ever met. I like that. I hope you feel better, so here's my number if you ever want to give me a call, no pressure or anything, but I mean, I've seen you in your underwear and have had a pretty good laugh with you, so I feel like we could be friends. I mean, here I am, standing in your apartment while you're sleeping...I should probably go. Wow, I'm somehow rambling even though I'm writing this on paper...I do that when I get nervous. Not that I am. It's 467-9002.

Khiara Banning.
P.S I totally think the punch was spiked with something.

I place the note on the table, smile at his sleeping form, and begin to walk towards the door until he says quietly, "God, I am so sorry. Just know that you're not alone, okay? Just because it is said, doesn't make it so. I won't let it. I'll never let it."

I sigh and smile. *He's dreaming.* "Good night Cael."

I walk out of his room and then out of his house, down the stairs and out into the night, which luckily is lit by the streetlights. I pick up my phone, sighing, and call Cara who has left me tons of text messages and a couple of missed calls.

"It's like you're going through the end stages of Alzheimer's. I took that guy Cael home and now I'm going home myself. I'm pretty sure both our drinks were spiked and it made us feel really sick, he had a fever and I think I probably do too. I have to walk home mind you, but God don't you remember what I tell you?" I say into the phone, annoyed.

Cara sniffles and I wonder what could be wrong. "I know! But I need you to come here right noooow! Damien is outta control and Victoria and him have been fighting, like, major bad! I don't know what's happening Khiara, but I don't like it! They keep mentioning you and I think she's jealous of you or something, but I don't really know, I can't make out what they're saying because of all the people here. My tummy really hurts and my house is a mess because they smashed so much in their fight! Please come! I will never force you to come to a party ever again and I'll make sure you're okay with the spiked drink situation, check your pupils and stuff...."

I sigh again, "Alright, I'll be there in...fifteen minutes."

She moans and I hear yelling in the background. "What? But baaaaaaaabe, I need you here noooow! Can I get somebody to pick you up? I don't wanna make you bus it here!"

The very small amount of busses we have in Serene Falls stopped running an hour ago. I tell her as much. "Oh! I'll call a cab m'kay? Where are you? This whole town is an hour long drive from the beginning to the end, so you can't be far." She hiccups or possibly wretches, to accentuate her sentence.

By the time the cab comes I'm exhausted and only slightly entertained that it's the same cab driver as before. We only have a few cab drivers in Serene Falls so it was a one in four possibility. Fun fact, the taxi station and the police station share the same building, that's how small this stupid town is.

I am not looking forward to going back to the party but when I get to Cara's place, it seems as though everybody has left. *Thanks Vicky and Damien, for having a turbulent relationship.*

"Thank God you're here! Help me clean up Kiki, oh please. I need it. You can take my car home afterward, I swear!" Cara pleads.

So, I help her with all of the smashed vases, a broken bust of her great grandfather, food strewn everywhere, dirty glasses, and more. Cara hands me her car keys and plops onto the sofa in her huge bedroom.

"I don't know why you just don't stay here. What is it with you and sleepovers anyway? You never liked them, even as a kid." She says lazily chewing a piece of gum and braiding her cat Missus Pussy Pants' fur. I feel sorry for her cat, the poor thing is treated like a doll and it is named Missus Pussy Pants (all capitals), which I know if that were my name, I'd want to die.

Also, Missus Pussy Pants is a guy.

"Night Cara, see you on Sunday," I say as I get up from her couch, startling the poor cat.

"Yeah, good night Kiki, you're the best. I mean it. Now get over here Missus Pussy Pants, I'm almost done!" The cat voices his discontent, but Cara ignores it.

I walk out the door and close it just after the cat runs out the room.

"Missus Pussy Pants you bitch!" slurs Cara.

I decided to take her bike instead of her car. I'm not so sure what happened in the car while I was at Cael's but when I opened the door, it smelled like sex and vomit, so I'm pretty sure Cara lent her car to people as a spare room.

When I get home, I'm so tired I can hardly stand. I almost don't even notice my parents' cars in the driveway, as I head towards the garage.

"I'm home!" I yell as I walk in.

"In here, honey!" yells Dad from the living room. I guess Mom is still out. My father has dark grey hair and big green eyes, and my mother is of Native-American descent. She was adopted and doesn't know her actual tribal background, though she has always had a suspicion that it's Cree.

"Hey! Is Mom still at work?" I ask, knowing it's a yes.

He gives me an awkward one armed hug and sighs, "Yes." And then as if sensing my disappointment, he says, "I know we're always gone Khiara, but you are very independent. You can take care of yourself, when we need to be out at all times of the day and night for work. You're old enough to understand, aren't you? We work hard so we can put you through school and so that you can get yourself nice things because you deserve them so very much, ma belle."

I nod my head as tears come to my eyes. I thought I was over being sad about them working all of the time, but to hear my dad talk about it just makes it worse for me because I know they love me and would do anything for me. But it's hard being alone all of the time.

When I was younger, they were able to spend more time with me, but as I started to get older, they took longer shifts. I guess they figured I'd be okay by myself since I wasn't a little girl anymore, but the truth is that it's very lonely.

My parents have always been pretty perceptive people, but it feels like they haven't figured out yet how much it means to me when I get to spend time with them like I did when I was a kid.

"Okay, Dad. I'll see you later." I kiss him on the cheek. "Love you."

As I head up the stairs and then into my room I notice Pug in his usual spot curled up on my bed. "Hey Butt-face, how life treating 'ya?" I say, smiling at him.

Pug grumbles and lifts his head to see me but won't get up. He is just too damn cute and I love him so much. Pug is the only pet I've ever had. He has always acted like a puppy though now I guess you can tell he's aged quite a bit since I first got him. He was already pretty old when we rescued him from the side of the road one day.

"Move over, pup," I say as I plop onto my bed and push Pug aside.

Smiling, I awkwardly slide out of my dress and kick off my high top shoes which I forgot to take off at the door. I relax into the depth of my queen sized bed with six fluffy pillows, which may seem like too many pillows but admit it, there's never enough. I climb under the covers, having decided against putting any pyjamas on because I'm so exhausted and fall asleep in just my bra and underwear in seconds.

~*~

I hear a voice, a male's voice, singing somewhere close by. I am walking down Valour Street and getting closer to my destination, the voice.

"The moon is bright and so are your eyes, in love I am with you. I see you smile and my heart skips a mile, in love I am with you." *I need to get there before he stops singing that lovely song.*

"Forever will my heart be true, it's you that I hold you dear..."

I begin to run until I get to apartment number 667. I walk in and it hits me; this is Cael's house. The voice must be him! I run into his room and see that he's sitting on his bed playing a beat up old guitar. He doesn't even notice me at first but then he puts down the guitar and smiles his heartbreaking smile at me, and somehow, I know that the song was for me.

I wake up with a start from the best dream I've had all night-where did Khiara go? I look around and try to get my bearings and look over at my dresser to find a note. I pick it up and read it, smiling at her awkward self-admission of being nervous and rambling on paper.

God, it must be five in the morning or so, I should really go back to sleep. But I want to see her; I *need* to see her again. Even though it's no longer my job, I must keep her safe. She's all that I have left and I will not let her stumble into the Battle alone.

~*~

I'm dreaming he's outside my window. He looks tired and I can tell he thinks I can't see him peering in. But wait- I'm awake…

I leap out of bed and run to the window, but I'm too late. He's gone. I must've been imagining it after all.

Six

The doorbell is what wakes me up from a deep, deep sleep.

"Who the hell is it at seven in the damn morning?"

Ring.

"Shut up!"

Riiiiing.

"Go away!"

When Cara's ringtone starts to play, I've had just about enough.

What could Cara possibly want from me at this time of day? It's so early! And I went to bed not long ago. What in the world is wrong with her?

"What do you want now?" I say into the phone angrily.

"Wow, chill much. We have school, you know that right?"

"What?" I yell, looking at my calendar to make sure she's joking, which of course she is.

"Hah. No, I just need you to come shopping with Janie, Chris, and me. We're getting our semi-formal dresses! And you're coming right? To semi-formal, I mean." Ah, Janie, the blonde Georgian Princess of itch with a capitol B, and Victoria's minion.

"I guess… ugh, I hate you. I practically just went to bed. I'll be out in twenty; I need a shower because I smell like cleaning supplies, vomit, beer and Missus Pussy Pants' fur, which by the way you should *really* clean, Cara."

"Don't avoid the question, honeybun. You're coming to semi-formal aren't you?"

"Yes," I sigh. "Apparently I am."

Twenty minutes later, I'm out the door and getting in the car with my best friend and two people I can't stand. I'm waiting for this day to get better.

"Oh, you look adorable Khiara! All dressed up. Super fancy, bless your heart," says Janie. I'm wearing skinny jeans, ballet flats and an oversized Flogging Molly tee shirt. My hair is pulled lazily into a messy bun and I'm not even wearing makeup except for some hastily applied mascara. *Yeah right, Janie.*

"Thanks," I reply, "but try not to *compliment* me too often today okay?"

Janie gives me a look that can be interpreted as, *whatever* or *oh screw off.* I'd like to think it means either or, just for the hell of it. Spice up my life with choices, and all that.

In the back next to Janie, Chris is absolutely, one hundred percent unhappy about something. He doesn't even want to be looking for dresses even though I'm sure on any other day he'd be happily running alongside Janie, whose pants he is dying to get into.

I lean forward in my seat, tired of looking at Janie's face and look over to Cara. She's yapping on her phone with her latest boyfriend; if you could even call him that.

Cara's chewing gum loudly as she speaks and I'd be tempted to smack her upside the head if I didn't know she did it on purpose to bug Janie. "I know right?" chew, "You're so amazing!" Chew, "I can't wait to see you! I brought people so we won't be alone and we'll have a double date." Chew, "Also, my best friend is coming, so you know, you get to meet her and stuff. Yeah, I know, but she's single. Maybe we could set her up with one of your friends. Okay," chew, "bye!"

I take the sunglasses that are resting on her head and put them on my own face, "Cara, do you think you could chew louder, I can't hear you."
Cara smiles and blows a big bubble, "No problem, babe." The bubble pops loudly in my face and Janie makes a disgusted noise. We laugh.

We pull into the parking lot of the local shopping centre and find a parking space near the entrance. We all get out as Cara explains that we're meeting the guy who she was talking on the phone to, in the food court. I guess we're getting lunch. Or breakfast more appropriately since it's only about nine o'clock in the morning.

As we get inside I notice that Chris's face looks no different from when we were in the car. I wonder what's wrong with him, but I don't want to ask for fear of Janie yelling at me to stay out of their business. It's too early for yelling.

Both Chris and Janie come from a strict religious background, and while Chris is ready for *everything*, Janie wears a purity ring. They've been together for four years which is a long time for any sex crazed seventeen-year-old boy to abstain from doing the deed, especially when his girlfriend is as good looking as Janie. I've always found it funny that she's such a snob, yet she's the daughter of a preacher.

We walk to a table where Cara's latest boy toy is sitting reading a book that I've already read. Five times. It's one of my favourites, 'Pride and Prejudice' so I decide to actually try to like this boy.

"Tristan!" Cara yells as we walk into the food court.

Cara gestures to Chris and Janie, "The other couple I was talking about. This is Chris and Janie." Then she grabs my arm and pulls me forward, "This is my best friend in the whole world, better than ice cream with cherries and chocolate sauce on top, Khiara. She gets me out of trouble and I get her into it, but she somehow keeps coming back for more." She smiles at me to see my reaction. I awkwardly smile back and she just looks thrilled.

"Everybody, this is Tristan. He's nice, he's gorgeous, and he's smart. Also, he's super tall. It'll freak you out when he stands up."

Tristan gets up and shakes my hand. Cara's right, he is quite tall. He goes to shake Janie's hand, but Chris who reaches out his hand instead, pulls her away as if to communicate, *back off.*

He's got dark brown hair that's been cropped pretty short and large arm muscles. He's pretty skinny in contrast to Cara but she looks so happy. Maybe this is for real; maybe she's stopped being so damn - I won't say it. She is after all, my friend.

"So, this is Khiara," he says in a voice that I can only describe as velvety smooth. "It's very nice to finally meet you, I've heard so much about you."

I nervously smile up at him, "Yeah? Well I've not heard anything about you so it's really nice to meet you, and I hope we'll get to know each other better today. You seem like a really good catch for Cara. You see, she's a bit promiscuous and I'm hoping this is going to be a long term relationship for you guys." *Oh no, I'm rambling.* "So it's just really great to meet you, I already said that didn't I, and uhh…" I bite my lip.

Cara pats me on the back a little too hard. "She does that when she's nervous, she just runs her mouth. If I were as promiscuous as she *says* I think you'd have already known that, seeing as we've been together for a *whole two months* already." Oh. This must be serious if she kept him from me for that long…

"I guess Cara told me about you before but I have a hard time listening, always in my own little world… and such…" I say, trying to salvage the mess I'm sure I have created.

Tristan sees through my lie and simply smiles. "Cara's changed a lot since we first met. She tried to get me to go out with her the day we met but I told her I wanted to get to know her. I guess she's not used to people saying no to her." Cara blushes and ducks her head. "So, we went out on a couple of dates and I guess we're official now since you know. I'm not surprised she didn't say anything yet, I'm sure she's wanted to tell you for quite some time."

Cara turns to me, "I have, my honeybun. I just didn't want to jinx it. You know me, I'm not usually the…long lasting relationship type. But this is different."

I smile at her. "It'd have to be for you to keep him from me. But you're lucky, I like him." Tristan smiles at this and Cara fist pumps.

"Well then let's get moving already! I wanna find a dress," says Janie, rather impatiently.

We walk around the mall a couple of times looking for dresses and I nod nonchalantly at everything Cara and Janie pick out for me. While Janie pretty much hates me, she's Cara's friend – when she needs a kick of girly companionship that I can't always offer – and she isn't always such an ass towards me.

Tristan seems to disappear at times but always returns when I least expect it. I wonder what he's off doing when he's not around us until I see him on a bench just outside of the store we've chosen, which is owned by Janie's aunt, reading quietly. I smile at that.

I turn around and notice that Chris is just standing there with that same stony expression on his face, and again I wonder what his problem is.

At one point, I decide to ask because it's just pissing me off not knowing. "Chris, what's up with the miserable face? Do you not enjoy seeing your girlfriend in revealing dresses? Or is my loser presence starting to give you a headache?"

Shaking his head he says, "That's not it, Janie's a babe, don't get me wrong here. I just *can't stand* Cara. I can't be around her but she's Janie's friend so I have to act like I enjoy her company. I don't hate you, and really Janie doesn't either, but she's not exactly one to let go of grudges. You spilled your drink on her when you first met her, remember? She was wearing her new dress." I roll my eyes.

"Why do you hate Cara so much?" I ask feeling obliged to do so, also ignoring the fact that Janie apparently hates me just because of something I did a couple of years ago.

Chris smiles wistfully. "Because she hurts guys like me. I used to be the *biggest* geek until high school, you know that. But when I met Janie, who was the nicest and prettiest girl I'd seen since, well, you know, ever, I just knew I had to be with her. She had moved here from Georgia and right into my heart. She was in the same church as me and everything. I had to get to know her better, but not as *me*. Not the real me."

He sighs, "That summer I bulked up, I lifted weights, I swam for hours, and I ran like nobody's business. My dad was so proud of me, finally becoming the Chris he wanted me to be, not a nerd that was in love with Star Wars."

"For the record, I thought you were pretty cool the way you were before. You used to actually talk to me in the halls," I point out.

He laughs a bit at that. "By the time we were all in high school after summer, I got up the courage to talk to her. She didn't even know who I was, only that I was hot and on the football team *and* in the same church as her. We went out on the weekends and I always brought her home before curfew. She seemed so nice at the time…and then she just started getting angry for no reason."

"What happened? How did she get to be the Janie we all love to hate today? I mean, the first day I met her after hearing about 'the new girl' all week I kind of got on her eternal shit list for spilling my drink down her dress…"

He shrugs. "She's nice underneath it all, really, but I think just really angry inside and I don't know why. She's just mean to you because you're so damned nice even when she's so mean to you. You're *genuine* I guess and she wants to be like that too. You don't have to fake who you are like the rest of us. I think Janie acts the way she does because she's tired of being her but at the same time, she wants to devote herself to the Lord just like a good girl should. I don't expect you to forgive her for being so nasty to you."

Nodding my head I let out a long deep breath that I didn't know I was holding. "I understand and yeah, I still don't forgive her. I know what you mean when you say Cara hurts 'guys like you'. But I know why, and even though I don't condone it, I can't stop her from dating people, and it's not like she's actually doing anything wrong with them. She's had a hard time with men, it's no secret. I don't expect you to start liking her or feeling sorry for her because she has daddy issues, but well, just to understand why. And actually, she hasn't dated anybody for a good couple of months. She might be past her phase, you never know."

What I don't tell Chris is that Cara and I found her father hanging from his closet in his study with dried tearstains on his cheeks and a look of pure hopelessness on his face. Not long after he was buried her mother brought in her boyfriend who she'd been seeing at the same time as Cara's father. That arrangement didn't last long though.

He's in jail under molestation charges - you can guess why. That is the reason she hurts guys like Chris, because all of the men in her life betrayed her or left her and she's trying to find a way to deal with that. I don't even think she knows that herself, or at least she can't admit it to herself yet, and every time I try to bring it up she gets really upset.

We stare at each other for a while and Cara breaks the silence. "Oh this is just perfect! I'm getting this one!"

And just as quickly as it started, our little heart to heart ended.

"Great!" Janie runs up to Chris and gives him a big hug, "What do you think about *my* dress choice?" She's wearing a golden ball gown, the typical dress that girls would choose for a semi-formal dance such as the one we're going to.

He says enthusiastically, "You're stunning -" but catches himself, "I mean, you look really hot, babe."

On Cara, is a dress the colour of a Granny Smith apple. It has layers of ribbon falling down from her chest and down her sides. There is a huge bow at the back of it, and it looks terrible on her. How am I going to tell her that the dress she chose completely does nothing for her?

Awkwardly, I put my hand on her shoulder and say, "Erm, Cara…that dress…you're really going to wear that?"

Cara laughs heartily, "No I've got the same dress as Janie but in red. This is disgusting but I wanted to get your attention. I've found the perfect dress for you," she grabs my arm, walks me to one of the changing rooms and throws me in, "it's in there, babe. I think you'll love it."

Sighing, I turn to look at the dress. It's gorgeous, elegant, and fairy-like all at once. It's strapless and goes down to, I estimate, just above the knees. The chest area has green and purple sequins, and just below that is a ribbon the colour of green leaves, that goes all the way around. In the middle of that ribbon is a flower of the same colour. Below that, is where the dress truly begins. From the waist down, layers of pink and light green mesh cover silk, which is a darker green, the same as the ribbon on the bodice.

After I put it on, I walk out of the dressing room and Cara squeals, "Oh, I knew that would look fabulous on you! I'm buying, my treat!" and takes out her wallet, "how much is it?

Checking the tag I almost die. "It's six-hundred dollars…"

Standing at the cash, Cara says, "Don't worry! I've got it, let me just swipe my credit card annnd…"

Smugly, the cashier looks at Cara and says, "Declined."

Cara doesn't even look defeated and begins to pull out one of her spare cards but I stop her before she can swipe it. "Cara, buy your dress. It's no big deal; I'll buy myself something cheaper later on."

She smiles at me. "You're sure? I wanted to buy you a dress as a thank you gift for being such a good friend…" but I nod my head and tell her to buy her dress. Gratefully, she hugs me and does just that. I think I just remembered why I'm her friend in the first place. At times when she's being like this, it's easy to remember, but at other times, it's also easy to forget.

After both Cara's and Janie's dresses are purchased, we decide to get some lunch. As we walk back to the food court, my stomach grumbles like mad and I frown. I really have to eat more these days. I decide that I want to get a blueberry bagel and a large Moxie cherry cola. Make that two cherry colas – I'm parched.

After we have all ordered our respective meals we decide to sit where Tristan was sitting when we met him. While walking to our seats, I notice that my shoe is broken. I sigh and bend down to examine it, placing my food on the table next to me. This is a huge mistake; next thing I know, I'm being tripped over and ice coffee has been spilled all over my shirt.

I turn around to give the person a piece of my mind, but everything I was about to say dies in my throat. There, on the floor next to me, is Cael. He's wearing a black hoodie and the same pants he wore when we met yesterday.

When he notices that it's me, whatever he was about to say dies in his throat as well. Instead, his eyes go huge and his face reddens.

Scrambling to his feet, he says, "Khiara! Oh my God, I'm so sorry about this."

He helps me up and passes me a napkin as if it were a peace offering. I'm just smiling like an idiot. Reaching for the napkin, I realize it's soaked as well. His face is a mirror image of my own.

"Cael, that napkin is, uhh, kinda soaked," I say and his face reddens even more than I thought possible. "It's okay. I'm in my hobo clothes anyway."

All of a sudden, I realize that Cara and the others, well mostly Cara, are waiting for me. Cael takes off his hoodie and hands it over to me. "You would look better in it than me anyway and it's the least I could do. Just take your shirt off in the bathroom and change into it, but before you do that, I think you should probably explain what's going on to your friends. Two of them look really annoyed at having to wait."

Laughing, I say, "Oh, no. If anything, Janie wants me to leave and Chris wants to leave himself."

Cael digests this and asks quietly, "Do you want to hang out then?" and I wish so bad that I could say yes because I really do want to hang out with him. But I told Cara that I'd spend the day with her, and so I have to.

I begin to explain to him, "Cael, I really wish I could say yes. But, the truth is, Cara wants me to -" but he cuts me off, "It's no problem. I get it; she's your friend. Well, I don't want to keep you, so I'll watch your tray while you change."

Seven

After I've changed into the hoodie and out of my wet, coffee stained shirt, I walk out of the girls' room to find my tray and Cael gone. I look around and note that he's sitting with Cara, Chris, Janie, and Tristan. Cara is blabbering on about something to him, and I know it's about me. I've never had a boyfriend before, not that he is my boyfriend or anything, and I know that she'll just assume that any boy she doesn't know that I happen to talk to is the biggest love of my life. She is like a stereotypical mom when it comes to things like this.

As I walk to the table, I get *that* feeling, the feeling that I've kind of grown accustomed to in the past couple of days, of being watched. I look around but only see people chatting and eating with their friends as per usual.

When I get there, Cara's telling Cael *all* about my life. Right now, she's launched into the epic story of my first non-training wheel bike ride. I fell and broke my wrist and Cara had to get some random lady to call an ambulance for us, earning the "stranger danger" talk from both sets of our parents. I was also ten years old, which is what makes the story so good to tell for her and embarrassing for me.

"Can you believe it? Ten years old and she still had training wheels on her bike? How pathetic is that?" snorts Janie. Cara shoves her in the ribs, "Hey, I bet you still can't ride a bike properly, so shut it, Janers."

Cael just smiles shyly at me as I sit down across from him in between Tristan and Cara. He says, "I think everybody learns at their own pace. Well, since Khiara's back, I may as well go..." but Cara won't have any of it.

Swatting him on the arm, she says, "Stay with us! Ki-ki needs a date for today. I've got Tristan here and Janie's got Chris. It's not fair to Khiara if you leave and we'd all love to have you. We've decided that we want to go to the movies so why don't you stay?" *I don't recall having any say about this...*

Tristan nods in agreement while Chris looks to Janie, who says in the voice she usually only reserves for me, "Yeah, why don't you stay?"

Chris smiles an apology at Cael, who just nods his head.

"If that's alright with you," he says, looking at me with pleading eyes. All of a sudden, I remember that he's probably never really had any friends around his age, or if he did they weren't very close ones. This must be really important to him. Plus, I also realize, I really want him to come with us. He makes me feel… something.

Blushing, I reply, "Of course I want you to come with us. I'd be crazy not to."

Cara claps her hands as Tristan drapes his arm around her. "It's great to meet you, by the way," he says to Cael, which makes me laugh and exclaim with laughter, "You've just met most of us too, you know."

I think this earns me points or something, because he holds his hand up for a high five. I smile and give him the high five, as he says, "No wonder you're her best friend. You keep everybody in check, don't you, Khiara? I like you." And somehow, I know in my heart that he means it. This guy is just so right for Cara.

Cara jumps at the opportunity to bring the conversation to the topic of her, "But not too much, right? That much like is reserved for me," and kisses him on the cheek.

"Of course!" He beams at her.

After a long walk around the mall (a couple of times over, since it's just one short strip), we find ourselves at the movie theatre just next door. It's hell trying to decide what to see even though there are only three movies playing but we all finally decide on a romantic comedy. I don't even remember the title, but it's probably something cliché anyway.

As we walk in, I remember that I hardly have any money and sigh because I'm thirsty. I want something sweet like a Coke, but the drinks here are *so* expensive because everything goes towards running the place. Sensing my thirst, Cara walks up to the concession counter – which is essentially an old desk with a popcorn machine, a fridge, and a little candy stand behind it – and buys me a bottle of Coke.

"Best friend telepathy," she says, handing me the drink, smiling like an idiot. She's so proud of herself that it's kind of cute.

"Thanks," I say, sipping thirstily and almost choking because I drank too fast.

After everybody has bought what they wanted, we head to theatre number two and get seats in the front row, which is the best view of the small projector screen that would rival any of the ones our teacher's in school use. The seating arrangement is Tristan, Cara, Janie, Chris, me, and then Cael on the end.

As the previews start flashing, I turn my head to see Chris and Janie already going at it, happily making out like they are the only ones in the theatre. If it weren't for the rest of our group, they would be.

I look further down and see that Cara and Tristan are also blissfully kissing away, but not in Cara's usual disgusting way, it's more just pecks on the cheek, and whispered words in ears. Kind of cute. But still, what the hell? Did they expect me to turn to Cael and start doing the same, though? I practically just met the guy!

I turn to him and see that he's watching me with a smirk on his face. He rolls his eyes and says, "Wanna get out of here? It's getting a little...erm..."

"Hot in here?" I supply. He nods, gets up, and offers me his hand, helping me up.

"Thanks," I say. We walk quietly to the back row of the theatre and both breathe in a big sigh of relief.

"It was getting awkward there," whispers Cael. I giggle and nod my head, "Yeah, it was."

We sit in silence as the previews flash by, simply content to watch. Cael is cool like that, not making me feel compelled to converse. After a couple of previews-the movie begins. It starts off with a big fight between the female protagonist and her current boyfriend. They're yelling, and throwing things at each other, making some big deal over nothing. I'm not even completely sure why they're fighting in the first place, though I think it had something to do with roller skates. I don't really care.

I feel Cael shift uncomfortably in his seat.

"Everything okay?"

He nods. "Yeah, I'm good. I just…well I guess I kind of don't like the movie."

Laughing quietly, I say, "The movie's only just started and already you don't like it? I mean neither do I but I don't like this kind of movie to begin with. What's your reason?"

Cael sighs, "Well look at the female protagonist. She truly believes that he's been cheating on her."

"Well, maybe he did," I say a little awkwardly.

Cael shakes his head. "I don't think so."

"We'll just have to see," I whisper ominously.

Halfway through the movie I realize that Cael was right. The movie sucks and the boyfriend hadn't cheated on her at all. I roll my eyes and turn to him, "Can we please leave? I'll but you a victory coffee."

Cael looks thoughtful, "Sure. Let's get outta here. But would you be up to taking a walk somewhere with me? I'll collect the victory coffee some other time."

"Anywhere but here is fine with me."

Ten minutes later, we're standing in the most beautiful café I have ever seen. "This is your shop? As in, you *own* this place?"

"Yup, I own it. Well, mostly. It's my business, but I don't own the space, I rent it. I saved up the money from my bookstore job and other odd jobs here and there. I've been emancipated for quite some time."

There are two large bookcases lining the back walls filled with so many books that you can't possibly count the number comfortably. Tables line the front of the room and in the center, there is a huge fridge partially surrounded by an island that holds about everything you could possibly want to add on top of your coffee or tea.

"In the fridge, I guess it's all milk and stuff?" I ask, feeling a little dumb for asking such an obvious question. He leads me over to the fridge and opens the door. There's every type of milk, including soy and non-lactose, and there is also every type of cream and creamer.

"This is amazing."

Cael laughs, "And it's about to get even better. Do you like cheesecake?"

Mock blanching I say, "Who doesn't!"

He leads me over to the back of the room where the books are, and there are stairs that lead to a little ramp. Comfortable chairs and couches are laid out with tables next to them and foot stools in front of them. We stop in-between the two bookcases where there is a door that I hadn't noticed before and Cael looks at me, "Are you ready?"

I nod and we step through to the kitchen. It is *huge!* "Oh my God!"

It's a kitchen like that of a restaurant which this space used to be as I recall. I thought they'd gotten rid of it but I guess not.

"We make our own baked goods to ensure the quality of the food," he explains. "This is strictly a pastry and baked goods only café. We don't do sandwiches or soup. That's why it's called *The Sweet Treat Café*."

Cael walks over to one of the many fridges lining the back of the room, "You have your pick, though I really recommend any type of cheesecake. It's amazing I think you'll love it."

"Cocky, aren't we?" I joke, but he just laughs it off.

In the end, I settled for a carrot cake cheesecake mix. "This is an emotional experience!"

Cael chuckles, "Careful not to drool everywhere, the big unveiling is in three days."

Through a mouthful of cake I say, "Really? Wow, I can't wait for everybody to see this place! It's going to be a huge hit, Cael."

"I hope so," he says as he runs his fingers through his hair. "I've worked really hard on the place and it took me a while to round up the kitchen staff. I still need somebody to work the cash register for me, and I need somebody to deliver the cake to the tables."

Seeing an amazing opportunity I say, "I can be a waitress, or work at the register on school days after class. I need a job, actually. I was fired from my last one…"

"What did you do before?"

"I worked at the town general store but I was accused of stealing one of my co-workers wallets and even though it was proved that I didn't, I kicked up enough of a storm for them to not like what they saw. All they did was say that they didn't like my 'attitude' and that they were letting me go. My neighbour's mom was my boss, fun fact. "

Cael digests this a little until he finally says, "Bring in your resume and we'll make it official. I'm still going to hire you, but I like to know who I'm working with and it's always good to know more about the person you're going to trust the cash with."

Astonished I say, "Really? No interview or anything?"

"If you want we can conduct one right now," he replies, a smirk on his face.

I take the last bite of my cake and nod. As I'm busy trying to make the cake last he asks, "What's your favourite colour?"

I swallow the cake finally, having chewed way too long and say, "Blue. But how does this have anything to do with my experience?"

"It doesn't, but I want to get to know you better."

Oh...

"What's your favourite animal?"

"All of them," I reply. "But my dog, Pug, trumps every single animal out there, even other pugs."

He looks at me strangely, "You named your pug, Pug?"

I blush. "Yeah, well, I did. Guilty of being weird and I like it that way." He smiles, and my heart does crazy things.

"What's your favourite food?" Cael asks next, his eyes dancing with laughter.

"Whatever batch of baked goods you've happened to whip up, because that cake was *fantastic*."

All of a sudden I remember his bookstore job, "Are you still going to be working at the bookstore?"

Laughing, he says, "Part time, now anyway. This shop used to be a project but now it's kind of my baby. When I met you yesterday I didn't want to let on too much about the shop because it's kind of a surprise for everybody in the mall. But now I'm really glad I saw you today and got to show you. It's kind of like fate, huh?"

I'm glad too. "Yeah," I say, staring at his mouth. *I wonder what it would be like to kiss those lips. Not that I want to kiss them; well I do, but I hardly know him. Oh lord, what* would *it be like?*

"I'm sorry, what?" he asks all of a sudden, brows raised in surprise.

Oh. My. God.

Did I say that out loud? "Uhh, I guess it depends…what did you hear me say?"

"Well, it depends whether or not you *wanted* me to hear it," says Cael with a grin.

My face must be crimson by now because I am totally embarrassed. "Did *you* want to hear it?"

"Yeah," he says, "I did. I really like you, Khiara, and I'd like to get to know you better. If that's okay with you. I feel like we were, I don't know - supposed to meet."

"You're my boss now," I say, a little awkwardly. "Are you sure you want to mix business with pleasure?"

"There is no pleasure in boring business, now is there?"

"No," I whisper, "I guess there isn't."

Eight

"Where the hell did you go?" asks Cara, as she and Tristan walk through my bedroom door, sit down on my bed, and wait for my answer.

Blushing, I realize that I'd forgotten to text her to tell her what was up. "I'm so sorry, Cara. I swear, I had every intention of texting you, but I got kind of caught up in hanging out with Cael. He's…" I search for a word, "different."

Tristan raises his hand as if he was in class, and I have to laugh at the sheepish look on his face. "Should I not be here right now?"

"No! I mean, no you shouldn't not be here right now…I mean you can stay!" I say awkwardly, feeling bad that we had all but completely excluded him from the conversation. "Sorry Tristan, I bet Cara didn't tell you how awkward I can be sometimes."

He smiles, "No, she warned me. I just didn't believe her, but I guess she was right. I've gotta say I'm kind of happy she was, because it makes for an interesting friendship."

Grinning I reach out and tousle his hair, "I'm glad we're friends then." He looks as if I've just made his day, and I can't help but laugh some more as his face turns a bright red. Maybe he doesn't have very many friends at his school. Cara had told me that he goes to this very prestigious private school about an hour or two from town, a very *posh* place tucked into the woods. It's a boarding school and he lives there, being originally from the city of Montreal over in Quebec, but he works at the mall in town for extra pocket money.

"I'm glad too. I was worried you wouldn't like me, actually," says Tristan, all awkward and cute, and right then I really see what Cara likes about him. I can only hope that they work out well because I like this guy for her. I just hope she smartens up and doesn't end up hurting him. I'll have to talk to her about it later.

Cara links one of her arms through mine, rolls her eyes, and says, "Well, we're all glad. Now, let's get down to business. I want ice cream and cheap thrills, and I *know* you guys don't have any of that here."

"You want cheap thrills? I can take my shirt off if you'd like." I say sarcastically, "But you need to take me out on a date first."

"Or, we could go to the amusement park and ride the Tilt a' Whirl until we puke," she says, already standing up.

Laughing, I say, "There's that option too, I guess."

Cara slaps my arm, "Shut up already and let's go. You can tell us what you did with Cael *the lover boy* on our way there."

We stand up and walk out of my room, momentarily forgetting about Tristan. Pug whines from my room as we open the front door, and Cara and I both almost collapse into a fit of giggles as we run back to my room to get Tristan.

"Hurry up!" says Cara, all excited and ready to go.

"I have no say in this, do I?" asks Tristan.

Cara and I both look at each other and smile, "Nope."

Once we get in Cara's car, I tell them all about Cael and his café and even about the day of Cara's party. Tristan listens intently and Cara voices her opinion on the matter.

"You got a job and a boyfriend all in one day? Skills girl, you've got skills."

Is he my boyfriend? I'm not really sure, considering we haven't even gone out on a date yet. "I guess so, at least for the boyfriend part anyway. I'm not entirely sure...I don't know him all that well, we've only known each other for what, two days?"

Cara slows to stop at a red light and once she's stopped, she applies a fresh coat of lip-gloss, "Well, find out then. Call him, invite him to come." She offers me her lip-gloss and I shake my head.

"Just call him, Khiara. It won't kill you!"

Grasping for any excuse not to call him, I say, "He's busy tonight, actually. He's got this thing to go to..."

"What thing?"

I bite my lip. "Just a thing, you know a function of sorts," I lie.

Tristan sighs and pats me on the shoulder from the back seat, "A function of sorts? You're a bad liar, Khiara."

"Yeah well…you suck," I turn around to stick out my tongue at him like a five year old that's just been told that she's not allowed candy. He grins at me, which just makes me more annoyed.

"We're here!" crows Cara an hour later, as we pull into the parking lot of Monster's Domain amusement park-located a couple of hours away from our town. We park close to the gate; hardly anybody is here because of the rain. Monster's Domain is one of the smallest amusement parks to exist with only one roller coaster, three small water rides, one Tilt a' Whirl, and some bumper cars, but it's a great place to be, and I think it even trumps Disney.

"Do you think they'll close the place if the rain gets bad?" I ask Cara as she twirls her hair with her finger absentmindedly while watching Tristan rifle through his wallet for his bankcard.

"No," she replies, "They'll just shut down the non-water rides. I mean, we're already wet because of the rain, so why not, right?" This reminds me that I should probably put my phone in the car for safekeeping, and like he's read my mind, Tristan says, "You two should put your phones in the car. Don't want them shorting out, do you?"

Cara shakes her head and I say, "Nope. That's just what I was thinking actually."

He smiles and says jokingly, "I read your mind. I'm pro at it, go ahead and test me."

"What colour is my bra?" I ask, giggling as his face goes red.

"Ouch!" he says as Cara swats him on the butt. "Answer the girl!" she demands. Tristan rolls his eyes, and shakes his head.

"Purple?" he says and my heart stutters. I force a laugh and say, "No, it's green. Tomorrow I'll wear purple and ask you again." My bra is in fact purple. I write it off as a coincidence.

As soon as we're past the gates of the park the rain picks up speed and they close down all of the non-water rides. We ride the log ride four times before getting fed up with it, and then move on to the other rides as the rain slows down and they re-open them.

"Yes!" shouts Cara, as we walk and she dances in the direction of the Tilt a' Whirl, her favourite ride.

Tristan shakes his head, amused as Cara runs off ahead of us, "Why is this her favourite ride?"

I shrug, "She likes to spin really fast. I think that's why she drinks so much. It's the same kind of feeling."

Contemplating this, he rubs his jaw, "I suppose so. I'm not one for drinking; it doesn't really affect me, no matter how much I drink."

I shrug again, "Yeah, well I wish that were the case with me. One drink and I'm half in the bag."

Tristan smiles, rubs his jaw again and says, "Well, now I know not to let you near the alcohol at the semi-formal."

"You don't have to worry about that. I'm glad you're coming though." I assure him, laughing as Cara trips and falls into a huge puddle. "It is not funny!" she shrieks but a second later she's laughing with me.

As we get to the Tilt a' Whirl, Cara does this little victory dance when she sees that we are the only people in line. We're practically the only people in the park (which, might I add is a very large place and with hardly any people in it, looks a little creepy). The guy at the controls of the ride gives Tristan and me a cursory glance, but his gaze lingers on Cara a little too long but Tristan doesn't even seem to care so I let it go. All three of us take our own seat since we're the only people on the ride at the moment - everybody else is taking advantage of the water rides - and wait for it to begin.

The control guy walks around to each of the seats, checking to make sure they all work and when he gets to mine his face suddenly changes from a mask of indifference, to a look of pure revulsion.

Startled, I ask, "Is there something wrong?"

He shakes his head, quickly composing himself, "There's puke all over the floor and you're stepping in it."

"Oh," I say, as my stomach grows queasy. "Thanks for letting me know." He shrugs, mumbles something close to, "It's part of the job," and walks off.

I get out and sit with Cara who doesn't bother to ask why I changed because she saw the whole thing.

When the ride starts, the queasy feeling doesn't go away, as it should. It gets worse by the minute. *I'm okay now, there's nothing gross about this particular seat,* I think to myself. But for some reason, I can't stop looking at the seat that I was sitting in. It's as if it is mocking me, which is stupid, because dirty puke-filled Tilt a'

Whirl seats can't mock, well, anything, and I know that. But there it is giving off this terrible feeling.

Next to me Cara laughs away, oblivious as ever to what's going on inside of me right now. I wish I could explain it to her, but I wouldn't know where to begin. Somehow, "That twirling purple chair made specifically for the amusement of people is terrifying me with its evil vibes," doesn't really sit well with me as a proper explanation.

All of a sudden, the chair starts to spin faster than all of the others, and I watch helpless as it starts to spin out of control, smoke rising around it. The ride suddenly stops, and we're ordered by the control guy, Brandy according to his nametag which I only just bothered to notice, to get off immediately. That one chair keeps spinning and smoke keeps rising all around it until I notice the telltale orange flames of a fire. Come to think of it, I never saw any puke when I was sitting in it, which brings up a very confusing question.

What the hell is going on?

"Sheesh," says Cara as we stand back and stare at the ride, "You have the worst of luck. It's a good thing the control guy..."

"Brandy," I inform her, and she shrugs. "Whatever. It's a good thing he noticed or that would have been you in there. Thank *God*."

"Seriously," says Tristan, as he wraps his jacket around my shoulders, even as I try to fend it off. He looks upward and smiles, "Thank God!"

"Maybe we should go home," Cara begins to say but I put my hand up in a gesture for her to stop. "I'm fine. We should go on at least one roller coaster. It's not late enough for us to go home."

Cara frowns, "We have school tomorrow, Khiara. I actually want to pass math class this term with more than the minimum mark. If I don't, you know I'll have to go to summer school and I'm not really into that sort of thing. I like *freedom*. So that I can you know, do stuff over the break. Plus if I want to get into nursing I need to get serious, which has been exactly as hard as it sounds."

The fact that she even bothered to study kind of surprises me, though I know she's wanted to be a nurse since I fell off of my bike when we were kids. "How much have you studied for this test?" I can't stop the apprehension from leaking into my voice.

She blinks at me, once, twice, three times, until she says, "Actually, for once I've studied a lot. Remember my convo with Paul? I plan to pass and I will. But you're right about the time;, it is too early."

Frowning, I say, "I didn't know how hard you'd studied for the test. Sorry…"

Cara smiles, hugs me, and says, "It's a rare occasion that you are an asshole and I am willing to forgive you, since you seem to be all *shook up*– to quote Elvis. Now let's go ride the Minotaur, and forget we ever had this awkward moment."

Tristan grins from the sidelines, "That's *my* favourite ride. I like the tunnel it takes you through before the big drop."

When we get to the roller coaster, the line is quite short with only about ten of us waiting and soon enough it's our turn. The Minotaur is the biggest coaster at Monster's Domain, and during nice days the line is packed with people. It's based upon some cheesy horror movie about a Minotaur that attacks a whole bunch of tourists in the woods while they go camping. I've seen it practically a million times with Cara and each time it gets funnier to see the fake blood oozing out of cuts that should be already clotted over, and the bad props that are so *obviously* put together on a very low budget. For whatever reason they made a ride based on it, and the ride is a million times better than the movie, *thank God*.

Once we're all seated and ready to go the cars begin to move forward and my heart starts pumping in anticipation. I'm no longer scared or worried; for now I'm going to enjoy the ride.

As it slowly moves forward, I can't help but let out a whoop of excitement, and then I can't stop. Cara, Tristan, and everybody else on the ride join in, and as we finally reach the top –my favourite part– we stop for a couple of seconds and overlook the whole amusement park. It's beautiful to see all of the lights down there.

Then we're pitching forward, super-fast, and this is one of my favourite feelings in the whole world because I equate it to the idea of falling in love.

After riding the Minotaur three times in a row, the rain starts again, harder than before, and we hide under the awning of one of the game stands. "Damn it!" yells Cara, as she pulls out her mirror to check her makeup, "I hate the rain sometimes."

Feeling childish, I push her out into the rain but she catches on and pulls me out with her. Laughing and getting soaked, we run around in the rain pushing each other and twirling and whirling to the beat of our own hysterical giggles.

Tristan smiles indulgently at us but he isn't safe because soon we have him joining us, whooping and hollering as we run around the park, splashing in puddles that are ankle deep. I decide that I like him.

He's a keeper.

~*~

By the time we get to my house, it's almost midnight. On the way home we stopped to get burgers from the only McDonalds within miles of us, giggling when the server ogled our wet clothes and messy hair.

I open the front door and take a tentative step in, looking around for anybody when I hear the light snoring of my Dad, and I know he's been waiting for me to get home for probably a very long time. I don't have a curfew so this must be important.

"I'm home," I say as I close the door and Dad's snoring stops.

"Come, sit with me Khiara, I have to tell you something." He says, eyeing me warily.

"I'm home before I usually am. Am I in trouble?"

He shakes his head and smiles warily, "No, you're not. But your mother and I, well, we hoped you'd be home earlier. We have something important to tell you."

Internally groaning, I sit down beside him on the couch, "What is it, Daddy? Can it wait until tomorrow?"

He sighs and I notice for the first time he looks his age, almost fifty. "I'm afraid not, Khiara. We feel we shouldn't wait any longer to tell you. No matter what, you know we love you. You do know that don't you?"

Startled, I say, "Of course. I love you guys too." He nods, like this is good progress but it's no secret that I love my parents, even though they're hardly home. They work hard and though it sometimes stings when they're away, I understand that they work hard so that we can live the way we do.

Dad sighs again, and opens his mouth to speak, but no words come out; a first for a big talker such as himself. Mom's soft footsteps pad down the hallway and soon she's in the living room with us.

"Hi beautiful," she says into my hair as she pulls me in for a hug. She smells like lemons and happy, familiar things and I ease into the hug, smiling. My mother has the softest russet coloured skin, big brown eyes, and light brown hair that is starting to grey at the top.

"Hi, Mom. How was work?"

"Don't ask," she replies, holding me at arm's length to get a good look at me, "I had a rough day. I came home early so we could talk."

"What did you guys want to tell me?" I ask and then feel bad as both their faces fall, like maybe they were going to back out if I hadn't have asked.

"Maybe we *should* wait until tomorrow..." Mom says, but Dad shakes his head and says, "Miranda, I think now is the time."

"We love you very much, Khiara," Dad says again. "But you need to know something very important." My heart beat starts to pick up. "We are not your birth parents. We should have told you earlier, maybe raised you to know this, but we didn't know any other way."

My heart skips a couple of beats. *What did he say?*

"Honey." says Mom. "That doesn't make you any less our daughter."

"What...I'm...I'm *adopted*? How could you not have told me earlier?" I hear myself ask.

Mom speaks up. "Well, you were born in Ireland, as far as we know. Your father and I had been living there for a while, after we moved out of France." My mother and father met while she was touring Europe and quickly fell in love and got married after only six months of dating. I knew that we lived in Ireland for the first year of my life.

She clears her throat. "We had been trying to conceive for a while and just when I finally became pregnant...I lost the baby just six months later; it would have been a girl. We'd named her Madeline, for your father's late mother. We were getting very frustrated with the situation, and we didn't know how to mourn for our lost child, so we fought. One day, after a very bad fight, you father opened the door because he was going to take a walk to cool down... and there you were. You were just lying there quietly sleeping, in an old cardboard box swaddled in blankets, and you couldn't have been more than a couple of days old."

Irrational anger pools in my gut. "So, what, you just adopted me like that? No paperwork or anything? You realize how ridiculous that is right? How impossible that sounds. It's just not plausible, I'm sorry. "

Dad smiles sadly. "We didn't sign any papers in the beginning. We took you to the hospital so that they could examine you. We didn't dare hope we could keep you as our own. They let us stay while you were being looked at by the doctor so we could hear the results of their findings. As we waited outside the neonatal unit your mother broke down in tears. We could not understand how somebody could just abandon a new born baby like that. We worried about you; you'd been so small and pale and your body was burning with fever. All over again, your mother and I were reminded of our lost baby."

He looks down at his lap and my mother whispers his name. "Jaques…"

I begin to shake and let out a long breath. My mother starts sobbing. "When they finally came into the hall to give us the news, we thought for sure you were gone- but they said you had a clean bill of health despite the fever you'd had earlier. We were so relieved, honey and they even decided that it was in your best interest to come live with us for a while. They knew we had all of the necessary means to take care of a baby. Khiara, we were so happy though we knew it was only temporary until they found a home for you. Only it wasn't temporary."

"One day we received a phone call stating that we could, if we wished, fill out the paperwork to legally adopt you. The whole process took a month to settle. We moved here not long after when I got my job working at the museum, so of course you wouldn't remember." My mother works at an art museum pretty far away from town restoring art as best as she can. She has her own painting business on the side that she runs out of a local studio.

I nod like I understand but tears still form in my eyes and soon they make their way down my cheeks, scorching. "So you're not my real parents?"

Mom and Dad look stricken, and instantly I rephrase it, "I mean my birth parents."

"No, ma belle," says Dad softly, his eyes filled with unshed tears.

Suddenly a thought occurs to me and I bit my lip nervously. "Who named me?"

Dad thinks about the answer for a bit and when he takes too long, Mom says, "A very nice nurse did. Her name was Morgan. She said that it fit you as 'the little dark one' or something, I assume because of your hair colour."

"I am sorry, I'm so sorry. We didn't know how to tell you, and every year we told ourselves that we would do it but we just couldn't bring ourselves to. But you're getting so big and we are so proud of you, and we just…" Mom trails off.

"It's okay. I know now," I say.

They each wrap their arms around me and I let myself fall into them, comforting me with soothing whispers and pats on my back, telling me that they love me. And I know they mean it, really mean it, and it feels nice to know that they chose to keep me when they could have given me up. But it still hurts to find out something like this after such a long time.

"Do you want to take the day off of school on Monday?" Mom asks, her eyes glinting with tears. "I'll be home until two and we can spend some quality time together until then."

"I guess," I say, wiping my eyes on my mother's sleeve. "I could use some mother-daughter time."

"Good," my father murmurs into my hair as he hugs me. "You guys need some time alone. Maybe we can have a day to ourselves too."

The next day passed with a blur of shopping for semi-formal accessories and eventually getting drunk and having a good time with Cara and Tristan who prompted me to call Cael while I was completely hammered – he didn't answer, which I rejoiced about – and laughed as I left an awkward message on his answering machine explaining the situation. Before I know it, I'm extremely hung over and it's Monday.

I wake to the smell of bacon, my mouth watering as I practically float down the staircase, towards the kitchen. Pug trots after me, sitting down by my feet as I plop into a chair at the dining room table, where my mother's set out waffles, syrup, butter, bacon, eggs, toast, milk, orange juice, and a cup of steaming hot tea. She really went all out.

"Mom, this is…fantastic. Thanks!" I say as I begin to pile my plate as high as I can. She's practically made enough to feed a whole small village!

Smiling and taking a sip of juice, Mom says, "Well, good morning to you too. It's good to know you still enjoy my cooking." Since she has to work so much she hardly gets to cook for me and when she is home, she's usually exhausted. My dad tries to cook when he's home but he's kind of terrible at it and I'm not much better. I can make small breakfast things but that's about it. When my mother cooks, it's like every ounce of love she has for me is put into the meal.

"So, what do you want to do today?" asks Mom as I plough through my breakfast.

When I'm done chewing, I say, "Anything is fine."

She thinks about this and smiles, "How about a makeover and mani-pedi at the mall?"

Even though I'm not much into that kind of stuff, I know she's really trying to fit in some girl time with me, which I appreciate considering I never see her and what I found out last night so I agree.

Mom squeals like a little kid at a Hannah Montana concert. "Great!"

Two hours later, I'm wearing the only pink article of clothing I have, a tube top that Cara bought for me last year on my birthday, and a pair of short shorts that Mom insisted I wear because it's so hot out. The only thing that resembles me are my signature black converse.

"Are you ready to go?" asks Mom as we get into her car, a sleek hybrid-something-or-other. She keeps telling me what type of car it is but I'm not that good with cars, so I always nod and mumble to give a semblance of caring.

As we pull out of the driveway, that stupid feeling of being watched has to pop up and no matter how hard I try to ignore it, it just won't go away. I close my eyes for an instant, and when I open them, Mom's slamming on the breaks, swearing.

"What is it?" I ask, confused and more than a little startled.

"I thought I saw somebody in the road. I guess not. It looked like that kid from your school…what was his name, Daniel or something? Though I don't know what he'd be doing running around out here during a school day. Damn near got himself killed."

"You mean Damien." I mumble.

Shuddering, I remember the day in the cafeteria when he grabbed my hand a little too hard and the way he looked at me as if I were a puzzle, as if I were something…I don't know. I haven't spoken to him since, anyway.

"Weird," I say as we turn into the mall parking lot. "Maybe he found out he was adopted too."

"Not funny," says Mom, but she laughs.

As soon as one of the spa-workers sees my nails, she titters and says, "You shouldn't bite such nice nails!" and starts vigorously filing them down to make them even. Apparently Mom's nails are perfect though, because they praise hers as if they're gold. They work on our hands first, filing them down, and then treating our cuticles. Afterwards, they let them soak in some type of liquid, and then they paint them with colours of our choice. Of course I chose black, making mom roll her eyes at me, but she keeps her mouth shut which I appreciate.

When they're done with our hands, they work on our feet, going through the same type of process with the nails, but taking all of the dead skin off of the bottoms of the soles. It tickles a little bit, but mostly, I enjoy the experience, and leave with a couple of bottles of nail polish that Mom insisted she get for me.

As we're walking through the mall, browsing, Mom decides to do a little Q and A session with me about school.

"So," she asks, "I hear you're passing French?" She asks all jokey, because she knows that it's one of my best subjects.

I nod. "Yeah, and all of my other classes too. Okay, well maybe not Gym, but there's still time to make it up."

"Is there anybody you *like*?" She asks, eyeing me with that you'd-better-tell-me-young-lady look that all mothers give. *What is it with moms?*

"No," I say a little too quickly, because she asks, "Who is it?"

I keep trying to avoid her gaze until finally she says, "It's Damien isn't it? He's a nice boy I like him. But he should be in school instead of running around in the middle of the road."

I shake my head, "No, it isn't. It's," how do I explain this, "somebody who doesn't go to my school. His name is Cael, and-" of course as I'm saying this, Cael walks around the corner and bumps right into me.

"Khiara!" he says, as he helps me up. "I thought you had school today?"

Mom's eyes get that wicked twinkle they get when she's excited about something, "She needed some time off," she reaches out her hand to shake his.

"Cael," he says as they shake and she looks over at me with that *stupid* eye-twinkle and introduces herself. "I'm Khiara's adoptive mother, Miranda."

"The only mother I've ever known and the best one in the world at that," I nudge her with a smile. I don't want things to be different between us and I want her to know that.

If he's surprised he doesn't show it. Cael becomes the perfect gentleman. "It's nice to meet you Mrs. Banning. It's going to be great having Khiara as an employee at the café." *Crap, I forgot to tell her about that...*

Mom thwacks me on my arm playfully. "*Oh!* Khiara didn't mention that she'd gotten a job! How wonderful! And especially since she's going to be working for such a nice boy such as you, Cael. And, please, call me Miranda, Mrs. Banning is so formal!"

Oh God, Mom.

"Well, we'd better get going, right Mom?" I pipe up, feeling intensely awkward. I need to get out of here right now.

Mom waves my away with her hand, "Nonsense, Khiara. I'd like to get to know your boss more."

"But we have that thing to go to." Again with the lame excuse! I need to get better at lying. "We don't want to be late."

Mom looks a little disappointed and Cael's trying to hold back laughter. "Well, it was nice meeting you, Mrs. - I mean, Miranda. See you around, Khiara. Are you free later on today maybe? We could have a proper *interview* since we had to cut our last one so short." Mom giggles at the way he says interview and I resist the embarrassing urge to happy dance in front of them both.

"She's free," says Mom, just as I'm about to answer, and as he walks off waving, she says, "You've got a boyfriend!"

"I'll call you later today! Oh, and by the way, I got your message last night. I'm glad you think my cake is fabulously-fantastic, Khiara." Cael says as he disappears around the corner. Oh man, so that's what I said. I silently thank the powers that be for the fact that I didn't say anything worse.

"He's not really my boyfriend…we've only met like, three times counting today," I mumble, my face turning red as she dances all around me. I didn't know my mother could be so…squeaky.

She says, "Well he should be, he's so nice! And handsome too," I shove my palm into my face, "and that Irish accent! So *lovely*!" Everything she's saying is true but I'm too embarrassed to admit it to her so instead, I just lead the way to the car.

Nine

Of course, when we get home Mom helps (forces) me get ready for my date before she leaves for work. I refuse to think of it as such until my phone rings, displaying Cael's number.

"Cael?" I answer, at the same time he says, "Khiara?" We both go silent and then laugh a little awkwardly.

It's Cael who talks first. "So," pause, "are you still up for that," long pause, "uhh…"

Oh my God, it is a date! Calm down calm down…Oh my God!
"Yeah," I say, trying to sound nonchalant, but my voice betrays me and I can hear Cael chuckle quietly on the other end. "I'm definitely up to it."

I run my tongue over my lips, trying my best not to lick off the lip-gloss Mom forced me to put on as Cael says, "Where do you want to meet? I can always pick you up, but only if you're okay with that."

"That sounds good. I live on McKinley Avenue. My house is the only house with shutters and a wraparound porch."

I can practically hear his smile through the phone, "I've passed by it a few times. I know the one."

"Good," I whisper.

"Yeah, good," he replies, also in a hushed voice. "I'll pick you up in about an hour."

Fifteen minutes later, the doorbell rings and I practically skip all the way to the door from the living room. As I get to the door, something stops me from opening it right away. Not only did Cael say he'd pick me up in an hour or so, but I also have that stupid creepy feeling nagging at the back of my brain. I feel watched, stalked even. And not at all safe.

I open the door reluctantly and only poke my head out. Damien is standing there, holding a whole bunch of papers and a tin of cookies. He's wearing a black suit as if he weren't headed home from school, but towards somewhere extravagant, somewhere extremely fancy.

"Hey," he says all smiles and good looks. "Can I come in for a second? I brought your homework and some notes. Cara offered to do it, but I said that since we live so close to each other, and it was on my way, it would be no big deal. I hope you don't mind."

My heart slows down and I open the door wider, "Sure, why not." I don't know why, but Damien makes me nervous in a way nobody *ever* has before. I kind of associate him with shadows, mysterious and out of reach. Like if I tried to grab for him, there would be nothing but air in my hands. I realize that sounds kind of strange, but nothing else seems to fit a good description for him.

He comes right in, and as he passes by me in the small doorway, I supress the urge to shudder. Internally though, my guts are completely twisted, making me feel like I'm going to vomit. "So, how much homework do I have?" I attempt to keep my tone as light as possible.

Damien smiles and walks into my kitchen like he's been here millions of times, when really this is his first time, and puts the cookie box on the counter next to the fridge. Damien reaches into the fridge and pulls out a Moxie cola, my last one actually (I go through about four cans a day sometimes) and pops it open. I'm too jittery to say anything about his boldness, and I rub my arm awkwardly. He takes a long swig from the can and burps when he's done. "Excuse me for my rudeness, but I was dying for a drink and niceties were not on my mind. Where were we? Homework, right."

Damien hands me the papers, "These are the notes Cara took for you. She photocopied a couple of other student's notes as well, but took extra detailed ones for you. You miss one day of school and Cara really goes all out for you. Got her taking notes, Banning, maybe you should stop going to school altogether!"

His words are amicable, there's no hint of contempt in them, but I still feel like he was implying something else with those words. He tries to laugh good naturedly but it sounds tinny to me, fake. *Forced.*

I look over the papers and smile at Cara's efforts despite my mood. I'll have to make a note to thank her later, take her out to lunch or something. Damien's eyes lock on mine as I glance up and he smirks at me and raises his eyebrows as if he were asking me a question. "What?" I find myself asking, my voice trembling as he continues to smirk at me.

Damien steps towards me, much too close, and he tucks a lock of my hair behind my ear. "I make you nervous, Khiara. Why is that? Have I ever done anything to offend you? I really like you. In fact – and you can't tell Victoria or she'll kill me – I've kind of got a little crush on you."

I gasp.

His smirk widens into a grin. "It's a silly infatuation, really. But you interest me. I find myself watching you from across the class; I know you've noticed. I'm not going to hurt you, Khiara, like you seem to think and don't try to deny it, I can read body language pretty well. I just…want to get to know you."

"I don't believe you," I whisper, and his eyes grow hard, his smile drops right off of his face. "You seem absolutely in love with Victoria and you've *never* given me any indication that you…feel that way about me."

He shakes his head and puts his hand over his chest. "You have my Scout's honour that all I want to do is be your friend, to get to know you. I mean I thought we were on the path to being friends already but I guess you've been a little conflicted. Please, don't worry. Will you please let me be your friend? I think I could show you a whole new side to life that you'd really enjoy."

No, I think. *There's something off about you.*

The doorbell rings just as I open my mouth to say something – I don't know what – and his face grows hard, his jaw becoming clenched. "You should answer that. It might be important."

I practically jog to the door and am relieved when I see that it's Cael. He's dressed in a normal green t-shirt with black jeans and his hair is messier than ever though I can tell he's tried to tame in into submission by the way he keeps patting it down. His unassuming clothing alone is enough to make me smile but the way he fusses over his hair honestly brightens my mood.

"Hey," I say.

Cael grins, "Hi. Sorry I'm a wee bit late, the car was giving me trouble." He peers around my shoulder at Damien, his expression becoming blank.

Turning around, I gesture to Damien, "I believe you two already know each other?"

Damien's face looks like he's tasted something sour, while Cael looks impassive. Cael reaches his hand out to shake Damien's, "Yes, we've met... *before*." I can't help but notice how he stresses the word before, like it holds something deep inside it. "We were good friends once. We grew up together."

Damien rolls his eyes and snorts, as if the story made him remember things he'd rather not, "Well, yes, but that was a long time ago. Things were different than they are now. I suppose I'd better leave you two at it then?" I wonder what could have happened for them to stop being friends.

"What happened?" I ask. Mentally, I smack myself. Why, oh why, do I have to blurt things out at such awkward moments? Damien motions to Cael to tell the story, looking weary about it.

He smiles a sad smile, "Well," Cael begins, "I guess we just got on the opposite sides of a fight we didn't know much about at first. We didn't really have a choice. It's hard to explain. We were young and stupid. Anyway, it's whatever now. No need to talk about it and ruin our d-" he pauses, "our day, hmm?" He almost said date. Almost. But he didn't.

Damien nods his head, smiles, and claps me on the shoulder, and turns to Cael. "Well, have a great time. Be careful with this one. She's pretty *special*." *Gosh, I feel dirty somehow...*

Cael's warm, strong hand finds its way to mine and he nods as Damien heads out the door and onto the street. "I will," he calls, "She's safe with me. Don't you worry."

~*~

Cael insisted on opening the passenger side door of his car for me. I tried to say no but he opened it anyway, helping me get in, ever the gentleman. Right now, we're still parked in front of my house, the engine idling. Cael smiles and says, "So, where do you want to go?" I shrug and tell him anywhere is fine by me, but he persists.

"There's nowhere at all you've got in mind? Like a *park* or something."

"Well, there is a park that I really like to go to, it's sort of a special place but it's kind of far from here, and we have to walk over a bridge. Have you been Facebook stalking me? How did you know?" I joke, but there's a slight amount of real curiosity in my words, because surely I didn't tell him about my special place, and even on Facebook, I only liked the park's page.

He laughs, "Cara swiped my number from your phone, apparently. Your mom called Cara and told her about tonight, and since Cara had taken my number down like a pro, she called me and told me where you might like to go. No stalking on my part, and I don't even own a Facebook account. There're too many people I'd rather not interact with." Well now I know why she took such awesome notes for me!

I feel my face turn three shades of crimson, "Oh…I'm going to kill her for taking my phone! This isn't the first time she's done this to me." One time, when Cara found out I had a crush on a boy named Jonathan in seventh grade she tracked him down and asked for his number. She managed to take my phone away from me in first period Math and slipped it back in right when the bell rang, and I caught her with her hand in my purse.

Another time, she wanted pizza, and knew that I had the number for Dominos on my phone. We were at a party, and she was drunk out of her mind, but she managed to take my phone from my pocket without me even noticing until I reached for it and it was gone. I spent half the party looking for my phone and as soon as the doorbell rang, Cara jumped up from the couch mid make-out session, handed me my phone, and went to pay for the pizza. The action itself explained the situation and I almost hope she choked on her food. That is, until I got some pizza in me and everything was forgiven.

"Facebook isn't worth the drama it brings. I hate social networking sites but they're so addictive, really." I say, as Cael starts the car.

He smiles at me and says, "So, can you take me to your special place? I kind of brought a picnic."

I feel my cheeks pull into what I think must be a pretty stupid grin. "Awesome," I say. "I'd love to show you my special hang out."

Twenty minutes later, we've parked the car, and we're walking across Pipton Bridge that leads to Elmridge Park. Not many people use the bike portion of the bridge because it's so high up, and there's a portion of it that's kind of broken. It's just a small part of the barrier that keeps the car and bike path separate but it makes most people nervous, so they rarely take this path. That never stops me and Cara or a couple of other nature lovers, though for the most part we're usually the only ones in the park.

Elmridge Park is on an island or sorts (a really, really small one) just off of Serene Falls, so the bridge we're on has a lot of water underneath it from the river and I've always wondered what would happen if I fell off.

Towards the end of the bridge near the island there are lots of rocks, and I know that if I was to fall there I wouldn't survive, or if I did I'd be seriously injured. I shudder at the thought and Cael misinterprets my shudder as me being cold so he stops walking, takes off his sweater and offers it to me. I slip it on gladly, not wanting to explain my thoughts. It's better that he thinks that I was cold.

Tying my hair up with an elastic band I usually keep on my wrist as the wind picks up, I smile brightly at him. "Thanks," I say. "You didn't have to do that. What if you get cold?"

Cael shrugs and runs his fingers through his black locks. "I don't get cold very easily. I have a high tolerance to it. It takes a lot for me to feel cold."

I smile and nod my head a little too enthusiastically, "Yeah, Cara is the same way. She could run around bare naked in the snow and not even have one goose bump."

His face grows thoughtful but he still has a small smile on his face. "That's pretty interesting. I don't know if I could do that. Maybe she's not human."

Laughing, I smack his arm playfully, "I've said the same thing to her before. That she's not human. She finds it hilarious and always declares that she's a werecat, you know, like a werewolf but only a cat. They're her favourite animal and she has one - I'm sure you saw him at the party, he's hard to miss. His name is Missus Pussy pants? He's this big ball of white fur." Aaand, I'm rambling.

He stops walking, "Are you nervous about something?" *Crap.*

"No?" I say, making my answer sound more like a question than anything. And the truth is I'm not sure why I'm nervous. I guess today has been a really hard day and in light of a creepy visit from Damien and my morbid thoughts about falling off the bridge, I'm just… anxious. But I can't really explain all of that to him so I smile and hope he'll brush it off. He doesn't.

A stubborn piece of hair falls into his eyes and he runs his fingers through his messy locks and frowns. "Did I do something wrong?" Of course he'd think he did something wrong!

I stop in my tracks, turn around to face him and put both hands on his shoulders. "No, no. You've been perfect, Cael. It's just -" here we go, "it's just that today has been a very tough day for me. I actually just found out that I was adopted this morning which is why my mother was acting so weird by introducing herself as my *adoptive* mother and why I didn't go to class today."

His eyes grow wide, "I am so sorry, I -" but I cut him off with a quick kiss on the cheek which instantly turns his face bright red. "Don't be. Now let's go before the day ends."

Once we reach the end of the bridge, I'm grinning like an idiot because we're holding hands, talking and laughing about simple things. We walk past the gate (there's a wrought iron gate at this end of the bridge because you're only supposed to be there during the day but it's never locked after hours) and towards my favourite spot. It's a small man made waterfall with a rock ledge over it to sit on and dangle your feet into the water above a pond where there's always geese and ducks to feed. I assume the waterfall is fed by a pump somewhere underground that takes water from the river to the pond and back to the river through another pump. Apple trees and intricately carved wooden benches surround the area of the pond, and the little waterfall is surrounded by rosebushes.

When we get to the waterfall, Cael reaches into his picnic basket and produces a soft looking blue blanket then proceeds to place it on the rock ledge so we can sit. I used to think that water would splash up onto the rock but Cara pointed out to me that it was designed to avoid that. It's a beautiful design, really, and I can tell Cael thinks the same as his eyes roam over the area appreciatively.

Once we sit down, he hands me the basket, grinning a lazy smile. "It's nothing fancy, I have to warn you. Cakes are my specialty, not sandwiches, but I tried."

I reach in and pull out a brown bag, which I assume holds the sandwiches. I open it up and the enticing scent of roast beef wafts out. I reach for a sandwich, which is made with big egg-bread buns, and take off the top piece of bread. Inside, it's stuffed with roast beef, lettuce, Swiss cheese, and tomatoes. Upon closer inspection, I see mustard on the piece of bread I'm holding and grin. I love mustard.

"I think you're going to have to add sandwiches to your menu, Cael, because this is absolutely to die for!" I exclaim, taking a monster bite and revelling in the amazing taste. As I chew, Cael laughs.

"All I did was stick some stuff into a bun and hoped for the best. I guess I have a lot of free time to perfect my culinary skills, but for now I think I'll stick to cakes and pastries," he says, watching me take another bite, or rather, stuffing as much as I possibly can into my mouth, with an amused expression. This makes me suddenly very aware of how I must look.

I swallow, wipe my mouth, and accidentally burp a little too loud for it to be considered lady like. "Oh…excuse me…I, uhh, I'm not usually this disgusting when I eat." *Yes you are…*

Cael shrugs it off with a wave of his hand, but I can tell he's fighting laughter. "No, that's okay. I find it kind of nice, considering I made that sandwich with the hopes that it would at least be edible. You're enjoying it and I'm glad." He runs his fingers through his hair and a small part of me recognizes that gesture as so, completely *Cael.*

I realize that he's not eating his own sandwich and I ask him why, not wanting to be rude, but feeling supremely awkward to be the only one eating, like a pig I might add. "I'm not very hungry. I eat at odd hours. I hope you don't mind. But, that being said I will have something to drink." He pulls out a thermos from the basket, and I wonder what's inside.

"This," he says as he unscrews the lid of the thermos, "is my victory coffee. You didn't even have to treat me to it. Simply being with you here in your special place is enough. Want some?" I do. Put that way, coffee sounds very enticing. I nod my head and gladly accept the cup he hands me from the basket and watch as he pours the hot liquid into it.

I take a small sip and then a bigger one. After I swallow my third sip, "Mmm, this is good!" I marvel.

He nods and sips his own coffee, content to stay quiet. As we sip our steaming cups, the sun slowly begins to go down and the lamps in the park turn on, one by one. After a while the stars are visible and we're sitting on the rock, looking up at the sky. As I finish my second cup of coffee, I put the cup down beside me and lay down on my back.

"Come, lay down with me. Let's look at the stars the proper star-gazer way. All of the pros recommend it," I say, with the hint of a yawn at the end of my sentence. I'm fighting it though. *I will not be tired! I will not give in!*

Cael lies down next to me, abandoning his coffee, and sighs as he looks up into the night sky. "It reminds me of home. You can see the stars perfectly where I'm from."

"Ireland?"

He takes a long time to answer me, but when he does, it's very quiet and I almost miss it. "Yeah, Ireland."

My hand finds its way to his and I'm glad when he accepts it. His hand is warm and his grip isn't strong, but it's comforting. I can tell that it could be strong if I needed it to be. But he's being careful. I squeeze his hand and turn to him and he squeezes back and turns to face me. We stare at each other for what feels like forever and it's nice.

Cael finally breaks the silence when he asks, so very quietly, "Do you believe in love at first sight?"

Blushing, I answer him. "Sometimes, why?" This is deep territory and even though I really like him, we just met and are already moving so fast.

"I know a story," he says. "It's about an angel who fell in love with a human. Would you like to hear it?"

I nod and a rush of relief flows through me as I realize he was just prefacing his story.

"His name was Camael, his calling was divine justice and love, and he was a very powerful Archangel. One day, as he was watching upon Earth, he came across a small village of farmers where a little girl had just been born. This little girl's soul was the brightest, most pure soul that had ever graced the earth and he found her so very beautiful." Cael's eyes have taken on this faraway look, almost as if he were living the story and not just telling it.

"You see, after Lucifer Fell from Heaven, there was a prophesy that the purest soul on Earth would be the one to bring the Great Battle between the sides of good and evil. All of the angels who had fallen and were repentant would be able to go home to Heaven if they so choose and the un-repentant would be forced to reside in Hell, having no choice to remain on earth at all."

"Camael fell in love with the girl as she grew older because as an angel he could see everything she could be, everything she could do, and it was *magnificent*. But God grew angry with him, for he was not supposed to love any human in that way. He was just supposed to do his duties."

I find myself gasping at how unjust that seems. Cael continues. "So he was banished from Heaven, and down to Earth. By the time he got there, nine days had passed since he'd last seen the child. He woke up weak, in a crater his body had created upon impact just outside of the girl's village, and though he was bloody and naked as a new born baby, he walked until he reached the village. It was the dead of night when he was found by the town's priest, who took him in. There he was cared for until he was strong enough to walk around town. The first two days he walked, he didn't see the girl and her family but on the third day – on the third day, what he saw was terrible. From a little house, her mother, father and older sister emerged, their faces stricken."

"What happened?" I ask my heart racing.

"She died. The girl's young soul had been reclaimed, and it was Camael's fault. He staggered back to his room in the priest's house only to find Naarai, the angel of children, waiting for him, holding the child's beautiful soul in her arms. It looked just like her, for the body is only a shell which carries our true essence. 'You should not be here,' he whispered to her."

"'I thought you might want to say goodbye. I know how you loved her.' Naarai responded." Cael squeezes my hand and I realize his words have moved me to tears.

"He began to cry and was confused at what this feeling was but when Naarai handed him the girl, he stopped. Her soul was sleeping peacefully, nestled in his arms. 'She will be brought back to His folds, Camael. God will not punish her any more for your mistake. The world is simply not ready for the Battle, and I suspect Father has other, hidden reasons as to the timing of her departure from the living realm just as you seem to have entered into it.'"

"Camael nodded. 'Why do I feel such despair? Is that what it is, to be human? To have water leak from my eyes and to feel…what is this?' he asked, his hand going to his heart as he handed the child back to her. Naarai smiled kindly, just as the priest walked into the room, unsurprised at the sight of the angel holding the baby."

"'It is heartbreak,' he said to Camael, 'it is human.' And then Camael finally understood. He was one of the Fallen. Cursed with a human-like body, he would live forever and he would not age. If he was wounded he would heal almost right away, the only thing left would be the blood that was shed. He could not die a *mortal* death."

"Naarai looked upon Camael one last time before taking the girl who had awakened and was staring up at him in wonder, and disappeared back into the folds of God, leaving him alone with the priest. 'You are repentant,' the priest said, patting him on the arm, 'I see that in you. Come let us pray for your forgiveness together.' Years passed and still Camael thought of the girl. He truly loved her because he could see her for who she was before even truly *knowing* her. He had truly looked upon her that one time and had fallen in love forever."

"Cael," I whisper. "That was beautiful. Where did you hear that?"

He smiles his sad smile, and squeezes my hand. "It's an old story and I…can't remember where I heard it." There was something hidden in those words but I don't want to question him about it. It feels invasive, somehow.

We sit there in the dark, holding hands and reflecting. Suddenly, I ache to know why he told me that story and asked if I believe in love at first sight. So I ask him. At first, he seems hesitant to tell me the answer, but then his signature smile dances across his lips and I can tell that he's going to elaborate. "I was just wondering, Khiara, if you would think it was worth it."

"I do," I whisper, looking into his eyes, trying to find something in them. "I feel like if I loved someone enough, I'd risk everything I had to be with them, absolutely."

"Me too," he says. For just a second, I can see something there, behind his eyes; something too deep, sad, and ancient to belong to anybody our age. But just as quickly as I glimpse it, it's gone, replaced by an emotion I can't quite place.

Cael sits up abruptly, letting go of my hand to run both of his own through his hair in a nervous gesture. "Damn," he says. My spine begins to tingle and the hairs on the back of my neck stand at attention. I get that familiar feeling, the one that brings dread into the pit of my stomach every time. The feeling of being watched by…

something. Cael almost growls, low under his breath, surprising me with the sound.

Alarmed, I ask, "What? Is everything okay?" *I know damn well it's not okay!*

He stands up and reaches down to pull me up as well, bringing our faces quite close. I stand there, a little stunned by the sudden close proximity of our lips and I can tell that it's distracting him as well, because he licks his lips a little and shuffles back nervously. "We should go. It's getting late, and uhh, tomorrow's still a week day. Don't want to be late for school because you slept in, do you? Also, your first shift at the café starts tomorrow."

I shake my head reluctantly, "I guess so…" but I'm not letting him off that easily. Picking up the basket, I sigh. I have to jog to catch up with his fast pace as he begins to walk towards the bridge, and once I do catch up, he grabs onto my hand and starts to run, me awkwardly tripping behind him as we make our way to the gate. As soon as we get close enough to see it, my heart speeds up; it's closed. Cael makes a sound between a sigh and a growl and I turn to him, still out of breath from running and whisper, "It's probably not locked. It's not past park hours yet."

He shakes his head, "No, it is. I can see the lock." Sure enough, when I squint, there it is. *Well crap. This is weird.*

"We're going to have to climb it," I say, resigned. I have climbed a few gates in my lifetime, all thanks to Cara, but this one looks a little harder than the ones I'm used to. Usually the gates are at least a couple of feet smaller, and are generally just gates to somebodies backyard or the school gate. Cara loves to go to school after hours for some reason.

With a look of surprise as if he hadn't thought of it, Cael sizes me up and nods once, "Right. We'll climb it then. But hurry, we don't want to get stuck here do we?"

No, we don't… I think to myself and Cael looks up like he heard what I said, but quickly looks back at the gate as if to dismiss having heard anything. "I'll go first," he says, but the way he looks at me is like he's asking my permission, so I say, "Yeah, sure." He begins to climb, and oh what an amazing climber he is! He's better than drunken Cara any day of the week.

As soon as he's at the top, Cael reaches his arm out. "Start climbing, Khiara. Hurry up, we don't have much time." When I get close enough to hold onto his hand, he hauls me up effortlessly and we jump to the ground together, hands entwined. He takes off running, pulling me with him and doesn't slow down until we're halfway across the bridge leading to the car. I'm so out of breath but Cael seems to be breathing laboriously for some other, unnamed reason.

"What were we running from," I ask between pants for air, my hands on my knees and head down.

Cael stiffens and forces out a quick laugh, "What do you mean?"

"The park isn't supposed to be closed for another hour and even then, they hardly ever lock the gate." I place my hand on his arm and squeeze. "You made us run like bats out of hell," he scoffs at that, "and, okay, I'll admit- I was getting this terrible watched feeling. I've been writing it off as nothing for far too long; it happens too much for it not to be real."

Cael's head whips around at this, and he says "Watched feeling?"

I feel my cheeks burn crimson. "Yeah. I've been getting it a lot lately, though I've noticed it for most of my life. I feel like somebody is watching me and their intent is not at all…good. I felt that just before things got weird back there."

Cael's eyes are hard but they soften as he looks into mine. "Do you feel it now?"

My voice is just a thin whisper as the hair on my neck stands up and my palms grow sweaty, but I manage to get out something that resembles a "yes" before he nods his head and takes my hand. "We need to get going," he says gently, "I promise I'll explain everything later. Okay?"

Cael walks me to my door. "Some first date eh?" he says sarcastically, as he rubs his arms. I realize that I'm wearing his jacket and move to take it off, but he smiles and shakes his head, "No, you keep it for now."

"What happened, Cael?" I ask, my voice trembling slightly.

He shakes his head, "It's complicated. I don't really know where to begin."

"You're not, like, a vampire are you?" I blurt.

His eyes become amused and he smirks, "Decidedly, no I am not. I'd rather not sparkle. If anything, I'd love to radiate a really cool glow or something that could overpower evil just by looking at it, I mean how cool would that be? It's simple but effective."

I duck my head, "Sorry about the stupid question. I just needed something to…"

"Fill the awkward silence?" he supplies.

"Yeah," I whisper. He brings his hands up to cup my face and his expression is unreadable, "I am involved in some really heavy things, Khiara, and with some pretty dangerous… individuals. I'm worried that it might get in the way of…"

Any chance for there to be anything between us, I think, knowing what's coming next. He's going to tell me why we're not going to work out in excruciating detail and I'm going to have to buy a pint of ice cream and call Cara to come over and comfort me.

That's not what he says. "But I want to give us a chance anyway. I want to get to know you and I want you to get to know me. But my life…it isn't an easy one. I have a lot of secrets."

"There's something about you," I say. "It's…"

"I'm not a vampire, Khiara," he chuckles.

"But you're something."

He looks me right in the eyes and whispers, "I'm me. And that is all I will ever be."

I remember the day we met, him telling me it wasn't safe for him to stay with me, that he wasn't supposed to be talking to me. He'd quickly covered it up by saying it was because he wasn't invited, but now that I think about it, half the people there probably weren't invited and they didn't seem to give a damn about that.

"I feel safe with you," I whisper. "I don't know why, but I do. I can't explain it."

His mouth quirks into a half smile, "Well, Khiara, I'll do everything possible to keep you safe; if you let me."

"I will," I whisper and he kisses me on the cheek, ever so softly.

"Good night, Khiara. I'll see you tomorrow at work."

Ten

The screaming won't stop! I'm in a hall of mirrors and a choice must be made- which way do I take? I can't concentrate with all of the screaming going on, and for some reason, I feel like whichever way I take will kill me in the end. My death is inevitable. "You must choose," *a strange female voice booms. I look left, and the screaming that's coming from all around me intensifies. I look the other way, and it gets even louder.* "There is only one way," *the voice purrs.*

"Death is inevitable." *The mirror closest to me starts to shake, the glass looking as if it were made of water, and then a dark form steps from it - a man. He seems to be completely made of shadow, and he is absolutely terrifying. I seem to be stuck in place, unable to move as he takes hold of my arm and his somewhat familiar voice drifts to my ears, a terrifying whisper of pure evil,* "Your time is up…"

I wake up feeling like I've been doused with a big bucket of cold water. My heart is beating erratically in my chest and my eyes can't help but dart around the room, looking for the dark things that have plagued me in my dreams. Actually, I feel around and notice that in fact I do happen to be wet; slick with a cold sweat that must have occurred during the bizarre nightmare I've just awakened from.

Sighing, I reach over to my bedside table to turn on my lamp and gasp at the time; it's three in the morning. I turn the light on, and make my way to my door and stop dead in my tracks when I hear a noise coming from the direction of my window. Turning around slowly, I scrunch my eyes shut and resolve not to freak out when I open them. It's probably a tree branch I think to myself. When I open my eyes, my heart stops at the sight before me. Damien is staring at me very intently through my window. I feel his stare like it's a cold, ugly hand tracing its way all over my body – defiling me.

He smiles and in the blink of an eye, disappears from sight. That's when everything goes black and I feel myself crumpling to the cold, hard floor.

~*~

When I wake up, the only thing that runs through my mind is, *my head hurts a lot. Holy crap my head hurts. Why does my head hurt?*

"How did you get on the floor?" asks Cara, who is standing in the doorway to my room eating an apple and staring at me in confusion.

I yawn tiredly and shake my head. "I don't know. More importantly," I groan as I sit up, rubbing my head, "who let you in and what are you doing up at this ungodly hour?"

Cara snorts indignantly. "We have this thing to go to, you know, school." *Oops...*

"Right," I mutter. I stand up, stretching my arms out and cracking all the good spots in my shoulders and back, and yawn again. "Thanks." She smiles and taps her wrist, "We don't want to be late. Hop in the shower, I'll make breakfast. Both your parents left for work but your dad said that he wasn't working late tonight, so he'll be home when you get back from your first day on the job to grill you for details."

~*~

Try not to make eye contact, try not to make eye contact- "Welcome to the Sweet Treat Café, what would you like today?" So far, my first day on the job has been pretty slow and of course Cara and Tristan are standing right at the counter, looking at me like proud parents. Would that make Tristan my step-dad? I chuckle at the thought.

"Can I get a butt-latté?" asks Cara, with the most serious look on her face I have ever seen. Our eyes meet and she bursts out laughing while Tristan says, "God damn it, Cara! I told you not to do that to the poor girl, it's her first day." I just smile, trying to hold in my laughter.

"Sorry," she says, her face turning red from laughter, "I couldn't resist," and I roll my eyes because her mascara is running down her cheeks her eyes are watering so much.

"Tristan, believe me, it's okay. I'll just spit in her drink," I say, and Cara instantly sobers as I say, "Now, what'll you be having so I can hawk a giant one *right* in it."

"You wouldn't," she says, grabbing a napkin from the counter to wipe her eyes, just as Cael walks up to the counter with a fresh strawberry cheesecake for me to put on display. He smiles at Cara and asks, "She wouldn't what?" then turns and winks at me, like he knows what we were talking about.

"Nothing!" both Cara and I say, at the same time as Tristan says, "Spit in her coffee." Cara smacks her boyfriend on the shoulder, and I glare at him. Cael just laughs, hands me the cake, and says, "Well, don't provoke her then." I place the cake inside the cake rack under the counter, and sigh. When I come up, Cael's smirking at Cara.

Cara gets a wicked glint in her eye, "Ooh! He's a keeper, Ki-Ki. Boy's got a sense of humour. We could definitely use him in our little group." Cael laughs and says, "That's good to know."

I look over at him, "Are you sure you can handle her? She's pretty wild." Cara frowns and sticks her tongue out at me and says, "Get me my latte, woman. I'm thirsty. You know how I like 'em."

I nod my head and roll my eyes at her and turn to Tristan, "And what would you like today?"

"Just a regular coffee would be great, thanks," he says, smiling, "I don't want to make your life any more complicated than it is."

"I *should* charge you fifty dollars, but that'll be eight dollars and fifty cents instead, please," I say, holding out my hand. Tristan hands me ten dollars and says, "Keep the change because you deserve the good tip for *exemplary* service." I roll my eyes.

After I ring up their purchases, I make Cara's - because only staff is allowed to use the latté machine lest anybody get burned messing up, and they stay a while to chat, marvelling at how awesome the café is, how cool it is that they can add whatever they want to their drinks and not get charged. Business begins to pick up not long after they leave half an hour later, albeit grudgingly since Cael ended up giving them free cake.

Near closing time, Cael's watching the front counter while I'm clearing off the tables when I pick up Victoria's familiar voice. I look in the direction of her voice and am shocked that she's standing at the counter, smiling away like her and Cael are privy to a joke that nobody else is.

"Hey there *Cael*," she says, sounding rather amused at something.

"*Victoria*," he replies, using the same tone of voice. "What can I get for you today?"

"I need something strong. You know, like a double espresso or something," she replies, smiling at him as if they were old friends. I guess it's very possible, if he and Damien used to be friends I'm sure they know each other by the way they sound so familiar with one another. I can't help but wonder who would want to be friends with a snotty bit - I mean girl like her.

"Ah," replies Cael, smiling at her with warmth that shocks me, "that I can definitely do." He moves to ring up her order, but unfortunately (for me) catches my eye doing so and Victoria follows his gaze, frowning when she sees me.

"Oh," she says in my direction, "I didn't see you, Khiara"

I give the table closest to me a half-hearted wipe and mumble, "That's okay I've been pretty busy."

Her frown deepens and she walks over to me, her blue eyes looking suddenly troubled, "No, I should have noticed you sooner. Sorry about that. I was a little preoccupied myself though, I guess."

"Right," I say, not quite knowing what to say. I pull my hair up into a pony tail and sigh then awkwardly gesture back to the table. "Well, I have to get back to work." She nods, satisfied – though her eyes remain troubled – and walks back towards Cael.

"Well," she says to him, her tone less light-hearted and jokey than before, "I guess I'd better get my ass in gear. I've got *somebody* waiting for me." I keep wiping the table like it's my lifeline and look anywhere but in their direction. I'm sure she's talking about Damien. "Here's your espresso," I hear Cael say and then he says something lower, something that I can't quite catch. It almost doesn't sound English and has a beautiful lilt to it. I begin to wonder what it is he said to her but try to ignore the pull of curiosity.

When about ten or so minutes pass, all of a sudden I feel a light tap on my shoulder. I turn to find Cael behind me smirking rather amusedly. His blue eyes sparkle with a laughter that he's trying to rein in.

"What?"

"If you keep wiping that table," he says, "you're going to go straight through it."

I look down and mumble, "To China. That was my plan."

Cael lets his laughter out and takes the cloth from me, "How was your first day on the job? That was officially the last customer of opening day!"

"It was great," I say, "I absolutely love working here. And it helps that my boss isn't a total asshole."

"That does help," he chuckles, but then stops and runs his fingers through his hair. "*Total* asshole? So does that mean I'm just a regular one then?"

"Let me take my foot out of my mouth and get back to you on that." I don't think it's possible for my face to get any redder.

Cael chuckles, reaches out and strokes my cheek, sending a trail of goose bumps where his hand gently touches my skin. "It's cute when you blush."

"Is it?" I whisper.

He blushes himself, "Yeah, it is."

"You know," I say, "I feel like I've known you forever. Talking to you is so easy."

Cael's smile fades for just a second as his eyes roam my face, "Forever," he says. He leans in real close and taps my nose. "You're right."

Eleven

As soon as I get home, Dad grills me about my new job (and about Cael) over dinner. But eventually he gives in and lets me go upstairs once he realizes that I'm not about to give away too much about my new relationship, if that's even what it is. Pug runs ahead of me and jumps up onto my bed as I enter my room and I sit down next to him then pat him on the head. Pug growls playfully as he wags his little tail, all cheerful and ready to play.

"Do you wanna take a walk?" I ask, as I suddenly hop up off the bed. "I think somebody wants to take a walk!" He growls and jumps up and down in place, confirming that yes, he definitely wants a walk.

Walking backwards towards my door, I gesture with my hands for Pug to follow, and he complies with full gusto practically flying off the bed and landing right in front of me. "Good boy, Puggles."

He barks in response.

As we walk down the stairs – more like I stumble down the stairs as Pug tries to trip me – my phone vibrates from my back pocket and Cara's ringtone echoes through the halls. Sighing, I pull out my phone.

"To what do I owe this phone call?"

She puffs out an overdramatic breath which sounds rather irritating over the phone. "I just wanted to call you to, you know, talk. But now that you mention it I do have something to ask you. I have to study this weekend at the library and I wanted to know if you were down to come. You could, you know, read and whatever while I plod through my Science textbook."

A smile tugs at my lips as Pug stares up at me adorably. "I'll come, yeah. What time do you want to meet up?"

"Pick me up for, shall we say, noon? My car has been doing weird things lately."

"That means the rest of the week I have to drive you to school, doesn't it? You realize I have to get to work in that thing, don't you?"

Cara squeaks loudly in my ear, "I know. I'm sorry. But yay! Thank you."

"Listen," I say, "I have to get going. I'm taking Pug for a walk and his legs are crossed. Plus, it's getting late. See you tomorrow, honeybun."

"See you tomorrow!" she crows happily and hangs up.

~*~

On Saturday as I wait outside Cara's house in my old, beat up, yellow Rabbit, with the rain pounding on the roof of my car as I snack on a granola bar and Cara locks her door, my phone vibrates from my bag with a text. It's from Damien.

Cara told me you guys were headed to the library. Care for one more in your party? I'm meeting Victoria there as well.

Instead of answering I just roll my eyes and put my phone back in my bag. I think about how this week has been pretty great; working for Cael is awesome and we've already hung out at his house after work three times to get to know each other. I've learned so much about him this past week and of course he has learned a lot about me too. I think we're really hitting it off, though I keep reminding myself we've only been on *one* date and we haven't even made our relationship official boyfriend-girlfriend status or anything.

Still, I like where we are headed. He's even texted me every morning to let me know the day's specials he's whipped up and it amazes me how he gets up so early in the morning to bake everything himself. I wonder how he does it. He's been looking for more employees but it's been hard to find somebody up to his standards. I'd help if I wouldn't burn the place down.

As I'm thinking about that, Cara gets into the car and says, "God is it ever getting colder and colder! Maine sucks, why on earth did my parents think this was the best place to raise a child? Anyway, I'm ready to study. I can do this. If I've been studying for that math test, *this* should be a piece of cake, right?"

Chuckling, I back out of the driveway and onto the road. "Totally, you can do this; it's just science. Science is essentially math right?" From my peripheral I can see Cara nod but she remains silent.

Ten minutes later we're at the library and I'm curled up in a comfy chair reading a random horror book and Cara sits across from me at a study table, muttering to herself as she flips through her textbook.

I must have fallen asleep, because an hour later I wake up to the sound of my book slapping against the floor.

"Drop something?" asks a familiar voice. I look up to see Victoria holding my book out to me, her face rather neutral. She's added blonde steaks to her black hair and I can't help but notice that it looks really good on her, and as I take my book I say so.

She smirks slightly. "Thanks. I did it as a kind of rebirth, so to speak. I'm trying this new thing out, whenever I feel like I'm going to beat the shit out of someone I ignore it and do something nice for myself."

I blink up at her, not sure if she's being serious or not. Victoria laughs. "I'm kidding, kid. I just got tired of the same old black hair, boring as ever. Haven't dyed it in a while, so I figured today was as good a day as any."

Her hair reminds me of something…someone far off in a deep memory that I can't quite recall. I shrug it off as a cough tickles my throat and works its way to the surface, catching Cara's attention.

When Cara notices Victoria she sighs loudly, "I'm trying to study here."

Victoria rolls her eyes, "We'll try to keep it down, Tinkerbell."

Cara sticks out her tongue and goes back to her textbook. I look over at Victoria to see that she's sitting down in the chair next to me. "So," she says, "we don't talk much."

I find myself chuckling at this. "That's because you hate me." She doesn't deny it, but instead smiles slightly as if I'd told her a joke. Today she's wearing a little yellow sundress which is odd because it's rather rainy out and pretty cold. I don't even see a sweater anywhere near her. I've never really thought about it before, but she always wears the oddest clothing. I've seen her on the weekends and days off wearing her school uniform, although with added accessories. But I have to admit, everything she wears seems to suit her, even if it's not always appropriate for the day.

"Anyway," she says, "you're in my history class. I was just wondering, because you missed class the other day, if you needed any notes. I know, I know, why am I being such a Good Samaritan? I'm not always such a bitch, and I remember the time you took notes for me when I was sick, so I thought I'd repay the favour."

I open my mouth to say no thank you but she simply hands me a small bundle of papers and says, "You're welcome, kid." This whole condescending kid nonsense is kind of annoying but she's being nice and I don't want to ruin the moment. Unfortunately, it gets ruined anyway because Cara decides it's the perfect moment to have a fit.

Cara angrily slams her book shut. "This is stupid. I'm going to kick some ass soon if I don't get outta here…this science shit is crazy!"

The librarian walks over to our little area and says, "You know, the pen is mightier than the sword. Instead of fighting, maybe try writing."

"What does that even mean?"

"You'll know some day when you wise your ass up," says Victoria.

Cara scowls. "Nobody asked *you*, Vicky. Also, you shouldn't yell in a library; it's rude."

Victoria's eyes narrow and she says, "You'd better watch yourself. I'm getting really tired of playing it safe around you. You'd better believe that I will kick your scrawny ass, pixie dust."

"Pixie dust? Is that the worst insult you can come up with? I mean, really?" Cara snorts. "That is just *weak*, Victoria."

Victoria stands up rather abruptly and saunters towards her table with a look that can kill. "I think you'll find," she says as she puts her face right in front of Cara's, "that it is actually rather spot on."

Cara rolls her eyes.

Victoria smiles and says, "Whatever. I, for one, have done all I came here to do. Now if you'll excuse me I need to find my boyfriend. He's somewhere in the building and I believe we have a lunch date."

Cara stands as well and walks over to me, grabs my arm and says, "I'm done here." So we leave.

"What a great Saturday," I mutter as we enter my car. "Oh don't overreact," says Cara, the queen of overreacting. I try to start it, and all it does is sputter uselessly. I try again, and all I get is more sputtering protests.

Could it get any worse? I think to myself. It begins to rain.

"Don't freak out," says Cara. "I'll call a taxi and we can head to my place. You can leave your car here overnight. Mr. Brown won't tow your car; he'll probably leave it be or bring it to your place for you. You're the only one in this God-awful town that has a Rabbit anyway." Mr. Brown is our local tow truck driver. He's a really nice guy and hardly ever tows people's vehicles unless they're really out of line.

"You're right," I concede. "Wonder what your mom's making for dinner? Better tell her I'm coming over." Cara sends her mom a text and soon we're on our way.

When we arrive at Cara's house, there are cars in the driveway. Upon entering the house, the stink of cigars hits us instantly and Cara makes an annoyed noise in the back of her throat. "Of course she'd have a business meeting now. Great. Head upstairs before she tries to force you to socialize, I'll get us whatever she's whipped up to appease her asshole associates."

Cara's mother works for the local law firm, and she sometimes has her work buddies over for "business meetings" which consist of absolutely no business, but lots of smoking, drinking and eating.

I head upstairs to Cara's room, sit down on her bed where Missus Pussy Pants is napping, and begin to absently pet him. He lifts his head up lazily and looks over towards me then yawns. I smile at him and blink slowly to show I mean no harm and he begins to happily purr. He gets up and comes closer to me, his body right up against mine and goes right back to sleep as I pet his soft fur.

Looking around Cara's room you'd think it belonged to a twelve-year-old. She still has all of her stuffed animals on a shelf above her bed, or at least the ones her dad gave her. There are pictures of us everywhere, at the amusement park, at the mall, at parks and at sleepovers (before I'd get scared of the dark and have to go back home); everyday things that mean the world to only us. They're plastered on her pink and white walls along with posters of her favourite bands and one or two pictures of her with her other friends;

but I'm in those too because she never leaves me out of anything though in most, I look kind of out of place.

It's a stark contrast to my boring beige room which has never really had a childish feel. Sure, I've kept some of my stuffed animals but I've never had any posters on my walls and the only pictures I have are on my dresser and they're of course pictures of my parents, Cara, and Pug. No, my room is the same as it ever was.

When Cara finally comes upstairs, she's holding a tray absolutely loaded with mini quiches, crab cakes, eggrolls, finger sandwiches, and assorted cheesecakes. Just looking at all of the food makes my stomach grumble and Cara laughs when Missus Pussy Pants jumps up and runs away from the sound.

Cara grins. "Let us dine!"

We stuff our faces until everything on the tray is gone, and drink water from Cara's mini fridge that she has beside her bed. After we've eaten, I text Mr. Brown to ask him if he could tow my car to my house to which he replies right away that it would not be a problem. So Cara and I hunker down to watch movies until the rain stops. She falls asleep around ten o'clock as we're watching a really cheesy re-make of Godzilla. I take my phone out of my pocket to see if anybody has texted me and am happy when I see that Cael's number is in my missed call log.

I get up and head for Cara's en suite bathroom and gently close the door behind me, sit down on top of the toilet seat, and dial his number.

He answers on the third ring, "Hey. How was your library day with Cara?"

I puff out a sigh. "Complicated. My car died on me, after we left because she and Victoria couldn't be civil for two seconds, it started raining, and now I'm kind of stuck here unless I magically produce some money for a cab. I don't feel like walking home in the rain."

Cael chuckles, "Well that does suck."

"Yes, it does. I hate sleepovers. They give me anxiety," I reply, stupid tears forming in my eyes. "I want to go home. I know it's childish and stupid but I can't be here right now."

I hear movement over the phone like Cael's shifting in his seat to get comfortable. "No," he says, "I don't think it's childish or stupid." I smile slightly, "Really?"

"Aye, I promise. As your boss and suitor, I give you my word."

I giggle at that. "Did you just call yourself my suitor?"

A mock gasp on his end. "And if I did, good lady?"

My heart flip-flops in my chest. "Isn't boyfriend an easier term?"

Now a pause. "Only if you, you know, think it fits." His voice has lost its teasing edge.

I smile so wide I feel as though my lips are going to fall off. "It does."

"Is your mood any better?" asks Cael.

"Yes," I say. "It's perfect."

Twelve

"Hello?" *I call into the scary darkness. My little hands are trembling, though they're tied behind my back.* "Mommy? Papa?" *Nobody answers me. I try to focus on how I got here but I just can't seem to remember. One minute I was outside playing with my tea set, and the next thing I know I'm here.* "Cara? This isn't funny! You know I don't like the dark. If this is about your doll, I'm sorry I broke her, it was an accident I swear, ask your daddy he saw me trip!"

"Shut up!" *booms a voice out of nowhere.* "Nobody is coming for you." *A flashlight turns on and illuminates the face of a man inches from my own face. He's real scary too, his dark hair is all dirty and stuck to his head and I can't help but think how nice of a colour it'd be if it were washed, and that he doesn't deserve pretty hair, being so scary and mean. His light brown skin is pretty too. It really isn't fair he gets to look so nice.*

"W-why'd you take me here?" *I ask, my voice shaking slightly with fear. The man's cold brown eyes roll and he says,* "If you must know, to deliver you to my boss."

A chill races down my spine.

"Wh-who's your boss?" *He deliberates a moment and answers with a rather smug smile,* "I call him Lucy for short. Do you go to church? You may have heard of him, although I must admit it's a rather skewed version of the truth." *I shake my head no and the man sighs.*

"His name is Lucifer."

I blink, unsure of whom he's referring to. The man next door has a cat named Lucifer but I know that a cat can't be anybody's boss.

The man balks. "Kids these days know nothing! Lucifer doesn't ring any bells at all? Okay then, we'll try this. Satan. The Devil.

God's opposite." *I gasp and he laughs maniacally. His breath reeks of alcohol.*

"That's n-not real," *I say, trying to steel myself. My eyes water,* "You're lying." *He shakes his head and clicks the flashlight off, plunging me into darkness once again.*

"Naw," *he says and I can hear him walking away from me.* "Not the way you've been taught." *His footsteps echo throughout the room, and I hear a door creak open.* "You just stay right where you are. I'll be right back."

Minutes that feel like hours pass by until all of a sudden the door creaks open. I'm so sure it's him I don't bother calling out for help. When the flashlight clicks on, I'm surprised to see a lovely girl staring back at me; her hair is dark as well but with pretty blonde streaks as opposed to the flat brown of the man. She puts her index finger to her mouth in the universal sign for shh, *and without turning the light off, she walks around me and unties my wrists. She then comes back around and smiles at me; and a warm happy feeling settles over me as she reaches out and strokes my hair affectionately.*

"Okay, kid," *she whispers,* "the cops are on their way. Your Guardian already took care of that."

"What?" I ask, confused.

She smiles, "Cam called the cops while I set you free. Now I gotta go distract my boy toy before he finds out I've helped you escape. Can't let him in on our little plan to save the world, now can we?" *I nod my head like I understand, but really I'm scared and just want to go home, and this nice (crazy?) lady helped me so I'll agree to whatever she says if it helps me get there.*

"Sweet darling," *she coos,* "I don't expect you to understand anything. Not yet. It's a shame that you'll have to forget this ever happened though. We'll meet again, though I'll have to be much nastier to you if I'm to help. I apologise in advance. I hope you stay on the side of the Light. Don't let anybody sway you. Your soul has the power to change the world, kid."

"I don't understand," *I say.*

"We have to go," *says a voice that makes my heart pick up, though not in fear. I don't really understand what this feeling is, but it's not bad, so I don't find myself panicking. I feel safer than anything else. I feel like I know this person...*

"Goodbye." *The woman places her thumb, middle and index finger in a triangle over my heart.* "We'll meet again, as I said – hopefully under much better circumstances."

Everything goes dark, and when I wake up I don't know where I am, but it's scary.

"Hello?" *I call into the scary darkness.* "Mommy? Papa?" *Nobody answers me. I try to focus on how I got here but I just can't seem to remember. One minute I was outside playing with my tea set, and the next thing I know I'm here.* "Cara? This isn't funny! You know I don't like the dark. If this is about your doll, I'm sorry I broke her, it was an accident I swear, ask your daddy he saw me trip!"

Minutes later, the police break through the door and-

The scene switches abruptly to Cara's bedroom. I'm watching the events as if I were a bystander. Cara and I are sleeping together in her huge bed curled up next to each other. We must be about five and six years old. I watch as my younger self begins to stir, and eventually wakes up. She looks around the room, and then her eyes focus on something and widen. I follow her line of sight and see a dark shape standing by the door. She tries to wake Cara up but she's a deep sleeper and just continues snoring.

Younger me then gets up and walks to the bathroom, hoping to escape whatever it is in there. Like I'm attached to her, I follow and step in before she closes the door. She walks over to the sink and washes her face and I feel myself being sucked into her body until we become one. I am five years old again, sleeping over for the very first time at my friend Cara's house, and I don't want to make a scene because I think I saw some kind of boogeyman. I splash some more water onto my face and look up into the mirror – and I scream.

I wake up.

Shakily I reach for my cell phone beside me on the couch, and shudder when I see the time. Midnight. I check outside and see that the rain is still going strong, and sigh. I stare down at my phone for a minute, debating what I should do, then I pick it up and click Cael's contact icon, hold my finger down until the text or call options pop up, and choose text.

R u up? I send.

Two seconds later he replies. *Yeah, just watching TV. You ok?*

No. Can't b here. 2 many nightmares…memories? I dunno.

My phone buzzes with his answer. *I can send a cab over and you can come here if you want. Or I can send a cab to bring you home.*

Can't go home. I don't feel like explaining anything to my parents right now.

Forty-five minutes later, a cab comes to pick me up. I left a note on Cara's TV where I know she'll see it, and she knows how I feel about sleepovers.

"Well then," says the driver, who I quickly recognize as the guy who drove me to and from Cael's house the night of Cara's party. "You're a regular, aren't you Mrs. Banning?" I politely nod. I don't question how he knows my last name. Our town isn't huge so eventually you're bound to know most of the workers. I've never seen him before and that means he must be new and replacing Jerry in his retirement. I know that he'll probably know the names of almost everybody in town by next month.

"You know my parents," I state, as we turn down Mercury lane.

"Yes, I know of your mother," he says brightly. "I've bought many of your mother's paintings from her site. She keeps her business card everywhere in town and eventually I had to see what all of the hubbub was about. I'm very glad I did. There's a lovely family picture on her biography page and I recognized you instantly. I hope to go to her studio in town."

The driver's nametag reads Fred, and his accent and beautiful skin tone hints at Middle Eastern descent. Perhaps Israel? "Here we are," he says as we pull up to Cael's place, "free of charge for tonight's best customer."

"Who's the second best customer," I ask as I pull out a twenty, which is obviously more than enough and hand it to him. "You feed your family, Fred."

"Thank you," he says, sounding touched as he takes it, but gives me the correct change instead of taking all of it like I intended. "But if you insist on paying for your fare, well I can't change your mind now can I?"

I smile. "I'm glad you moved here, Fred, and replaced Jerry. You're going to be the most requested cab driver in no time."

"There are only a few cabs anyway," he says, chuckling, but visibly pleased.

Cael is standing outside in his pyjamas holding an umbrella, and he opens the door for me and helps me out. He walks me to the door and gestures for me to go inside. I smile as I walk in and see a steaming hot cup of coffee waiting for me on the living room table where I've sat the last couple of times I was here. I walk over to it, plunk down on the couch, and close my eyes and sigh.

The door closes and I open my eyes as Cael sits down next to me. He smiles. "Coffee's for you, if you were wondering. Unless you wanted tea or hot chocolate…" his smile fades a little, but when I pick the coffee up and shake my head it returns.

"Coffee is *absolutely* fine with me." I take a sip of the delicious stuff and place it back on the table.

"So," I say, "what's on the tube?"

"Late night re-runs and infomercials. It's lady's choice tonight." He passes me the remote, his blue eyes filled with good humour.

"I'll take infomercials for two hundred, please." I flick through the channels until I find an infomercial worth watching. A lady is excitedly explaining how to cook with this new kitchen set we can get for only ten small payments of twenty-nine-ninety-nine!

"See," I say, "It's like watching a cooking show." I take a sip of my coffee and smile at Cael, who nods.

"Exactly. It's entertaining."

We sit for a while, watching the lady cook with the "amazing" pots and pans and cutting things with the "just superb" knife set. Eventually, I find myself growing sleepy and I yawn.

"Tired?" asks Cael, who yawns himself right after. I nod my head, but then shake it. I don't want to fall asleep and have such terrifying nightmares again. Cael's eyes narrow and he asks, "Those dreams you had. How bad were they?"

I look down at my thighs and sigh. "Bad. I think they might have been memories but they're too strange to believe you know? But they feel so familiar…"

"What were they about? If you, you know, don't mind me asking." I wave my hand in a gesture I hope comes across as *not at all.*

"When I was in grade two, I was kidnapped. It's why I hate the dark so much. I never remembered much of how it happened. I always remember waking up in total darkness, and then being found not too long after by the police. They always said it must have been some stupid kids from out of town playing a prank because a call came in about my whereabouts." Tears fill my eyes.

"Tonight though, I dreamed that it was a man who kidnapped me. I can't remember what he looked like anymore but he seemed so *familiar*. He told me that he was working for…*Satan* and that they wanted me dead." Cael remains silent, looking pensive.

"And then," I continue, "there was this girl. She saved me…and somebody else. She said his name and it…it was the angel from the story you told me about. He was the one who phoned the police while the girl untied me."

Cael's Adam's apple bobs as he swallows. "That's rather scary isn't it? I wonder what made you dream about it?"

I shake my head and lean into him. At first he seems surprised, but then his arms entangle me and bring me closer. "I don't know. It felt so real, like it really happened. But that's impossible."

He nods his head in agreement. "Impossible."

"When that dream ended another began. You know how I told you sleepovers give me anxiety? I think I remembered why…but I can't remember much about that dream. Only that something scared me, I guess I saw a shadow in the mirror when I was washing my face and it traumatized me."

Cael kisses the top of my head. "I'll keep you safe from your nightmares tonight if you want."

I try to smile through a yawn. "How?"

He gently pushes me aside and stands up. "Wait here," he says as he leaves the room. He comes back a couple of minutes later with a huge fluffy duvet, a sheet, and some pillows. I giggle at the rather large load of things he's carrying and offer to help him but he promptly drops them on the floor.

"We can make a fort."

Thirteen

I slowly drift awake in the early morning to the sound of soft snoring. Not wanting to open my eyes I lay there, quietly trying to remember where I am.

Groggy, it takes a couple of minutes for the memories to come to me but when they do I smile. They're like pictures at first, snapshots of the fun we had; *Cael laughing at my expression after he threw a pillow at my head, and then our crappy attempt at a couch fort.* Then they start to move together like a reel. *He was tickling me and I kicked over my coffee cup and I felt such horror and embarrassment at first. But then our laughter continued as he said it didn't matter and continued to tickle me anyway.* I replay the moments that lead up to when I eventually must have fallen asleep, and I lie there in our terrible attempt at a couch fort, listening to Cael's snores, feeling his chest move up and down under my head with his breaths, and I realize something. This must be what it's like to be slowly falling in love.

~*~

I never thought anything like this could be possible but here it is, this situation that has my kind-of-human heart beating fast and hard in my chest; the chest which her head is currently resting upon deep in slumber, her breaths even and deep. I find myself smiling as she mumbles something incoherent in her sleep and shift my arms around her a little tighter. She sighs into the embrace as if there's nowhere she'd rather be. There is nowhere I would rather be either than right here, right now. I will protect her and I will find a way to break her curse. The Battle will be fast upon us and I need to find a way to tell her soon.

"Father," I whisper. "Please help me find a way."

In response, thunder rumbles in the distance and the rain pelts the windows and roof harder. My heart lurches. I know that He cannot help even if He wanted to. God can only do so much.

But still, it's nice to know He wishes He could do more. Curses only have so many loop holes.

~*~

My eyes pop open at a sudden movement underneath my head. I scan my surroundings and realize I'm still at Cael's. Yawning, I sit up and stretch as he does the same.

"Sorry to have woken you," he says, running his fingers through his sleep-messy hair. "I was about to get up to put the coffee machine on. Do you want some? I also have tea and hot chocolate if you'd prefer." His voice is still thick from slumber.

Gratefully, I smile. "Coffee would be heavenly, thanks." Another yawn is stuck in my throat when panic strikes me; I must look like a total mess! I stand up rather abruptly. "Uh, I'll be right back. I have to go to the bathroom."

Cael smiles a knowing smirk and nods his head. "Aye then, I'll go start the coffee."

It takes everything I have not to run to Cael's small, tidy bathroom but when I get there I close the door behind me and take stock of my reflection in the mirror above the sink. I don't look half as bad as I thought I did which is probably saying something. My hair is a greasy mess, there's dried drool in the corner of my lip, and what little makeup I'd put on yesterday is miraculously un-smudged but my eyes are red like they always are when I first wake up. I look like I could pass for a racoon with my dark circles and I have a dull ache in the back of my throat.

Sighing, I splash some water on my face and decide to put my hair up in a sloppy bun using the hair elastic I always keep around my wrist just for emergencies like this. When I'm done, I don't look half bad. *The bags under my eyes can almost pass for designer…*

I exit the bathroom and walk down the hall to the living room to see that Cael has already taken down our fort and folded the blankets and sheets. "Did I take that long fixing myself up?" I ask.

The coffee machine beeps letting us know that it's full and he laughs. "Does that answer your question?"

For the next couple of hours –we got up at around eleven– we sip our coffee and talk about random things, what I'm doing at school, what we're both currently reading;. I'm reading Mary Shelly's *Frankenstein* and Cael's reading a book of Yeats's poetry that he picked up at the bookstore he works at, which finally I – after such a long time, I realize – remember is called *Yes To Books.*

When one o'clock rolls around my phone buzzes with a text from Cara asking if I want to go extra accessory shopping – her words, not mine – for semi-formal with her and even though I want to say no I agree because I basically ditched her last night and feel bad about it.

My phone rings right after I send my agreement. "So you're really down?" she asks.

I roll my eyes and turn to Cael, who smiles and rolls his eyes too prompting me to chuckle. "Yeah, I'll come with. Maybe I'll find a dress. But first, how are we going to get to the mall? If you've forgotten, the Rabbit isn't working anymore. Mr. Brown towed it to my place."

Cara grumbles, reminding me of Pug. "Yeah, I know, I'll drive. Don't worry, my car should get us to the mall and back without too much protest."

"You'll have to pick me up from Cael's. I'll give you directions; it's not too far from your place."

"Yes ma'am! Though in this town, nowhere is very far from my place." She agrees to pick me up from Cael's in twenty minutes, giving her enough time to pick an outfit for the day.

"I guess this will be goodbye until tomorrow," says Cael after I hang up.

My heart thumps in my chest a little faster and a lazy smile rises to my lips. "Yes, well," I say as I lean in and kiss him on the cheek, "unless I want to lose my job I'll see you at work at the usual time."

~*~

Dutifully, Cara picked me up exactly twenty minutes after we spoke. We drove to the mall and that is where I find myself right now, standing in front of a full length mirror in the same green and pink dress I tried on what feels like forever ago. It still looks as beautiful as ever on me and now that I've been working and received my first pay check, I've finally got the money to buy it. We've been at the mall for at least three hours and so far Cara has found absolutely nothing in way of accessories.

She practically shrieks when I come out of the fitting room with the dress slung over my right arm. "I'm so excited for you!" she says. She offers me some lip-gloss which I refuse as always before she coats her own lips in the stuff, "I don't want to give you my cold," I explain.

She waves my explanation away and smiles at me. "You are going to look so beautiful, honeybun. Hopefully I find some nice accessories soon because we've been in his mall way too long. I'd settle for a crappy fake diamond necklace as long as it looked good. Honestly, you'd think there'd be *something* in this place for me."

"Semi-formal is like a month or something away and we have lots of time to go shopping, you know," I say, swatting her arm playfully.

Cara smiles at me and shakes her head like she pities me but says nothing as we walk towards the cash register. "What, is a month not enough time?" I ask.

When we reach the cash, a girl of about six years old begins to cry from her seat on a bench just outside the store. Her mother is standing about six feet behind me, looking at a royal purple gown, ignoring her daughter's tantrum. My head starts pounding with a sudden headache and I find myself sighing.

Cara sighs as the cashier rings up my purchase. "There can never be enough time, right up until the day of the dance I will search for the perfect accessories. Maybe I should go somewhere out of town. There's more variety. Hell, I might even find a better dress! Imagine?" My turn to shake my head which she pointedly ignores. "Well you never know. I'll let you know how it turns out if I end up going."

"You do that," I say as we head out of the store. "In any case, I'm done for the day. My head is pounding and I need to get home to take a shower." Cara frowns at me, reaches out and touches my forehead and her frown deepens. "Babe," she says, "you're a little warm."

I shrug. She punches my arm, hard. "You could have *told* me you were sick. I'd have postponed this for another day. It's not like the dress would have gone anywhere, nobody our age really comes to this mall to buy their stuff anyway– they all go to freaking somewhere out of town."

"I did mention that I have a cold..."

Her face scrunches up even more, concern palpable. "Yeah, but a cold is a cold. This kind of fever doesn't usually indicate a simple cold, babe." I keep forgetting that Cara wants to go into nursing.

"Well I feel like crap. I just want to go home and rest. I mean I'll probably feel better after I take some pain meds and a nap."

Her frown deepens even more. "I'm coming over to make sure you actually get to bed." I think of the first day I met Cael and smile, remembering that I did the same thing.

"Okay, you're going loopy," says Cara, "What's with the idiotic smile?" She feels my forehead again and shakes her head.

"Nothing. Just remembering something."

"Riiight," she says, taking my things from me. "Let's just get you home."

~*~

I wake up to Cara's voice. "Get up. You've slept long enough, babe."

I open my eyes to see that it's light outside and I glance at my alarm clock and realize how much I've slept. It's six in the morning. My heart jumps into my throat. "Holy shit, Cara. Why did you let me sleep for so long?"

From her perch at the foot of my bed she shrugs. "You clearly needed it. I tried to wake you up to get you to eat, but you just drank some water and went back to sleep. How do you feel? I figured I'd wake you up early so you could shower and stuff, but if you still feel sick..."

"No," I sit up immediately. "I feel better. Thanks."

Cara beams at me, obviously proud of herself. "Good. Your parents were worried but I told them not to worry too much. They both left for work not long ago. I stayed the night; hope you don't mind."

I shake my head, "No, no it's fine. Really. I appreciate it actually." I stretch my arms above my head and reflexively yawn. "I guess I need to take that shower. I must smell like a homeless person."

She laughs and tells me that I do and I realize that she's acting too chipper for somebody who was up taking care of their friend all night. I know for a fact that she's usually rather grumpy when she's tired. Something is off. "Cara," I say, "have you slept at all?"

She stands up and walks towards the door, "I should probably make breakfast. Do bacon sandwiches sound good to you?"

"Cara."

"Is that a no?"

"Is there something wrong, Cara?" I ask, my heart starting to beat too hard.

Her face falls. She toys with a lock of red curly hair and she looks at the floor. She mumbles something which I don't understand.

"What?" I ask. She repeats herself a little louder but I still can't hear her. I ask a third time and of course she yells at me.

"There was someone at your window last night!"

I wish I had the power to stop time to properly think about what she just said, but I don't, so all I can do now is freak out.

Standing up, I walk over to her, ever aware of our height difference because I have to look up at her. "There was a person in my window last night? How could you not wake me up to tell me that there was a fucking person in my window last night which, by the way, you need to get to by climbing a God damned tree?"

Cara's voice warbles when she says, "It was a guy...and he..."

"He what, Cara," I say, realizing that she seems genuinely upset.

She shrugs. "He looked a lot like your least favourite person. And he looked angry. When I got to the window he'd probably jumped down and run away. I stayed in your living room last night, your parents helped me get all set up, and I'd come in to check in on you every once in a while and one of those times...yeah. I didn't tell you because maybe I'd hoped it didn't actually happen." She's crying now, and when I hug her she crumples into my arms like a child.

"I'm sorry I didn't wake you but you were so sick. I don't know why Damien would be at your window but I was so scared Khiara. He looked about ready to hurt you."

"I think," I say slowly, not wanting to offend her, "that it was a bad dream. You must have fallen asleep and not realized it. Damien has no reason to be creeping on me when I sleep. He might be a little strange, and I may not like him or even *trust* him but I don't think he would do that. That goes to a new level of creepy." She nods and hiccups back her tears.

"Go take your shower," she says, still clearly shaken. "I'll get on those bacon sandwiches."

Fourteen

"Are you kidding me?" I say as I get to my locker. It's open again, and as I search through its contents I find that though nothing's been taken as usual, something has been added instead. On the little hook I usually keep my mirror on (I took the mirror off recently because it was dirty so I wanted to take it home to clean) is a necklace pendant. The design is simple yet beautiful, intricate brass wings wrapped around a ruby heart as if protecting it by simply cradling it.

"What on earth?" a whisper escapes my mouth without my permission. I don't know how long I stand there before Cara nearly stops my heart by tapping my shoulder.

"Uh," she says as I turn around and slap her hand away while simultaneously stuffing the necklace in my pocket with the other hand, "everything okay over here?"

We seem to be at a standstill until she frowns and looks down at my pocket. "Wanna explain what's in there?" My cheeks heat up something terrible and I shake my head.

Cara reaches out slowly and panic builds in my chest, "It's nothing, Cara, seriously stop." Her eyes narrow, "Khiara, with you…with you it's never nothing. Now explain."

Sighing, I reach into my pocket and produce the necklace. "This was on my mirror hook. My locker was open again, nothing was taken as usual…but," I clear my throat, "I don't know why someone would leave this only now? Why break into a locker repeatedly, take nothing every time, and then finally decide to leave me with this?" I dangle the necklace out in front of us and Cara takes hold of it.

"This is beautiful," she breathes as she examines it. "But it's also *really* sketchy. I mean I'm all for secret admirers but the whole breaking into your locker thing is like, out of hand. And then just poof, they decide to give you a little gift. I don't know, Ki-ki, I don't like this."

"Neither do I," I murmur as she hands it back to me. Placing it in my pocket I turn around and reach into my locker for my books just as the warning bell rings.

"Let's just get to class," I say. "We can talk about this later."

By the middle of the school day, we still haven't had any time at all to talk about the necklace. It has been burning a hole in my pocket all day and as I sit in History class, I can't help but reach into my pocket as Mr. Burnette drones on in that annoying voice of his about nothing to do with the lesson. As soon as my fingers touch the necklace, something strange happens.

Everything in the room completely stops. It's like suddenly everybody but me is frozen in place. From the seat next to me, Jake Pellinger's finger is halfway up his nose. Mr.Burnette is in the middle of gesturing towards the board where there's a crude drawing of a cat walking under a ladder right next to a list of some of the most influential people in history. Most of the students have a bored look plastered to their faces and as I look around the room, I can actually make out the dust motes in the light of the window, frozen as if mid-dance. I find that I am hyper aware of everything; every breath that fills my lungs every blink of my eyes.

And then it all goes back to normal as if nothing's happened and I'm left with a very confused and probably hysterical look on my face.

Mr.Burnette stops gesturing at his ridiculous drawing. "Miss Khiara," he says, concern colouring his voice, "is there something the matter?"

I can only blink up at him and whisper, "There's something *very* wrong with me."

"So," says Lucille, the school's guidance counsellor from the chair across from the couch I'm sitting on. "Tell me why you're here today. I'd like to hear your feelings before I give any input."

"It was just a panic attack," I mumble. She jots something down in a little note book. "I think really I'm just stressed out, is all. I'll be fine." That's a lie because I am pretty sure I may be going absolutely crazy but I can't tell her what I think just happened. I'd be sent away for sure, shipped out to the hospital all the way in the next town over. Our town is so small it doesn't even have a mental health ward in the hospital.

Lucille smiles kindly at me, her warm brown eyes crinkling in the corners. She has a nice smile, comforting and warm, and it makes me *want* to tell her all of my problems. "Honey," she says, "are you having trouble at home?"

I shake my head. "No. It's nothing like that. I'm just stressed about school and work – it's hard to do both at the same time without stressing out."

She writes in her notebook some more. "Oh," she says, "you're working? Yes, doing both will definitely cause stress." Her red hair is messy and keeps falling into her eyes and I'm reminded of Cael when she pushes it out of the way. Except he's never frustrated by it, unlike Lucille, who seems like her hair is the bane of her existence.

"Do you want my elastic?" I offer her the band I always keep on my wrist. Lucille smiles and shakes her head, "No, thank you. I just got a perm and it didn't really…well it looks awful," she concedes. "But we're here today to talk about you, not my hair disaster."

I sigh. "I'm fine. I promise. I just need to learn how to deal with panic attacks and how to manage my time."

An hour later, I'm sitting at the lunch table having arrived ten minutes before the beginning of lunch about ready to punch somebody in the face, cry, or both. Lucille and I went through various breathing exercises and stress management techniques. It was truly not fun.

Cara sits down across from me, her tray filled with cookies, a very small plate of lasagne, and an even smaller salad. To complete the tray of un-healthiness, she's got a Coke and a chocolate milk to drink. Cara sees my expression and instantly hands me the Coke and her meagre salad.

She says, "You should probably have something to eat. You look like you want to die." I nod and gladly take the food. In my awkward state, I'd forgotten to get food for myself. She gives me a pointed look and whispers, "I keep thinking about when I thought I saw…you know, and ever since, I've been getting really creepy vibes."

Victoria and Damien sit down at the other end of the table and both give us a cursory glance. Janie and Chris arrive not long after them, Chris carrying a tray with both of their meals on it. Their presence effectively silences Cara and she swirls her fork around her plate, not even bothering to eat her food.

Taking a bite of lettuce covered in some God-awful salad dressing, I close my eyes and try to pretend that the weird things that have been happening are products of my overactive imagination. Just as it's beginning to work, that stupid tingle goes down my spine and I know, I just know that I'm being watched.

When I open my eyes, everybody at the table except Cara is looking at me.

"Are you okay, kid?" asks Victoria, actual concern lacing her voice. Everyone turns to her, confused, and she frowns. "What? She looks like somebody has her cornered with a gun. It's disrupting my lunch to see her look so pathetic."

Janie laughs and raises her hand to give her a high five, but one look from Victoria and her hand hangs awkwardly in the air and she looks like she's been slapped.

"Sorry," she mumbles, "thought you were being serious."

Victoria chuckles at her own private joke, "I was being serious. Doesn't give *you* an excuse to be such a cun-"

"Whoa there," Cara interrupts her. "I'm all for swearing but I think y'all need to calm down."

With a smirk Victoria says, "Y'all? This isn't the south. I mean you Native Mainers all talk funny, but really?"

Janie turns her usual snark towards Victoria, a rare occurrence. "Last time I checked, you were from Canada and shouldn't say anything bad about this great country."

Victoria narrows her eyes and abruptly stands up, slamming her hands down on the table. "You have no idea where I come from, where I've been, or where I will go."

Damien pales and slowly rises from his seat, his brown eyes tense. Placing his hand on his girlfriend's back he says, "Come on, hon." He turns to the rest of us, "We were up late last night." Both Cara and I visibly cringe.

"I'm fine," says Victoria, and then she turns to me. "But I know something is up with you and it's pissing me off. You should *probably* fix it."

Fifteen

When I arrive at work, I'm pleased when Cael tells me it's been a slow day and that he's found somebody to work part time.

"Her name is Lisa," he says. "She's a friend's daughter."

I smile and think about where I've heard that name before. "Lisa Foster?"

Cael nods, "Yeah, she goes to your school. I guess you've met before? Her and her father moved here a couple of years back around the same time I did. I grew up with him and his daughter has become kind of a niece to me."

"Yeah, I'm supposed to help her with her French."

He smiles warmly, "She's a lovely girl. Lisa will be coming in today, actually. Maybe you can show her the ropes."

I find myself grinning at the prospect of seeing her today because she really was very sweet. "Maybe today I can help her with her French on my break too."

Cael claps his hands together, "Excellent idea. I'm sure she'll be thrilled." His messy hair falls into his face and without thinking I reach over and gently push it away. His electric blue eyes meet mine, then trail up and down my whole body and heat instantly rushes to every part of me as they leave a trail of goose bumps in their wake.

"I should get to the cash," I whisper. He nods, but his eyes hold a mischievous glint to them that matches his grin. "Yeah, you should I suppose. Nobody is manning it. Luckily there are no customers." Winking, he leans in close and kisses the tip of my nose then walks away towards the kitchen.

"Oh," says a voice from behind me, "that was uhh, intense."

I whip around, and Lisa is standing there with cheeks that are as red as roses. "Hi, uhh," she says, "I see that you and my uncle are enjoying yourselves."

It's my turn to blush, but I can't stop the dopey smile that's plastered onto my face. "Hey. I'm supposed to show you how things are done around here. It's really not so hard; I've been working here since it opened."

Her head bounces in a bubbly nod. "I can't wait to get started. "Well then," I say, "there's no time like the present. How about we start now?"

Lisa almost bursts with palpable excitement.

~*~

In between training Lisa for a bit, which proves not to be difficult at all because she is a very fast learner and a natural with the customers, and helping her with her French on break, I fall fast in love with her quirky attitude. Even though she's only thirteen she acts so wise sometimes and is extremely composed when she has to be.

Cael is manning the cash and waiting on tables while Lisa and I work on her French verbs when I suddenly remember about the necklace that's in my pocket. It's been stored in the back of my mind since I got here and I almost completely forgot about it – but now it begs for my attention. I reach into my pocket and as soon as my fingers touch it, it pulses with a strange heat. I look around the room. Thankfully, nothing freezes this time and I wonder if I'd been imagining it all along – but no. I know what I saw, even if it sounds insane.

I pull the necklace out of my pocket and look it over. The red ruby of the heart sparkles beautifully in the light of the café and the brass wings that cradle it suddenly seem so frail compared to the beauty of the stone.

"Wow," marvels Lisa. I look up to see her staring at the necklace with a look of complete awe. "Where did you get *that?*"

I bite my lip. "Oh, it's actually kind of a funny story."

"I'm sick of conjugating verbs anyway. Let's hear it then." Lisa looks at me expectantly, like Pug when he's waiting for a treat. I sneeze – stupid cold.

"Okay," I say, unsure where to start. "Well, from the beginning of the year till today my locker has been randomly broken into a whole bunch of times. That's not even the strangest part either. Every single time it's been broken into, whoever has been doing it has never once stolen anything from me. Not once!"

She gapes, "That is so weird!"

"Right?" I nod. "So today, when I got to my locker before the first bell and saw it open, I was like beyond pissed off, because again, nobody took anything. But – and this is the strange part – where I usually put my mirror this necklace was hanging, like some weird gift."

"That's messed up!"

"I know," I whisper.

Cael picks the perfect moment to sneak up on us, and scares me half to death when he says from behind me, "That's a really special necklace you've got there."

"God!" I practically shriek, "scare me right out of my skin why don't you?"

He chuckles. "Sorry, it's a bad habit."

Lisa points towards the necklace. "It's so…*shiny.*" Cael nods and absently runs his hand through his hair.

"You said it was special?" I say hesitantly, "what did you mean?"

He crinkles his nose, a thoughtful motion that makes me smile because it's something I do as well, and takes a moment before answering. "Well," he says, "I can't tell you much, but what I can tell you is that necklaces like that are incredibly rare. There are many counterfeits for fashion purposes, but they are useless. They say that necklaces like that are crafted by God himself."

Lisa's eyes are full of wonder, her mouth slightly agape as Cael reaches for the necklace. I hand it to him without a word and he examines it. He whispers something in that beautiful lilting language I've heard him use a couple of times, and then turns to look me right in the eye.

"Khiara," he pauses, "you should put this on."

Narrowing my eyes, I ask, "Why?"

He shrugs like it's no big deal. "Well extra protection is always a good thing, I think."

"I don't know," I whisper, and then louder, "it just showed up in my locker."

Cael nods his head, "Yeah, I heard you talking to Lisa about that."

"Such an eavesdropper!" Lisa says and smacks him on the arm. He smiles good-naturedly and shrugs again.

"I believe everything happens for a reason," he says seriously. "If that necklace ended up in your locker, you're supposed to have it."

Unable to believe what he's saying, I exclaim, "But it's so creepy!" Lisa nods emphatically and says, "Sooo creepy."

"I don't know," says Cael thoughtfully. "Maybe somebody noticed your locker was open again and decided that you needed some protection. I mean, it's just a superstitious legend about a ruby necklace, right? It's probably not even true."

I look down at my lap and think for a second about what happened with the necklace in class and the strange pulse of heat. If what Cael's legend says is true, somebody thinks I'm in trouble and this necklace is supposed to be for my protection.

"Cael," I look up from my lap, "do you really believe that?" He sighs and oddly, he and Lisa exchange a look I can't interpret.

"I can tell you this much," he says, his mouth quirking into a small smile I can't help but return. "I'm still not a vampire." He winks at me and Lisa giggles so hard she snorts endearingly.

"You've mentioned," I say drily, only slightly aware that nobody is manning the cash though there is nobody in the café anyway which explains why Cael was eavesdropping in the first place.

"I will tell you everything you want to know," he says as he crouches down to my eye level, reaches out, and strokes my hair. "And it will be soon. But right now," he says, "right now I can only tell you to trust me."

Even though this makes absolutely no sense, even though I've only known Cael for a week and a half and I have no idea what is going on…I feel deep in my soul that I would trust this boy with my life. "I do," I say. "And I'm glad that you're still not a vampire."

I turn to Lisa and ask, "So, you're not a vampire either right?"

She shrugs. "No promises."

"So," I say to Cael. "I should put this thing on, hmm? For protection."

He holds out the necklace, "I'll put it on you, if you want."

I nod, "Okay. Put it on then."

Sixteen

A soft rain pounds on the windows of my room, and as I close my eyes I know that I'm safe.

Two weeks have gone by since I got the necklace and so far I haven't taken it off. The minute Cael put it on me that day an overwhelming feeling of safety instantly flooded me. He'd smiled at me and asked how I felt and I just couldn't help but reply honestly. Cael smiled at me then, and told me *again* that he'd explain everything when the time came. I just have to trust that what he's said is the truth.

He's my boss, my boyfriend, and a possible supernatural being. I can deal with that, I suppose. For the most part, it's been really great between us. We've been together for about a month and though there is an *obvious* elephant in the room – the secrets he carries – I can't deny that I'm really falling for him. I've always hated it when I read books where the main character falls I love right away but this is something more than a shallow attraction.

There is something between us that I can't ignore and I won't ignore. This is much bigger than young love; I'm certain.

As I drift off to sleep, a shadow of light plays behind my eyelids, but I know that it's nothing to worry about. Nothing can hurt me. I am safe.

~*~

It's Saturday and semi-formal is soon and I still don't have any accessories to go with my dress. I don't really want to go because I won't have a date – unfortunately Cael is busy that night until pretty late – and going stag to a dance is something I don't look forward to doing.

"Dad," I say as my father buttons up his fall jacket, "did you ever go to school dances back in France?"

He stops unbuttoning his jacket and walks over to where I'm sitting down on the couch. "Yes," he says, "I went to dances. They were not as fancy as the ones you have here in America, but yes."

"We're not *too* fancy, Dad. This is the state of lumberjacks and farmers." I lay my head on his shoulder and he puts his arm around me.

"My sweet, is there something troubling you?" He asks

I nod my head. "I'm worried about going without a date to the dance."

Mom walks into the room and smiles at the pair of us, "I see you're nice and comfy."

Dad chuckles, "We are having a nice talk about the upcoming dance. Khiara is worried about going without her boyfriend."

She sits down on my other side and puts her feet up on the coffee table. "Oh? I went to lots of dances without a date in my day. I had lots of fun; I'm sure you will too. How come Cael can't come?"

"He still works part time at the bookstore. His boss won't give him time off that day."

"Well I'm sure he wishes he could be there with you." Mom says, patting my leg.

I nod my head, "Yeah, he feels bad he can't come."

"Well I hope you find something today when you and Cara go out shopping." Just as mom says that the doorbell rings twice in fast succession, and Cara walks in, Tristan in tow.

"Hello simple peasants, the queen has arrived!" She crows.

"Come, darlings, sit with us a second," says Dad. He nods at Tristan who smiles and nods back at him, and he scoots over for Cara to sit next to me.

"So, what is today's plan, Petite Reine," he says to Cara, who beams at his use of her nick name. It's something he's called her since we were kids; it means *little queen* in French.

Cara stops chewing her gum to pop a bubble, and then smiles at my dad. "Shopping out of town. Maybe we'll take a drive to Moosehead Lake, just for fun."

"Lovely," says Mom. "Well I hope you find what you're looking for but if not, don't worry too much. You'll find something eventually, if not today." She stands up, "Come on now Jaques," she says to Dad, "let's get to the gallery." Dad leans over Cara to kiss me on the cheek and gets up to follow Mom to the door.

"Have a good day, kids. Drive safe. Oh, and Tristan?" says Mom.

"Uh, yeah?" he replies awkwardly. No matter how many times he's met my parents over the last month he can't get over the fact that they've taken to him so quickly. But how could they not? He is one of the nicest people in the world!

She smiles at him and he blushes. "Take care of my girls." With that, her and my father head out to her studio.

"Okay then," says Cara. "Let's get ourselves some great accessories!"

~*~

Cael and I have created a game, kind of like twenty questions, except for every question one of us gets wrong, the other has to make a game show buzzer noise. It's the day before the dance, or should I say the night before – it's about ten o'clock at night. I should have been home from work a while ago, but nobody is home and I really don't want to be alone tonight.

Cael, Lisa, and I have stayed long after work was over and we're supposed to be helping her with her French work, but of course we've decided playing our little game is way better than doing that instead. It's Lisa's turn to ask me a question. She squirms in her seat while she thinks, her red tartan leggings standing out against the soft brown of the seat she's sitting in.

"Okay," she says, her freckled nose crinkling, "Did you lose your virginity to *anyone* yet?" The way she says anyone, I know exactly who she is talking about, even as her eyes drift between Cael and I.

Cael chokes on his coffee.

My face turns bright red.

I want to hide under the table but she's looking at me as if it's the most important question in the universe. So, I answer.

"Nope," I say awkwardly, looking anywhere but both of their faces. "I have not. I've been with him for a month, so…and uhh, you have to be ready for sex…and oh God I don't know how to explain this…"

"Darn," she says, "because from what I've heard, everybody in the grades above me has already had sex," and I swear to God I didn't know Cael could live off of breathing just coffee because he is still choking on his drink and hasn't died yet.

"Who told you that?" I ask as I awkwardly pat Cael's back.

He waves me away, not unkindly, and chokes out, "Her father."

"Oh," I say, my face still not quite recovered from the nuclear bomb of a blush that my cheeks are broadcasting live to the world. "Well, he uh," I say, "he's probably thinking of somewhere else. This town is kind of…kind of sleepy – no not sleepy, what's a good word?"

"Normal?" Lisa supplies, and I nod, thankful for the way out.

"It's Cael's question now!" she crows happily, and he and I exchange a look as she thinks of a question to ask him.

"So, how old are you?" she asks him, and I let out the breath I was holding because that's such a mundane question to ask somebody she considers an uncle, but Cael stiffens.

He shrugs, but if he was going for nonchalant it didn't work. "My birthday is actually in three months."

Lisa frowns. "Avoid the question, whatever."

Cael smiles and ruffles her hair, causing her to sigh. "I think we should probably head out, guys. Tomorrow's a big day for Khiara and it's not getting any earlier, is it?" he says.

I look at my phone and gasp – it's almost ten o'clock. "Oh crap, yeah. I really need to get home."

Lisa hops off of her chair, runs around the table, and flings her arms around me in a hug. "I bet you're going to look so pretty tomorrow. You *have* to take pictures!"

Cael stands, brushes some cake crumbs off his pants, and walks up to us. He adds his arms around the two of us, "Yes," he says. "Pictures are a must. If I can't be there because of my arsehole boss, I want to at least live vicariously through your photographs."

"Don't worry," I assure the two of them. "Cara will take every opportunity to take pictures of absolutely *everything*."

Our hug breaks up and we all walk towards the back exit. "Cara scares me sometimes," says Lisa, but she's smiling. "She's funny and she reminds me of my dad. They have the same sense of humour. You should come over one day; I think you would like him."

"You and your dad are close, huh?" I ask.

She nods her head. "I never knew my birth mom. My dad always tells me I look like her but I wouldn't know. We have no pictures of her or anything. She just gave birth to me for my parents and disappeared."

"You look like *you*," says Cael, and he slips his hand in hers. "And you're beautiful."

I find myself shivering in the cold air outside; it'll start snowing soon if it keeps being this cold. Winter in Maine is harsh and unforgiving and I absolutely hate it. Why couldn't I live somewhere like Florida? I rub my arms, currently only covered by a thin sweater because I'm an idiot.

When we reach our cars, Cael's and mine respectively, we all say our goodbyes. "See you at school," says Lisa, as she climbs into Cael's dark green Nissan Sentra. I wave, and she closes the door. Cael gives me a quick kiss on the forehead and a promise to text me, and hops into his car.

An hour later I'm lying in bed, Pug snuggled up against my back, just falling asleep, when my phone buzzes not once, but twice. One text is from Cael, telling me to have a good day tomorrow.

The other is from a number I don't recognize, but I know somehow that it's definitely meant for me.

Be careful tomorrow.

I will. I don't know who sent this, but my gut tells me it's the same person who put the necklace in my locker, and that can only mean one thing; I'm in danger.

Seventeen

Semi-formal is finally upon us. Cara and I are standing in my bedroom just finishing the last touches to our respective looks, though I haven't looked in my mirror yet because Cara won't let me.

When I put my ruby stud earrings on to complete my look, Cara appraises me with a huge smile. "You look gorgeous, babe!"

I turn around and stare at myself. Wow, she's right – I do look gorgeous. I love how Cara's done my make up; my eyes are done in smoky greens and pinks, lined with black. My eyelashes look incredibly long, she used *so* much mascara, but it looks like they could actually be naturally like that. My lips are a soft pink, coated in lip gloss.

Squealing like mad, I hug her close to me. "Cara, whatever you did, it's amazing. You should be a make-up artist!"

Obviously this has made her day, because she squeals along with me and says, "Really? Screw nursing, I'll make a splash in the make-up world! But my Mom…"

She doesn't have to finish the sentence. Her mother was a make-up artist before her father hanged himself. She quit and got a job at a law firm because he used to work across from her at her make-up job, and they'd gotten lunch every day at the mall. Her mother can't look at a make-up artist without feeling guilty. But then again, she can't look at Cara without thinking of him and feeling guilty.

Awkwardly, I smile at her and loop my arm through hers, trying to help shake the feeling of guilt she carries with her wherever she goes. She's like a sister to me, so when she's in pain, I'm in pain. "Shall we?"

The dance is being held in our school's gym, so when we pull into the driveway, it's hard to find a parking space.

When we get inside, I notice that everybody has the same type of dress on except me and a few other people. *Of course...* if there's a certain way to be dressed at an event, you can bet that I will not be wearing the same type of thing as everybody else. In this case, almost everybody is wearing a flowing ball gown type of dress.

But I love it. I *will not* let this good moment be taken away from me.

When Cara notices Tristan, she grabs my arm and starts to run towards him, pulling me with her. It doesn't matter that he's not supposed to be here because he doesn't go to our school. He showed up just for Cara's sake. *Because he really likes her,* I think to myself.

He wraps his arms around her as soon as she lets go of my arm, "Hey beautiful!"

Smiling and bouncing, she hugs him back, all excited about the dance and about his presence. Tristan's eyes find mine and all I see in them is kindness. He smiles at me and nods his head once at me in greeting. "Khiara, don't you look...different. I don't mean that in a bad way – just that I'm pretty sure you're the only person who isn't wearing a ball gown." He looks down at Cara and kisses her head.

I reply, "Thanks! You look awesome too, how did you afford that tux? It's got to be, like a thousand dollars?"

He just shrugs and says, "It's a rental."

I nod my head and all of a sudden feel the need to turn around because that feeling of being watched, the one that I've grown accustomed to, is back, and I find Damien staring at me from across the room. Victoria's glaring at him while he glares at me. He looks like he's studying me like a complicated puzzle, and she looks like she wants to rip his eyes out of their sockets. I look away.

I never did eat those cookies he gave me... I think to myself. *He really creeps me out.*

"Hey, why don't you guys go dance. I know you're itching to. I'll be fine, I actually brought my book," I say, gesturing to the dance floor.

Cara's face lights up with pure delight saying, "Really Ki-ki?" at the same time Tristan says, "You're sure?" I smile, nod, and push them out onto the dance floor like the good friend that I am.

I find a seat near the stage so I can keep an eye on them, where a horrible wannabe punk rock band is playing so I can keep an eye on them and pull my book out from my purse. I begin to read it, for the hundredth time in a row. *Flowers for Algernon* has become one of my favourite books in the past two weeks. I get to page twenty-two when Victoria makes her way towards me.

Eyeing me reproachfully she says, "Stay away from Damien. He'll just end up hurting you in the end."

Taken aback, I say, "Excuse me? But don't you think it's a little odd to be telling me that *your* boyfriend is going to hurt me. What, do you suspect him of cheating? Because I'd never agree to anything like that, he's all yours Victoria. He gives me the creeps anyway."

All of a sudden her face softens like it did in the library and her eyes take on a pitying look to them, "Look, I know *you* wouldn't hurt a fly unless you had to. But he's just not a good person, Khiara. He'll want to hurt you soon. Yes, it's true that I act like I don't really like you, but I have my reasons and suspecting you of stealing my...*boyfriend* is not one of them, believe me. That's a little too juvenile for me." I frown and look down at my book. She's telling me to be careful...could that mean – "Stay away from him. That's all that I ask," she says, cutting off my thought before turning away and walking back towards Damien and her friends. She doesn't even wait for me to answer her; she just simply walks away.

That was awkward... I think to myself, as Cara and Tristan waltz across the dance floor to a totally un-waltz-able song. They're so cute together and he makes her a better person, not that she's a bad one. He's what she needs in life, more than I could have ever done for her, even if she *is* my best friend.

As I sit there, trying to get back into the book, everything suddenly stops, like it did in class, only I know for a fact that my necklace is not the cause. I look around the room. The only other person, who is not paused as far as I can tell, is Tristan. He lets go of Cara and walks towards me.

"You know, you're right. I do really like her," he says.

"How did you do that?" I say, pulling my knees up to my chin. It's happening again, oh God.

"Relax, it's only temporary. I just needed to talk to you in private and this is the only way to do it," he says.

"But *how!*"

"I just...can. I'm not so sure how, exactly, but I can do some pretty strange things. But believe me when I say it's okay. It doesn't make me *any* less human, Khiara."

Another voice, from across the room joins us, "Well, yes, it does actually. It makes you more Angel than anything, Nephilim." Victoria slowly walks towards us with a grace I hadn't noticed she possessed. How is she un-frozen? I don't know how any of this works, I mean it only happened to me once and I almost lost my mind.

"It is technically wrong for us to couple with humans to create…well, your kind," her face scrunches up into an expression of pain, but she wipes it away, fast.

She turns to me. "I'm sorry you had to learn this way, things are supposed to be much different, and I thought Cael would have told you all sooner, considering the circumstances." *Cael? What circumstances? Man, I knew something odd was going on between them the other day…*

As I'm trying to work everything out (because this is crazy) Tristan's face is as white as a sheet. "What did you call me?" he whispers.

"Nephilim, I think…" I supply, just going along with the insanity. Things like this don't happen in a span of minutes to normal people. Things like this just don't happen. And yet…

Victoria stops walking when she is an inch away from Tristan's face, staring him down. "You are the product of a human and one of The Fallen. Now, at least you can understand the aversion some people feel towards you, while others simply cannot get *enough* of you. Like your girlfriend. She is attracted to the real you, don't worry about that, but the real you happens to be a little more angelic than human. Your glory appeals to the little nymph. She likes *shiny* things."

He shakes his head, but I can tell by his face that he believes her. He knows it's true and I guess now so do I, as impossible as it sounds. I guess now I know how he guessed my bra colour so easily.

"Victoria, are you a good angel or a bad one?" I somehow ask through all of my confusion. It feels like something I should ask for some reason.

She smiles, and I think for the first time it's a genuine smile directed towards me. Turning to me, she says, "I'm on the fence when it comes to everyday living. But I suppose if you really want to know – and I guess you must – when the Battle comes, I will be on the side of Light."

Battle?

"Why did you mention Cael?"

"I think deep down, you already know the answer to that. I'm sure you've noticed some pretty odd things about him. He's never really been good at hiding his true nature…but then again, I've been here longer than he has." She jerks her head towards Damien, "Longer than him too, though not by much. *Don't* trust him."

Cael's voice echoes through my mind, as he tells me the story of the angel that fell in love with the human girl…he looked so sad after he told the story. *"There was an angel, an angel of Love. His calling was divine justice, and he was a very powerful angel."* I think about the weird happening with the necklace and everything strange that has ever happened to me – especially recently – and I feel the necklace pulse with warmth.

I want everything to go back to how it was, I think.

And then everything is just as it was.

Tristan is gliding across the floor with Cara, Victoria is chatting away with Damien, and I'm sitting here with my knees up to my face feeling like a fish out of water. Victoria catches my eye and winks and a cold shiver is sent throughout my whole body.

Tristan and Cara stop dancing when they glance over and notice my facial expression. They make their way over to me, sit down next to me, and both put their arms around me.

"What's up, babe?" asks Cara.

Tristan makes a funny face, "You feeling alright?"

I nod my head, suddenly extremely tired, and unable to explain what just happened to Cara without sounding insane I say, "Yeah, but I just had this really messed up dream. That's all."

Tristan's face becomes a mask of many different emotions, "Well, I'm sure you don't want to talk about it right now." But I understand what he's really saying; *we can't talk about it here.*

I nod again, "I just…" but a very drunk Damien cuts me off.

"Look at you!"

I look up at him. He's standing right in front of us pointing down at me. "You're one of a kind, did you know that? But what I really mean is that you're a *freak.* A freak that will be alone the rest of her life because you're," he pauses to think of the word, "cursed."

Heat floods my face as I realize that most everybody has stopped chatting and dancing to watch what's going on here and tears find their way to my eyes. He really must be dangerous. Something big is happening.

My heart feels like it's going to burst through my chest *I. Can't. Process. This.*

Damien keeps spewing things at me about curses and some type of war, and I force myself to stop listening because there are too many missing pieces to this puzzle. Tristan gets up and punches Damien square in the jaw, saying, "I think we've had just about enough of you," but it does nothing to him except make him laugh and walk away, Victoria quickly shooting me a strange look before following after him.

She said she was on the side of the light but I don't know what that means. I don't know what battle they were going on about, and frankly, I'm about ready to pee my pants like a toddler and throw a fit.

That punch should have broken Damien's jaw with its sheer force. But it didn't.

Cara rubs my back, "Come on, let's go. This party is lame anyway; we'll have our own at my house. Mom's out late tonight."

I open my mouth to say something, *anything*, I can't quite find the words to convey what I really want to say. So I get up and run straight for the door ignoring both Cara and Tristan's voices as they call my name.

I run as fast as I can.

I burst through the big double doors of the gym and into an onslaught of icy rain. My dress is instantly ruined and my makeup is completely smudged beyond repair. My hair is stuck to my scalp from the rain, but I don't even care anymore, I just want to get away from here. The fear and uncertainty I feel right now is worse than anything I have ever imagined, and it has burned its way into my very core.

I run until I end up on Valour Street. When I get to his house, you can't tell if it's tears or rain, or even both, running down my face but either way I know I look horrible.

I don't even care.

Knocking on his door, I wait, feeling impatient. I'm about to knock again when he opens the door, standing there in his boxers and nothing else; sleep is deep in his eyes. I remember that the dance only started at nine, and it must be almost eleven by now.

"Khiara? What time is it?" asks Cael.

"Late," I reply as he rubs at his eyes.

"It's cold and wet out, come in," he says, and I make my way inside into the warmth. I just stand there, in the doorway, unsure of where to start, until he looks me over and says, "You know what? You're going to take a hot shower. Stay right there and I'll get you a towel."

He leaves the room, and a minute later, he comes back into the room with a fluffy green towel. He hands it to me and points me to the bathroom, "Go do your thing, don't let me bother you."

When I get into the bathroom, I'm about to close the door and it's only then that I even remember my manners.

"Cael?" I say quietly, my head peeking out from the doorway of the bathroom.

He must be in his room, because he doesn't answer me right away, so I say it again, "Cael?"

This time, I hear his bedsprings creak – he must've been sitting on his bed playing his guitar or something, and he walks into the hall. "Yeah?"

I blush at the sight of him in his boxers even though it's not the first time (though the last time he was barely conscious) and thank him. He just smiles and goes back to his room and says, "Anytime."

When I get into the shower I let the water rush over me and am filled with a sense of calm. I let my mind drift as I rub the shampoo into my scalp and the soap onto my body, washing all of my troubles away. His shampoo smells like lavender and honey. When I step out of the shower, I feel *so* grateful and relaxed. I dry myself off with the towel he gave me and go about looking for my clothes, which aren't there, having been replaced by a pair of boxer shorts and a plain black tee shirt.

I slip them on, open the bathroom door and quietly pad down the hall towards his room. When I get there, I find that he's sleeping. I don't quite know what makes me do it, maybe it's the way he's snoring lightly, or maybe it's the small amount of drool that's running down his chin, but he just looks so vulnerable that I crawl into bed with him. This isn't our first sleepover but it's our first in his bed.

He starts a little, at the movement I suppose, but he sleepily wraps his arms around me and sighs, "Hey."

I wipe the drool off of his chin. "Hey yourself," I say as I snuggle deeper into him.

He yawns, "So are you going to tell me what happened tonight? Or am I going to have to guess."

"Guess," I laugh quietly as he yawns again.

"Did you…trip and fall into the punch?"

I make a game show buzzer noise, "Wrong answer. You lose this round. Which was the only round," it's my turn to yawn, "I'm exhausted."

He smiles, "Just go to sleep, we'll talk about it tomorrow."

I don't know how long I wait to say it but after a while I whisper, "Are you the angel?"

No response.

"From the story?"

He waits what feels like forever, until finally, his signature sad smile appears on his lips, and he nods his head, the movement sending that stubborn piece of hair over his closed eyes. "Yeah," he whispers back, "I am."

"What does that make me?" I ask. He closes his eyes. "Please, all of this weird stuff is happening and I know you said you couldn't tell me right away but I think it's time, Cael," I whisper. "You told me to trust you, but you need to trust me too."

"You're the girl," he says, opening his eyes and looking deep into my own. "You're the purest soul on Earth. You're the one I fell for and I have never regretted it. I will *never* regret it."

Eighteen

Bacon. That's the first word my mind supplies as I sit up, yawn loudly, and sniff the air. *Definitely bacon.* I look around the room and the events of last night come back to me in a whirlwind. Thank the lord we have the week off of school.

Oh God…I look around the room again, and take it in this time. The words "*I will never regret*" float around in my mind as I look at the wall where it's written in so many different languages. I now know what they mean.

I get up and walk towards the enticing scent of food, my panic slightly ebbed as my stomach takes over the task of thinking for my brain. "That smells good," I say as I walk into the kitchen, only to see that Cael's been rather busy. Pancakes, bacon, eggs, toast, and fresh fruit are set out on the small kitchen table.

"I figured you would have questions. So I thought food might distract you for a bit," he admits with a sheepish look plastered on his face. His hair is still messy from having slept and his blue eyes seem impossibly light against the backdrop of his black curly hair.

I shake my head, "It won't distract me. I can ask and eat at the same time."

He smiles and rolls his eyes, then runs his hand through his infuriatingly unruly hair. "Of course. You're taking this awfully well, you know."

I smile, albeit shakily. "Give me time. I just woke up."

He walks over to the coffee maker and pours some coffee into a huge mug, then goes to the fridge to add some milk. "I figure a big cup will be good. We have a lot to talk about."

Nodding I sit down at the small kitchen table where the food is laid out buffet style. I pile some food onto the plate he's put down for me and thank him when he hands me the huge mug of coffee.

"Soo," he says, looking everywhere but at me. "I should probably be honest with you."

I take a huge gulp of coffee and then sigh. "That'd be nice, yeah."

"This isn't the way I wanted to tell you but nothing is going the way it is supposed to." He looks at me finally, his eyes so, so sad.

"The day we met at Cara's party was a mistake. I'm…I'm not supposed to exist for you, not yet."

I put my coffee down. Narrow my eyes and bite my lip. "I don't understand…"

He sighs. "You were born in Ireland; your birth parents were Irish travellers, Maria and Ewan O'Leary. You were sick, and the midwife didn't think you'd make it through the night – and you probably wouldn't have."

Chewing on a piece of bacon, I nod again. "Yeah," I say once I've chased the bacon down with a sip from my mug. "My parents told me I was really sick when they found me."

Cael winces and shakes his head. "Well yes, you were. But that was after…"

"After?" I prompt.

His voice softens as if to lessen the blow of what he's about to say. "That was after you were cursed by the Goddess Morrigan. Your birth parents were selfish people, Khiara, and the Morrigan preyed on them, as she does selfish people. She is a Goddess of War and often takes the shape of a crow because they are natural tricksters. In the world of Gods, she is known as the Crow Goddess."

"Wait, what the hell? I don't understand…" I whisper, my food and coffee forgotten. "You're not making any sense."

Cael looks at me with eyes filled with a misery, ages old. "There is much that you still don't understand, and that humans shouldn't *have to* understand. There are many lower Gods and Goddesses but there is only one Almighty. He is the one we all refer to when we say God, but the truth is so much bigger."

"Did he create everything, then? Like the Bible says?"

A brief smile, "No," he says, "He didn't. There is truth in every religion but none of them *are* the truth. The Bible and books like it, they're just stories humans used to explain things they know little of. Things evolved mostly like you think they did. Science properly explains many things, but of course much of the world has yet to be scientifically discovered yet because you don't have the technology.

What we call Gods and Goddesses, are simply beings that formed naturally in the cosmos who found a home on Earth just at the dawn of its life. As for our God, He was…elected you could say, to protect and watch over humans, even after they have passed. He *did* create the Angelic race though, in *your* image, not his. So you could say the human race is older than the Angelic race, and our language, which is based off of the original language of the Godly entities."
Somehow despite my confusion I motion for him to continue.

"Earth was divided into three realms upon God's decision to watch over the humans,: the world of the living and the *physical body*, the world of the dead which is actually split into two halves, Heaven and Hell, and lastly, the in-between or Limbo as it's affectionately known. The latter two are realms of *spirit* that simply cannot be seen by most people, although there are those who can see beyond. See, before God decided to watch over the humans, spirits were flying everywhere once people died, all willy-nilly, and it was pretty chaotic. He intervened very early on, mind you. The other Gods and Goddesses govern over whatever they please, and there are multiple entities that work together to oversee things. Finally, there are the five Gods of the elements that the Fae worship, which they are referred to in the Faen language, as simply Mother Earth, Grandmother Spirit, Father Fire, Sister Wind, and Brother Water. They bear different names for different human cultures, mind you, but they are close to the Faen people."

"Fae? As in fairies?"

He nods. "Yeah, they have existed alongside humans since the dawn of man. Most look just like humans and are roughly the same size and stature, but there are some that are so small they could fit in the palm of your hand. When they die their bodies succumb to their particular type of magic so if they were a Water Fae for example, their body would simply dissolve into water as soon as they were placed into a river. Their soul will either be reborn or remain part of the environment."

"That's beautiful…"

"It is indeed," he says.

"How did…your kind come into being?"

"God called upon his heart when he was first elected to govern over humans and created us. The only difference is we are made of pure light and do not have physical bodies for our souls, unless we are banished to the physical realm, and we are supposed to serve only God, our Father." Three fingers on his right hand twitch, as if he were about to make a gesture, but he stops himself.

"So I was cursed," I whisper. "Why?"

"Morrigan came to your parents as a nurse named Morgan. You see, when you were born, your pure soul was like a beacon, and Angels – Fallen and otherwise – Gods, and people able to see what they should not, knew that something was up. She knew that you were very sick and would probably not make it and thought it was quite a shame. She asked your parents if they could be rich and young forever but would have to give you up in exchange, if they'd do it." Tears form in my eyes. I know the answer.

"Your mother said that you would be dead soon anyway, and your father agreed. Morrigan was angered by their lack of compassion, and cursed both your parents, and you. She gave your parents immortality, but no riches, and you…I'm so sorry." He whispers the apology like it could possibly help put my life as I knew it back together. "You were cursed to have no soul mate or Guardian."

Everything seems to shatter into a thousand pieces after that. I'm vaguely aware of calling Cara to come pick me up and to bring me some clothes, of Cael apologising to me over and over again, but I can't understand words anymore. I can't look at him anymore. Can't understand why this would happen to me.

Once I get into Cara's car, I apparently tell her where to go, because she nods her head and starts to drive, but I can't remember where I told her to go.

When I finally come back to my own mind, I'm standing on the Pipton Bridge, looking down into the water.

"Wanna talk about it?" asks Cara, gently putting her hand on my shoulder. I shake my head. My phone vibrates in my pocket but I ignore it.

"I want to explain, Cara, but I don't know how." I look at her. "I'm scared…"

My phone vibrates again.

Somebody calls my name in the distance; Cael.

"He followed us," says Cara. "I need to know what happened, I'm worried about you, Ki-ki."

I can see him at the beginning of the bridge, the wind whipping around his already messy hair, this way and that. "Please!" he shouts.

We don't move from our place in the middle of the bridge, and wait for him to come to us.

Cael's eyes are wild with panic when he reaches us. "Please. I really need to tell you something. It's important."

"Why should I listen to you when all you did was keep things from me for so long?" I know how irrational I'm being because the situation is a lot more complicated than I can even fathom, but I don't really care if I'm being honest. How could he not have told me earlier about everything?

He seems suddenly aggravated. "I just wanted to keep you safe! You don't understand! I was supposed to keep you safe and I…" his voice breaks as it cuts off, his electric blue eyes pleading with me.

This just irritates me, again irrationally but I still don't care much – maybe I've lost my mind? "Keep me safe? What are you, my Guardian Angel or something? I mean *obviously* I don't understand!"

I can see that my words have hit Cael like a slap in the face because he knows that one of the rules of the curse means that I'm to have no Guardian, I can tell just by the tears that well up in his eyes.

But then he says, "I-I was…but not anymore." He reaches out to me, but I don't take his hand because of the shock coursing through my body. This situation keeps getting more convoluted as time goes by and I just can't keep up.

"What?" is the only thing I can possibly think to say.

He retracts his arm and raggedly runs his fingers through his hair. "I *was*. But I didn't do a good enough job. I didn't keep you safe. I let my own emotions get in the way, and I interfered when I shouldn't have. Remember the first night we met? That empty, sick feeling you got? I got that too. For you, it seemed like I'd contracted some type of bug, I'm sure, but to me, it felt as if my whole body was on fire and that something so very precious had been *ripped* from me. That was our tie being severed, my Guardianship being taken away, and for the first time, you truly felt alone, didn't you? Because of that stupid, *fucking*, curse."

"Why?" I ask. He just stares at me, his chest moving up and down and up and down, so rapidly that I'm almost afraid he'll start hyperventilating.

I reach out a hand to meet his, that's been hanging in the space between us. His tears finally spill from his eyes. My heart does something like a flip in my chest.

"Because I *love* you!" he says, his voice rough, raw. "You could hate me for what I am and for what I've kept from you but I need you to know that I love you, and I have since the moment I laid eyes on you; on your *soul*. It's the most beautiful thing that I have ever seen, ever will see, and I will *never* stop loving you, Khiara. I love everything about you, even your flaws, because you're *human* and I will *never* be human, *ever.* My body will never *feel,* the way yours does. If I jumped right now…"

I gasp as he points to the water, picturing him plummeting onto the rocks that lay just below the surface.

"I would heal within minutes. If I were to get shot, it would knock me down but the bullet would disintegrate from my flesh and all of my wounds would close up, as if they had never happened. I have been alive for far too long but I only started living the night we met."

I don't know what comes over me but I walk over to him, take his face in my hands then pull it towards me and kiss him on his full, beautiful lips. I kiss him for every time that I have ever wanted to but was too afraid to do it. At first, he doesn't kiss me back because I think I've caught him off guard. But then, he lets go and kisses me back with a fierce passion. It's a heart stopping, world spinning, crazy kind of kiss. It's wonderful.

It's like truly breathing for the first time.

And *yes*.

Yes, if there was ever doubt in my mind before, it's gone now because I am in love with this boy, this *angel*, that I've only known for about a month but who's protected me my whole life. I think in some way that's why I felt like I've known him forever.

I have, haven't I? Hasn't my soul always somehow recognized him?

A startling amount of wind picks up all of a sudden, and I hear a loud clap of thunder which makes me yelp and open my eyes, all thoughts of passion thrown from my mind. The first thing I notice is his expression of apprehension.

"Sorry…"

"Was that you?" I ask, my voice shaking a bit. I don't actually know what he's capable of.

He gives a nod, and then a shake of his head, and then another nod. "Kind of. It's uh, well, I caused it." Then he blushes and looks down at the ground, "Would you believe me if I said that right now, God is really, really pissed off with me?"

I nod my head, because at this point I can't *not* believe.

"He can't give me another chance at being your Guardian, and because I blew it, He is really angry but He ordered the Gods of thunder and rain to show us a sign."

Another clap of thunder resounds, as if to agree with Cael's statement, and then it starts pouring rain.

"He's also kind of rooting for us. I'm not the only one who has a weakness for you, it seems." In seconds we're soaked from the cold rain.

"He's got a funny way of showing it," I hear Cara mutter. *Oh crap, Cara!*

"How long have you been here?" asks Cael and I at the same time, both blushing profusely.

Cara shrugs, like it's no big deal, "As you might recall, Khiara called me in a catatonic state to come pick her up and ordered me to drive her here. I'm just the chauffeur." She puts her hands up in a very *I surrender* kind of way.

"So…" I say awkwardly. "You saw all of that?" Cara nods and then shrugs her shoulders.

"I guess you're probably wondering why I'm not freaking out about the curse?" she asks then.

Cael laughs breathlessly and looks between Cara and I, "Kind of. But I have a hunch as to why this is no big deal to you." Cara smirks and replies, "Yes, well all in due time I guess."

I chuckle, "She'll go along with pretty much anything."

"Yeah," she says, laughing. She sounds somewhat sarcastic when she says, "Could it get any weirder?"

"Actually," Cael takes in a deep breath and looks me right in the eyes, "you are the one that's supposed to bring about The Great Battle between the sides of dark and light because of how pure your soul is. That's what I was trying to tell you before you left. I'm so sorry, Khiara. It wasn't supposed to be like this, but the curse…it complicated things."

Well shit…

Nineteen

Cara, Cael, and I are sitting on Cael's couch. I just explained to Cara pretty much everything she missed – which admittedly is a lot more than I wanted to keep from her and it feels great to finally come clean about what's been happening to me.

The television is on low playing an old black and white romance movie.

Cael made us some hot chocolate because by the time we got to his place the rain turned into hail and we were already soaked through to the bone. Our clothes are currently in the dryer and Cara and I are wearing borrowed pyjamas from Cael's closet.

"So, about your accent, you're obviously not really Irish are you?" asks Cara, voicing something I've wanted to ask since I figured out what he is.

"No, I am not technically Irish," he says, "I sound like this because it was the site of my Fall. It's simply coincidence that Khiara's two incarnations were born in the same country. It could have been anywhere the second time 'round."

"I don't believe in coincidence," says Cara in a mater-of-fact kind of tone, crossing her arms. "I think something happened when you held her first incarnation's spirit."

"What do you look like as an angel?" I enquire, curious.

He takes a sip of his hot chocolate and smiles. "Pretty much like I do now, except I have wings and glow," he replies. I smile, remembering something he'd said to me after our first date.

"Can it overpower evil simply by looking at it?"

"Yes," says Cael, his eyes full of laughter, "that would be my Glory. Its shine overcomes evil." He turns to Cara and says, "I shit you not." She bursts out laughing and Cael smiles his sheepish smile, and I know everything is right in the world again.

"Can we see your wings?" I ask, tentatively.

He shakes his head, "No. They're made of spiritual matter. You can only see an angel's true form if you are dying. Let's hope you never see them." He whispers the last part solemnly.

"Where do they…go. Like, how do you walk around and not hit things with them. Can I feel them?" I ask, and he laughs at my round of questions.

"They exist in two different places at once, I guess, kind of like myself. In this particular plane, I appear human but to other angels who also inhabit both planes, I appear in my true form. I don't know if you could feel them," he replies thoughtfully. "Every shirt I own has very thin slits in the back so I don't have to bind them; the slits are so thin you can hardly see them. Why don't you give it a try? I mean they're *here*, you just can't see them because you're human."

He stands up and turns his back towards me. "Give it a go," says Cara, eagerly waiting to see if I can actually feel them.

"You can try too," he states. "I'm curious if it affects you."

"If I can feel them, Cara probably can too," I say, stating what I assume is the obvious.

Cara frowns but nods her head, and I wonder what those secrets she mentioned are. Cael's head whips around and he says, "She'll have to tell you herself."

"It's very rude to listen in on people's thoughts, you know," I say. Cael laughs and turns around again so we can resume our little experiment.

Cara reaches out towards his back and the disappointment she exudes is palpable. "Shit," she mutters. "I can't feel anything! Cael, can you feel me touching your wings?"

He shakes his head no. Cara's phone rings and she excuses herself to the bathroom to talk to Tristan and I think to give us some alone time.

I reach out expecting not to feel anything but instead, my fingertips meet with the softest thing I have ever felt. Cael stiffens under my touch but doesn't push me away, so I run my fingers across the silky-soft feathers of his wings and try to imagine what they must look like.

Under my touch, I can feel his wings quivering; he is visibly shaking as well. "Are they curled up against your back?" I ask. He nods his head. "Are you comfortable with them that way?"

"It's…" his voice cracks and he has to clear his throat, "it's kind of like having to consciously flex a muscle, or suck your stomach in all day. Eventually you forget how uncomfortable it is and you grow used to the feeling, and when you're alone, you just let it go. Whenever I'm alone, I can unfurl them, but in public I have to keep them close to my body. You can't *possibly* understand how good this feels right now."

"Why don't you unfurl them now?" I suggest. He takes a second to think the idea over and he nods his head.

"Okay," he says as I take my hands off his back, "but you should probably prepare yourself for it." He turns around to face me, and he cups my cheek with both of his hands. "Are you ready?"

I nod.

"Alright then," he whispers, and all of a sudden a current of heat rushes into me, a small gust of warm wind that picks up my hair for only a moment. The T.V. turns off and then back on again and the lights flicker.

Cael takes my hand and places it seemingly in mid-air, but I can feel his solid wing beneath my hand; it's unmistakeable. He closes his eyes in pleasure.

"Turn around," I whisper, in complete awe. "I want to feel them both."

He sits down next to me and presents his back to me, his wings brushing up against my body as he gets situated on the couch. "Sorry," he says. "They're kind of big. Usually I have the whole couch to myself."

I reach out and run both my hands along each wing, taking in their delicate softness. "It's alright. They're beautiful," I breathe.

Cael chuckles, "You can't even see them."

"I don't have to," I say. "I just know. I can feel it."

I continue to explore the invisible expanse of his wings and I feel him lean into me ever so slightly, encouraging me to continue. "You don't understand how good this feels. Imagine the best massage you could ever get and then multiply that times one-hundred, and you wouldn't even be close to how amazing this feels."

Of course, Cara picks this time to interrupt us. "Holy shit!" she exclaims. "The air around you guys is tinted blue!"

I look around the room, but I can't see what she's talking about, but Cael laughs, deep and rich, and wonderful. "Oh," he says.

"That's an after effect of unfurling my wings, my Glory shines through. Humans can't see it because it's a part of my true form."

Cara looks as though she's a deer caught in the headlights of a car. "I uhh," she says, looking between Cael and I. "Err, well, the thing is, I'm only *half* human. The other half is Faen; Nymph, actually. Specifically my identifying element is fire. Hence the red hair," she points to her head.

"Don't be mad," she pleads with me when she sees my surprised expression. "I've wanted to tell you, but we're not usually supposed to tell humans what we are unless we have a good reason and I haven't found one until now."

"What's the reason?" I ask, somewhat hurt by her admission. Everybody seems to be keeping things from me.

She sits down next to me and Cael turns to face us, his wings curling around my body in a hug-like gesture along with his arms. "Because," she says, "my dad used to tell me bed time stories about this human girl who would change the fate of *everything* one day. She would rise up as a warrior of the Gods, and it was our people's job to make sure she reached her goal. My mother thought they were just made up fairy tales because she didn't know what we were, no pun intended on the fairy part, but I realize now that they were meant to prepare me. My dad and grandma used to take me to these gatherings where all of the adults would talk to us about it to keep us quiet."

My eyes grow wide in astonishment. This can't mean what I think it means…"To prepare you for what?"

"Protecting *you*. There are no truly Dark Fae, Khiara; only Light. And you, you are *pure*. I can't believe I never noticed before. I guess I should have known, it's just, you're so…"

"Boring?" I supply. Cael's wings tighten around me, and he brushes a piece of hair from my forehead with one of his hands, while reaching down to hold one of mine with his other.

Cara snorts. "No, not *boring*. You're just *you*. We met by pure chance. I never expected that I'd be fighting along with my best friend. Or at all. This makes my awesome fictional bed time story task so much more appealing now that I know it's legit. I never expected the girl from the story to be real, let alone turn out to be you! I just thought it was some bullshit elitist Fae story they tell kids to make them feel special. Every race has them."

"Does Tristan know you're half Nymph?" I ask, and she shakes her head. Fleetingly I wonder if she knows he's Nephilim, but I figure that's for him to tell her. Cael squeezes my hand in what I take as a silent agreement and I realize it's nice not to have to voice my thoughts for him to hear them.

"I know I have to tell him," she says. "I just don't know when. I don't want him to react badly, you know? My kind, we're pretty sexual…hence the word nymphomaniac. We have an allure, and in my case since I'm half human, I just come off as extra flirty…and you know, kinda promiscuous. I've always tried to tell you it's just in my nature. But when we mate, we mate for life…and I don't want to scare him. I feel like he's the one."

"I don't think you'll scare him off," I say as I crinkle my nose in thought. "He really likes you."

She smiles and then suddenly she makes the face that I have grown to love over the years. It's her I-have-an-idea face. "I could invite him over," she says. "That way he'd have you guys here and you could tell him everything too! We'd all be in on it, like a team."

I turn to look at Cael, who shrugs. "He's welcome to come over, if he wants. I'll put the coffee on."

I smile as Cara picks up her phone and begins violently texting, her fingers flying across the screen of her smartphone.

The doorbell rings and suddenly Cael's warmth disappears as he gets up to answer the door.

"Hey," says Victoria's voice from the front door. She walks right in and sits down next to me as if we're best friends and Cael looks helpless to stop her. I remember her mentioning that she's been here longer than him and I assume her hierarchy is higher up than his. "Can I join your little party? I'm sick and tired of babysitting Damien. I've got a friend watching him currently, so I've freed up a substantial amount of time before I have to go crawling back to that pathetic idiot."

I nod my head and open my mouth to say something when Cara says, "What's she doing here?"

Victoria turns to her and says, "Any problems you have with me, know that I am not who I have presented myself as. I am known as Verchiel, Angel of Affection. I fell in love with a human who lived in Egypt in 500 BCE and I was banished to this realm because of it. I did not know it at the time, but I was betrayed by one of my own.

The man I loved took me in and cared for me and we eventually had a family together, one daughter and a son. That's all I'll say on the matter."

"What were their names?" I whisper, and she turns to me.

"It doesn't matter now. They're all dead."

"I'm sorry," I say. "That's awful."

"Who betrayed you," breathes Cara.

Victoria frowns and says, "His Heavenly name is Douma, Angel of The Silence and Stillness of Death. Damien. He is the one who betrayed me in Paradise and he's the one who put out the order to kill my family out of jealousy. He had been the one to comfort me right after it happened and I was distraught and scared. I didn't know that he was in love with me at the time and he tricked me in to falling in love with him by pretending to care about the loss of my family. I never thought that he'd do something so wicked and cruel. In Heaven he was one of my greatest confidants, the one I told everything to. I didn't know that he'd go Dark."

"Including the fact that you were in love with a human…" I whisper.

She nods. "I found out years later. Of course I pretended that I didn't know and I still do. He thinks I'm not on the side of Light. It'll be a good day when he realizes that I have fucked him over for all he's done."

"Well then," says Cara. "Cael, get the girl some coffee because she's just earned my respect."

Twenty

When Tristan gets to Cael's, he's pretty confused as to why Cara is sitting on a couch next to somebody she can hardly stand on a good day. When his eyes meet my own, I can see he's remembering the other night and what Victoria said to him. Cael gets him set up with a coffee and everybody goes quiet, the only sound coming from the T.V. which is on pretty low.

"Clearly I've missed a lot," he says to nobody in particular.

Smiling sheepishly, "You have no idea," Cara says.

"Soo," he says. "I guess you guys want to clue me in on something? Because that's the reason I called Cara in the first place. I have something to tell her."

Cara bites her lip and her blue eyes meet mine. I nod my head, smile, and even throw in an exaggerated wink to break the tension.

"Well, I guess I should start first," says Tristan. "Try not to freak out and just listen to what I have to say. I'm not...I'm not human. Well, I am, but I'm not exactly a full one. I've always known that I could do some pretty strange things, but I always figured it was just...I don't really know." He clears his throat. "My father was a Fallen Angel but I know next to nothing about him because he left my mother when I turned two. My mother is human."

Cara smiles slightly, "That's uh, not so bad. I mean, I just found out all of this stuff exists thanks to these two," she points at Cael and Victoria, "but it's nice to have a little continuity I suppose."

Tristan opens his mouth to say something and Victoria cuts him off. "Yes, as you know, I am not human. And neither is he," she nods in Cael's direction. "We are of the Fallen, on the side of Light."

"I liked it better when you talked like a regular teenager," mutters Cara, throwing some serious shade at Victoria with her eyes.

Victoria smiles, "Yes, well, sometimes I need to work on not killing people who get on my nerves. Pretending to be a teenager gets hard sometimes. So watch it."

"Stop being so violent!" laughs Cael.

Victoria chuckles and Cara sticks her tongue out at her. I guess old habits die hard.

"Okay," says Cara. "So now that you've put things on the table, I have to tell you something. And then maybe Khiara might want to also add in some…important information, since this has become a weird supernatural pow-wow." She twirls a lock of red hair and takes a deep breath. "I'm *also* not fully human."

The shock that shows on Tristan's face is intense. I feel as though it's a tangible thing, a cloak that's wrapping itself around his being. He looks around the room and takes everybody in.

"Is there *anybody* here who is a normal human?" he whispers. Oddly, I can relate to how he seems to be feeling.

I raise my hand. "I'm human. But can you define normal?"

He shakes his head. "I guess not." Then, to Cara, "I just…wanted somebody to balance out the non-human part of me. I'm not *natural*."

Tristan stands up. "What *are* you?" he almost shouts at Cara, his voice frantic and like a slap directly to Cara's soul, because he looks almost disgusted – which is ridiculous because he just admitted that he isn't even fully human.

Cara's eyes are wide and filled with tears but her jaw is set and I can tell that she is very hurt, maybe angry. "I'm half Fire Nymph. My father was of the Faen people. My mother, like yours, is human. She cheated on him and he killed himself."

Tristan looks at me. "And what's wrong with you? You're human, but there's obviously something off about you too. I could feel it when we met."

I'm about to tell him the whole curse thing, when Cara stands up and grabs Tristan by the shoulders with both of her hands, and gets right in his face. "There's nothing *wrong* with her and there's nothing wrong with me or anybody in this room. We are just different, and so what? Why is that so bad? I'm not that much different than you are. I'm still a person; we all are. Race doesn't make anybody less of a person."

"Damn," says Victoria, surprised.

Cael lets out a low whistle.

Tristan shakes Cara off of him and stumbles towards the door. "I just wanted somebody uncomplicated, normal, *and human.* I knew you were a bit of a lush when we met, but I liked you because you seemed interesting. I just…I need to think about all of this. I just need some time."

"But –"

"I'll text you later," he says, and soon he's out the door. Cara runs to the door and I follow after her, but it's already too late. He's gone. The only sound is the wind which is cold and smells like the promise of snow. Winter is coming. Good bye fall.

~*~

Cara and I are sitting on my bed. I put together some snacks but I seem to be the only one interested in actually eating them, as Cara's just taking out her frustration on one of the low fat blueberry muffins.

"I don't deserve this muffin! Stupid *low fat muffin! I shouldn't be eating this; it's for skinny people. I'm so fat! I should be eating like a fatty! Buy me some McDonald's!"* It's no use arguing with her when she's like this, so I stay quiet as she screams herself hoarse.

"Are you done now?" I ask as Cara puts her head in her hands and begins to cry. I try not to let the sympathy show in my voice because I know she'd be annoyed if I did, but she doesn't notice and nods, miserably.

I smile at her, and she smiles back at me and blinks her tear-thick lashes, "Sorry," she says. I roll my eyes, "Don't even worry about it. So you're half Nymph and your boyfriend is half Angel. You guys should be on a show together. The premise would make a lot of people pretty interested." I bop her on the shoulder, "He'll come around. I think he's just scared. I mean he just found out he's not fully human a couple of days ago and he thought you'd compensate for that. It's stupid, but I get it. He'll call you, Cara;, he really likes you."

She hiccups and then burps, prompting us to laugh like idiots and then she's snorting, which is making me laugh harder. When she calms down enough to talk, she says, "Thank God you're not one of those stereotypical heroines who keeps her best friend in the dark. I would hate you. Really, really hate you. And I wouldn't have been able to tell you about what I am."

"Heroine? Screw that, Cara. I'm probably going to die, for all we know. And stereotypical actually is a pretty good word to describe me. I'm just a regular, average looking teenager who's had the fate of the entire world as we know it thrust upon her. Call me Mary-Sue."

Cara nods her head, "Mary-Sue it is! I can be you're right hand gal, Merry-Jane."

I wipe an imaginary tear from my eye, "What would I ever do without you?"

She shrugs and pulls me into a big bear hug, "Don't think about that, Mary-Sue. Mary-Jane's got your back." She pulls back and holds me at arm's length, "Seriously though, *don't* think about it because I'm *not* going anywhere. I'm going to fight by your side."

She holds out her hand, which is wet with tears and snot (and yes, I let her touch me with that hand) and a brilliant red flame appears in her palm. "I promise."

Twenty-One

As it turns out, Nymphs are bad with rejection, being such affectionate creatures. I knew Cara always took things a little too hard but I never realized that it was in her *blood*. I just thought she enjoyed being dramatic, because she's always said so. But that was part of her cover-up. And I now know why she wants to go into nursing so badly; she has a small amount of healing knowledge passed on to her from her father's adoptive mother, who she always referred to as Grandma Coal, because of her coal black eyes and hair native to the Sprit Nymphs (go figure, I didn't know Spirit was an element). She lives close to Portland, and hasn't visited Cara since her father died, though Cara has gone out there at least once a year to visit her in her forest home. I've been on only a few of those trips. She was always very kind to me and insisted on my calling her Grandma Coal as well.

At Bren's (Cara's father) funeral, Grandma Coal took my hands in her own and thanked me for being there for Cara. She told me I could visit with Cara anytime but I never wanted to ruin their time together so I only visited every two years instead of every year, to give them time to bond.

It takes two days for Tristan to finally realize how much of an idiot he was being. Two days of Cara clinging to me like a toddler that's been refused candy clings to their parent in hopes of getting some. When he finally calls her she almost jumps off of my bed in excitement.

"He's calling! What do I say?" She flails her arms like a madwoman until eventually pointing at the ringing phone.

"How should I know? Just answer and hear him out."

"No."

"Cara, it's going to stop ringing soon. You should probably–"

She answers. "Hello?"

A minute passes then two, then four, then six and so on as he talks to her. Her face goes through a range of emotions until after fifteen solid minutes of silence on her part, she bursts into tears.

"Is everything okay?" I ask.

"He says he wants to know everything."

~*~

"You know," I say to Tristan as he walks into my room, "I wanted to break your face."

"I know," he says, rubbing the back of his neck. "I freaked out and fucked up." I walk over to him and punch him in the arm.

"I deserved that," he says.

"Yes, you did," Cael says from his perch on my window seat, his eyes full of laughter. He got here about ten minutes before Tristan. Apparently Cara texted him to come on over and he extended that invitation to Victoria, who is currently sitting on my bed like she owns it.

"Now that we're all here," she sighs, lazily stretching out like a cat across my still sleep-messy sheets (I didn't expect to have anybody but Cara over or I would have at least made my bed), "I suppose we should get started."

Cara rolls her eyes. "Get started on what? I updated him on everything over the phone."

Victoria frowns but nods her head anyway. "Good. Then that saves us time. We're going on a field trip today."

Cael hops off the window seat and walks toward me. "We figured since we're all in one place, we may as well break out the big guns. If we're going to get through the Battle intact we're going to have to build relationships with the people fighting on our side. And we also figured we'd start with a mutual friend of mine and Vicky's –"

"I like it when you call me Vicky," Victoria says. "It's much better than *Victoria*." I make a mental note to refer to her as Vicky from now on.

"Anyway, our friend is a good guy," says Cael. "His name's Liam and he'll be instrumental in helping keep you alive during the Battle. He's extremely strong and powerful."

"Let's get this show on the road!" shouts Vicky as she pops up in a sudden burst of energy. "There's going to be food there and I'm hungry."

Cara, Tristan, and I exchange an awkward look with each other. "Okay then," I say.

~*~

Vicky glances at me with a strange look on her face as we walk up the steps to a cozy looking bungalow twenty minutes away from town, tucked into the forest off of a dirt road. The property has everything it needs to keep warm out here for the harsh winter that is on its way. There's a huge stack of firewood next to the house that will last them quite some time if they burn it wisely.

It's pretty cold today so we all decided it was best to wear sweaters – of course not Vicky, who doesn't seem to mind the cold.

"What?"

She sighs, "Don't be nervous okay?"

I laugh, "What, does Liam thrive off of fear?"

"Kind of," she says as she pulls me towards the door of the small house.

"Really?"

She chuckles and I realize that she was kidding. Tristan, Cara, and Cael are not far behind us.

As we walk through the back door into the little kitchen/dining area, I'm struck by how cozy it is inside. The appliances in the kitchen, which is painted a cheery canary yellow, are all new but you can tell they've been used. The kitchen table is small and round, enough for about four people, but there's an island where some chairs have been placed I assume to accommodate more people.

Liam is sitting at the table reading a magazine. His bare arms are covered in tattoos, angelic symbols I think, and his hair stands straight up in a black mohawk. His skin is a nice brown and I notice that his eyes are a deep green when he looks up at us. He looks as if he could be of Asian descent, maybe India. I make a mental note to ask where he Fell.

At first glance, he looks absolutely terrifying, but when I look through the kitchen to the living room, I realize that his appearance is just that, an appearance. There are toys and gaming consoles in the living room, an indication of children and the walls are painted a nice shade of orange. The two couches that occupy the space look as if you'd sink right into them if you were to sit in them.

"Hi," I manage to say.

He looks up from his magazine again, nods at me, and says gruffly, "You're the one?"

Awkwardly I run my fingers through my hair, a gesture I guess I must've picked up from Cael. "Yeah, I guess so."

He smiles and beckons me over, "Come, sit. Do you want anything?"

I try to answer but he just gets up and smiles warmly. "You like pizza?"

"Um, yeah, I do," I answer a little bewildered.

"Is cheese okay? My daughter's allergic to the spices they use in pepperoni and V here hates anything with vegetables so I just ordered plain cheese," he says.

I smile, encouraged a bit. "Yeah, that sounds great."

Tristan, Cara, and Cael walk in and he asks Tristan and Cara the same question. They both tell him it's perfectly fine.

Liam claps Cael on the back and they exchange one of those man-hugs, "Hey, Cam."

"Nice to see you again, Leliel," says Cael, using (I assume) Liam's angelic name. "A week is too long to go without seeing you!" he says sarcastically.

"Cam?" asks Cara, looking at Liam expectantly.

Liam smirks, "Camael, *angel* of Divine Love and Justice. But of course that's not what he's going by these days."

"Oh," Cara takes a moment to think about it. "That would make sense, then. I'll have to start calling you that," she says, teasingly poking Cael in the ribs.

Cael smiles good-naturedly, his blue eyes sparkling. "I like Cael just fine, thanks. It makes me feel…" he trails off in thought for a second. "It makes me feel more human."

"Well you know, you're not," says Liam, very matter of fact. He pulls Cael close to him again and grinds his fist playfully onto the top of his head. "You're my little brother of sorts, and I'm sure as hell not human, no offence to present company, half or whole."

He chuckles, "My daughter is half human so I'd be a real hypocrite if I discriminated against humans. Which is *whyyy*, you have permission to call me Liam. I have to keep up appearances."

The doorbell rings and from somewhere in the house, "I've got it," cries a female voice. I instantly recognize it; Lisa.

She comes scampering down the hall and into the small part of passage that divides the living room and kitchen. Lisa's in an old pair of black sweat pants and a comfy looking green camisole, and there is a huge smile on her face. "I'm so happy you're here!" she squeals, clapping her hands.

The doorbell rings again, two times in fast succession. She laughs and smacks her hand against her forehead. "Right, the pizza. Don't want to leave the guy hanging."

Dashing towards the front door at an inhuman speed, her blonde hair trailing behind her, she reaches the door just as the pizza guy is on his third ring. "Impatient much?" she says when she opens the door, handing him a twenty and telling him to keep the change.

"It's going to snow soon, you know," he replies dryly. "But thanks for the tip."

In her excitement, Lisa slams the door in his face and runs with the two pizzas towards the kitchen.

"Okay, now everybody is here!" she says excitedly.

"Not everybody," says Liam. "Wake Sam up, he should be here for this."

She rolls her eyes but does so with a smile on her face. "Okay. He'll be grumpy though, he hasn't been sleeping much."

"Lisa go wake up your brother," he orders. She sighs and leaves the room momentarily only to come back out holding the hand of a small boy with the most beautiful head of blond, curly hair I have ever seen. His skin is a gorgeous colour – not quite white but not brown either. His shirt has a blue dinosaur on it.

"Hi," he says rubbing eyes that are so green it should be a crime. The intelligence they hold for such a young child is unbelievable. "My name is Sam. I'm five."

"Hi Sam," I say, bending down to his height "My name is Khiara. I'm seventeen."

He smiles at me, showing perfectly dimpled cheeks. "Your soul is pretty," he declares. "But your face is pretty too. I'm glad." Sam extends his little chubby hand. "Nice to finally meet you."

I shake his hand. "Well it's nice to meet you too."

"Are you sick?" he asks, as we all gather around the counter while Liam hands out plates and Lisa doles out the pizza.

"Well I have a cold." Suddenly I'm feeling kind of self-conscious and nervous; how can such a small boy be so perceptive? "Why do you ask?"

Sam's face falls a bit and he whispers, "I can feel it. It's a heavy kind of sick, a strong one. Do you wanna lie down in my bed? It's kind of small but you'd fit just enough." *Oh...*

"It's okay," I reply, my voice quivering a bit. "I'll be alright." His green eyes crinkle in concern.

"Sam, stop bothering our guest or she'll never want to come back," Liam scolds though not harshly and Sam laughs then scampers over to him arms raised so Liam can pick him up.

"I'm sorry," he says. "I just noticed."

"This kid," Liam says. "This kid is a special one."

Once we're all seated on the couches with our cups full of juice or soda – we decided the living room would be a suitable place to fit all eight of us – and our plates full of delicious pizza from our town's only pizza parlour (and really, it's just a mom and pop deli that also sells overpriced but tasty pizza), there is much to discuss. Liam has already been brought up to date on who Tristan and Cara are, and about how much we all individually know, which apparently isn't much in the grand scheme of things.

Liam clears his throat, and begins talking. "When Lucifer Fell and took at least one third of the angels that were in Heaven with him, willing and unwilling, and he vowed to do away with anything that belonged to...we'll call him *Man-Deh* which is his name in the Angelic language. The closest pronunciation is the Hebrew word for God, but it isn't exact either. It translates, *roughly* to 'life-breath' which is kind of appropriate since he breathed life into the Angelic race."

"Rumours started flying around that he was preparing anybody he could find, anybody who would listen, and corrupting them. As time went by, more and more were following him. The repentant Fallen who he brought with him were targeted and killed unless they joined him. He forced angels to take advantage of innocent civilians and the Nephilim race was born. He ordered the Nephilim killed if they were too weak and more like their human parents. This was before the rise of the people of ancient Mesopotamia. And this was before the angels in Heaven began to fall in love with humans or became enamoured with the idea of free will."

"What happened then?" I ask at the same time as Cara. She smiles at me and bumps her shoulder against mine, a smile on her face. "You owe me a soda," she says, and I can't help but laugh.

Liam smiles, rolls his eyes at us like he would his own daughter, and continues. "Well, eventually there were just as many repentant Fallen than there were Lucifer's followers. We call them demons, but they're exactly like us, just Dark. Rumours of a prophesy began in Heaven and made their slow way to Earth. The purest soul would set us free, but only after a war between Light and Dark."

"You," breathes Cael, looking at me as if I'm the center of his universe. "The purest soul ever born; almost Angelic, but still human."

Is it possible to blush with your whole body? Because I think that's what's happening to me, I send my thoughts straight to him. He smiles and sits back, never breaking eye contact, his pizza forgotten. Sam takes advantage of this, and swipes Cael's last piece, shoving it happily into his mouth.

"Your pizza's fallen victim to my brother," says Lisa, from her seat on the floor next to the couch Cara, Tristan, and I are sitting on.

Cael shakes his head, still smiling and simply shrugs. "Let him have it."

"That's the problem when you've been given the body of a teenager for eternity, the hormones are inescapable no matter how long you have been alive," says Vicky with a smirk. "Leliel here is lucky he was cursed with the body of an actual man, unlike lover boy and me. I'm in perpetual puberty."

"How old are you?" asks Tristan.

"You mean in years? I'm old. The 'age' of my body is and will forever be sixteen; when we wake up after the Fall we have a vague knowledge of how old the physical body we've acquired should be. Though, I know I look like I could pass for fourteen on a good day."

"Yes, well, that's great and all, but we have business to get to," says Liam, a tinge of annoyance clear in his voice. "Khiara, your soul should have awakened to its duties some time ago, but unfortunately that curse put on you by Morrigan seems to have caused some trouble and… *Cael* here interfering when he shouldn't have, well that hasn't helped either."

Cael's fingers run through his messy hair and he sighs. "I am well aware."

"Okay then," says Liam. "Khiara, your soul must awaken to its duties and for that to happen, we have to teach you as much as we possibly can about the war between our kind, and about what you must do to rouse your soul. It was supposed to happen naturally, or so said the prophesy, but as mentioned, that doesn't seem to be an option. The Battle is in a couple of months."

"I can help," says Sam, his big eyes gleaming with hope. "I know that I can!"

Liam shoots him a stern look. "Sam, you have to be careful."

The small boy frowns, his whole face falling. "But daddy, I *know* what to do."

"No!" says Liam, this time a lot harsher than I think he intended to, because instantly he seems to regret it. "Sammy, I know you want to help. But you…" he pauses, sighs, and looks around the room as if he's at a loss as how to deal with his young son.

"Not to get all up in your business," says Cara awkwardly, "but uh. What exactly is going on?"

Tristan raises his hand as if he were in class. "I second that."

Everybody in the room turns their eyes to Sam, who by now has big tears falling down his cheeks and is trembling from the effort not to make any noise as he cries. His hands are balled into chubby fists, and his cheeks are blotchy, a patchwork of red and pink. "I *know* things," he whispers quietly.

"You know how I said that Sam was special?" Liam says, putting a hand on his son's head. "Well, I meant it."

"He's Nephilim," says Tristan, "like Lisa and me…isn't he?"

The room falls silent and Cael whispers to my thoughts, *brace yourself, and please, don't feel sorry for me. I have enough of that from the others.* "Lisa," says Liam calmly. "Get out the book."

"Aw but it's gross and heavy!" she grumbles. Still, she gets up from the floor and walks down the hallway into one of the various rooms, returning shortly with a large leather bound book that looks like its weight would dislocate my shoulders. The effort she's showing though is a lot less than I would be, being a mere human.

"It's made from the skin of the wings of one of the most beautiful and kind angels in existence," she explains, making Cara, Tristan and I cringe a little. Lisa thumps it into the coffee table. "Well," she amends, "she doesn't exist *anymore*, as far as we know."

"What was her name," I find myself asking, a strange stirring in my chest overpowering the pleading look Cael is giving me, and his voice echoes in my head again. *Please. Your sympathy would be the worst sting, like lemon on a fresh wound. Please understand that I can't even bear to think about her normally.*

"Her name was Samael."

Twenty-Two

Vicky's voice fills the room. "Samael and Camael were created together and while Camael's glory was blue tinged with white, hers was a deep shade of magenta, tinged with olive green."

Cael squirms in his seat, obviously uncomfortable. *I can't, I can't, I can't,* he chants to himself, not realizing that our minds are still connected. Images of a beautiful blonde woman, who is almost his mirror image if not for the colour of her long hair, flash through my mind and I realize that they're Cael's memories of her from before and after his Fall.

"They were twins. While Camael was an angel of Divine Justice and Love, Samael was an angel of Death and Temptation. They acted in tandem, Samael taking people's souls who fell to various temptations, and Camael judging whether or not they deserved to go to Heaven, Hell, or Limbo, embracing them lovingly in his warmth if he found their soul was filled with enough good." She continues.

"When Lucifer Fell, he took her with him, although unwillingly on her part, and Camael was left without his twin and best friend to do the job of two."

"Until he Fell because of me," I whisper.

"Yes," says Liam. "Of course now others have taken their places, as…as it goes for all of us. They took on our duties on top of their own."

"What happened to her," I ask, holding my necklace. If ever there were a time I wanted time to stop, it would be now, because the look on Cael's face is pure pain. I bite my lip nervously.

Don't, whispers Cael in my thoughts. But the question is already being answered.

Liam shoots an apologetic look towards Cael. "She was tortured for hundreds of years by Lucifer's followers because of her repentant nature. Eventually somebody stabbed her and left her for dead; only she *didn't* die. I'd Fallen just seven years before she found me and had made my way into the Himalayan mountains. I had been taken in by some Buddhist monks who thought I could use my strength to help them build a new wing to their monastery and in turn they gave me shelter, food and taught me about their religion. How's that for irony, eh? Buddhist monks and an angel working together! They knew there was something different about me but never pried. I suppose they had their suspicions about what I was, but they were good people."

"Where is it that you Fell? And what century?" asks Cara. "You look like you could be from India, which would make sense geographically, if the monks were Buddhist, and in the Himalayas…but it could also be in Tibet."

He smiles fondly at some memory that seems to flit through his mind, but doesn't answer her questions. "If you know your history well, then you'll understand this; it was the same century as the American Independence."

"I was working on a wall that had cracked during a storm, when one of the monks came to me, telling me of a crazy white woman who kept asking for me." His smile fades somewhat. "Samael finding me wasn't a coincidence. We all seek out our own kind when in distress, and of course she was in much agony. See, the only way one of us can die is if it is another angel to harm us but it has been known to fail in the past…and when Lucifer had his men stab her and leave her for dead, they did more than just that."

Tristan is sitting at the edge of his seat, his short hair stuck to his scalp from sweat. The story must be getting to him as much as it's getting to me. "What did they do?"

"They ripped off her wings," Lisa whispers, gesturing to the book.

Cael looks like he is going to be physically ill and he stands up abruptly, and wordlessly walks out of the living room and into what I guess must be the bathroom, all the way there thinking, *I can't, I can't, I* just *can't. I'm sorry.* Our mental connection is cut off. I realize that he knew we were connected and was giving me a private glimpse into his mind willingly.

"Don't follow him," says Sam, quietly, reading the look on my face. "Uncle Cam just needs some time to be alonesome."

"Don't you mean alone?" says Lisa, smiling despite the very awkward and intense situation.

Sam shakes his head, his blonde messy curls bouncing around like springs. "He need be alone. And lonesome. He needs to feel it, 'cause he keeps it in too much and doesn't think of it. Alonesome."

He puts his hand over his heart, "It's his feelings. I'm not wrong; I can feel it, in here."

Liam sighs tiredly and continues the story. "Of course because the monks cared for me as if I were one of their own, they took Samael in as well without many questions. I nursed her back to health which took a good year because of the shock of losing her wings. We had been good friends in Heaven, her Camael and I, and though all of the angels were close, there were special bonds of course."

"Samael and I fell in love and after another year, we left the monastery and travelled the world, much of which she had seen and was eager to show me. It was truly wonderful. We knew that two angels cannot conceive children together, but still, we tried. We had a friend who worked at an IVF clinic and we even tried to get her pregnant using…"

He looks towards his son, "other men's specimens. Nothing worked. Eventually we decided to get a surrogate mother instead and that is how Lisa came into this world. Meanwhile, we reconnected with Camael and even Verchiel who crossed our paths a few times, though we had to be careful when it came to contacting her. We corresponded as regularly as we could since we moved around a lot. We settled down here almost two years ago."

"What about Sam? You conceived him the same way?" I ask.

"No," he says quietly, his voice quavering a bit. "Sam is our miracle baby. His kind shouldn't exist. He is the product of two Fallen angels. We don't know how it happened. There has always been talk about his kind but everybody usually assumed it was just myth."

Lisa opens the book. "Mom loved us but she just up and disappeared two years ago. And then we were sent this book and…"

Cara's eyes are as round as saucers. She stands up, walks towards the book, but stops abruptly, her brow crinkling in confusion. "It glows. It's very faint, but it still glows."

"I can see it too," I muse, cocking my head to the side like Pug does when he's confused or studying something.

Lisa seems surprised but nods her head. "I forgot the Fae can sense things that most humans can't. I guess your necklace helps you see that, Khiara. That's why we think she's still alive. Mom wouldn't have left on her own accord, and the fact that this book came a week after her disappearance is even more evidence towards the fact that she *has* to be alive."

Tristan scratches his head thoughtfully and after a minute of appraising the book, he asks, "What *is* the book anyway?"

"Well, that's the thing. Only Sam can read it. For some reason it looks blank to everybody else." Lisa twirls a piece of blonde hair around a finger for a second and bites her lip; we share a nervous habit. "Sam," she says, "read them the first page."

Sam walks over to her, looking so young, so small, and he takes the book as if it weighs as much as a feather. "Okay," he says, opening the book to the first pages.

His small voice suddenly seems much deeper, when he reads, *"The Rephaim race is the purest in existence; it is the offspring of two of the Fallen. They must be guarded, as they are hunted for all they can do. Rephaim are the closest to God and should not theoretically exist, yet they do, and have the potential to change the world."*

"It's a book all about what Sam's kind can do," explains Liam. "They can do everything angels can do and more. They can bring things back to life. They have the potential to be like Gods. For all intents and purposes the Gods are aliens and angels are creations of an alien race in the image of humans. But the Rephaim race is *native* to Earth. They are almost like Earth-born Gods. Do you know what Lucifer can do with this knowledge?"

"I can only imagine," I breathe. "So who sent you this then? Samael went missing then a week later you get this book and the cover is made from her wings *and* it just so happens to be about your son's kind. That is not a coincidence."

"We think it's a warning," Vicky says with a sigh. "Somebody must have forced a member of the Fae race to divine the future all those years ago after ripping Samael's wings off and found out that she would give birth to Sam. It's the only way it makes sense and it makes even more sense that they would abduct her a while after Sam was born."

Cara nods, "She's right; my grandmother taught me a bit about the art of divining, though I'm crap at it since it's not my element." She looks at me sheepishly – I keep learning more about her than I thought possible since I thought I knew everything about her.

"But," she says, "the future is not always concrete; it's all about chance, especially when it comes to birth. They must have been very advanced."

Tristan says, "So then the question arises. Where is she?"

"That's the problem isn't it? We don't know. We've searched, and even Sam has tried to find her, but he's still young and we have to limit the use of his powers, lest he's found and taken away," replies Liam, sadly.

"And that's why I can't help? Just 'cause Mommy went missing and I can't find her doesn't mean I shouldn't help if I can," says Sam, "because I can help Khiara with what she needsta know!"

"No," says Liam. "It's too dangerous. I won't hear any more of it, and this is the last we'll talk about it until we find a way to find your mother, *without* you using any of your abilities."

Sam puffs out a world-weary sigh, pouts, but nods his head. "Okay."

I cough a bit and my head begins to throb with a slight headache, and sensing this, Sam looks over at me, his green eyes wide with concern. "You can still nap in my bed if you want," he says.

"I'll be okay," I reassure him.

"You sure?" asks Cara, who begins to study me as if I were some math test she needed to ace. "You look really pale, K."

"I promise," I say. But really, I'm not so sure that I'm not trying to reassure myself as well.

Twenty-Three

Cael is quiet when he finally emerges from the bathroom, his eyes swollen from tears, and his voice hoarse from the strain of crying. "I'm alright," he says to nobody in particular, as he sits down next to Sam on the couch and pulls his nephew by blood in close for a hug. I can see the resemblance between the two now; the messy hair, the shape of their eyes.

He hardly says a word as Liam and Vicky explain their plan to awaken my soul. They will teach me as much as they know about the war and Cara will help in any way she can now that she knows the stories her father told were true. They will show me how to fight against not only angels, but Nephilim too, and potentially even rogue Fae, though Cara thinks it's impossible.

My soul will have to figure the rest out.

When we leave it's snowing lightly, not enough to really warrant heavy jackets so we're fine with our sweaters – everybody except Vicky who is now complaining about the cold.

"Tinkerbell," she says, addressing Cara. "Gimme your sweater. You don't need it anyway do you?"

Cara flails her arms dramatically. "Well no, not technically. But I love this sweater, it's fuzzy and comfy."

"And it's mine," I remind her, though I don't actually mind since we're always borrowing things from each other.

She rolls her blue eyes. "That is *beside* the point! It's a sweater that I am enjoying the comfy-ness of. Damn it!"

"Oh just take it off," says Tristan, peeling his own sweater off and rolling his own eyes. "I'll give you mine."

"Ach," says Vicky, making a gagging motion. "You guys are sweeter than syrup." But then she stops walking altogether.

"Everybody go back to the house," she commands. "Now!"

All of a sudden, just as Cara is about to complain, growling comes from behind our car.

Cael, who's been quiet since we left, narrows his eyes and looks around as if he's sure there's something he's missing.

"*Camael*," Vicky whisper-shouts. "You need to get your girlfriend inside; pronto."

Cael nods and turns to me with panic displayed clearly on his face. "We need to go back in," he repeats Vicky's words, his voice still thick from crying and lack of use.

Cael clears his throat. Nods. "Come on," he says, taking my hand and leading me back towards the house.

All of a sudden the back of my neck tingles, and the feeling of being watched, that feeling I'd almost forgotten about, is like a punch straight to the stomach. Damien. *Douma*. He's here.

The growling grows in intensity and Cael breaks into a run, towing me along with him, Cara and Tristan not far behind us.

As soon as we reach the back door, he shoves me inside, and Cara and Tristan follow. He opens his mouth to say something to me, but an angry scream from Vicky stops him and he pushes me deeper into the house and slams the door shut, rattling the glass. He runs off at an almost unnatural blur of speed, disappearing around a corner.

"The house is protected," says Liam from behind us, gesturing towards the living room. "Nobody can come in unless we want them in here."

He gets out six cups and puts the kettle on. "I'll make some hot cocoa for everyone." I sit down at the kitchen table, watching him get to work putting cocoa in each cup, carefully measuring out the right amount, putting some chocolate syrup into the smallest cup – Sam's.

He looks at me with his piercing green eyes and smiles, so fatherly and kind. "You look like you could use some extra chocolate in your cocoa as well."

I smile a bit. "That would be great, Liam. Thanks."

Ten minutes pass and suddenly Cara is in the kitchen, terror on her face. "Hey, uhh do you want *him* in here? Cause he's sure trying real hard to get in!" she shouts, pointing at the door where Damien is suddenly standing, bloody and dishevelled, fighting to open the door.

"Don't worry about him," says Liam calmly. "He can't get in."

Abruptly, Vicky is behind him grabbing him by the throat and squeezing savagely, yanking him away from the sliding door. She too is covered in blood and her lip is burst and seems to be healing at a very slow rate.

"Get away from there," Liam says gently, handing me my cocoa. "You don't need to see this."

Cara listens and goes back into the living room where Lisa is sitting on one of the couches, cradling little Sam in her arms while Tristan tells a story.

But I don't follow because I can't see Cael and somewhere in the back of my mind, we're still connected; but I can't feel him there anymore. I didn't know he was still there until…until he wasn't. As Vicky and Damien disappear from sight, I begin to panic. *Where is he?*

Before anybody has time to stop me, I thrust open the door as fast as I humanly can, and my eyes roam over Vicky and Damien, who are now fighting just next to the huge pile of fire logs.

When they land on Cael, lying on the ground unconscious, covered in dirt and blood, my heart squeezes painfully in my chest. The scent of burning hair wafts over to me and then I hear Damien scream in pain, only to be cut off into low growls.

He's shifted into a dog, I realize. It probably speeds up his healing to change forms.

I gag at the odour of his burnt hair.

Taking hold of my necklace, I close my eyes – then everything goes still and I'm running to Cael, running like I'm in a marathon sprint and I'm about to win. Details around me become fuzzy as I run towards him.

I kneel next to Cael on the dirt covered ground and assess the damage. He doesn't appear to be cut anywhere, but his cuts could have healed already which is good; they would have to be shallow to heal so quickly. The blood could be anyone's and I pray to whoever cares that it isn't his. Just because he can heal doesn't make his pain any less real to me.

He looks so peaceful, as though he could be sleeping if he weren't covered in blood, twigs, leaves and dirt, and if his clothes weren't ripped to shreds and his hair dishevelled even more than usual.

I reach out to touch him but that proves to be a mistake. As soon as my hand touches his face to move his hair out from over his eyes, I'm being pinned down by the biggest red fox I have ever seen, with very familiar blue eyes. Everything seems to still be frozen outside so I momentarily don't understand what is going on.

But then it speaks.

You idiot, it thinks to me in Cara's voice. *If you hadn't have gone outside and done that weird time freezy-thing, which by the way doesn't work on the people inside of the house, fun fact, I wouldn't know I could do this. As cool as being a giant fox is, I really wish you'd have stayed inside. I burst out of my clothes for this shit.*

I'm sorry, I think back because it's all I can muster. I cough and instinctively wipe at my suddenly runny nose.

She barks out something that resembles sarcastic laughter. *Get inside now. I'll carry him in; just place him on my back. And then you're going to have to un-freeze everything and let icky-Vicky do her thing.*

I drape Cael's body over her back but I'm so preoccupied with getting to the house that I lose my hold on my thoughts, and somehow everything un-freezes too early. Cara has to grab me with her teeth to drag me inside the open door as Vicky and dog-Damien resume their fighting.

Only when we get inside do I realise that my necklace isn't on me anymore; it's just outside the door. It must have ripped when she dragged me inside.

"Shit!" yells Liam as he pushes me towards the living room where both Lisa and Sam are now sobbing and Tristan is looking appropriately terrified, holding the scraps of Cara's clothing that she must have burst out of.

"Move back, I need to get it now! That necklace is supposed to protect you and without it you are as vulnerable as a new born fucking baby."

He moves to get it, but not fast enough. Almost instantly a big dog – Damien, I have to remind myself – whose long black hair is drenched in blood and matted with clumps of dirt, appears as if out of nowhere and scoops it up, bounding off into the forest.

Seconds later, Vicky stumbles through the door into the small kitchen where everybody has now gathered.

"Fucking… hell, kid. You… have a damned death wish," she pants, looking at me and then promptly passes out right on the dining table, blood seeping out a massive cut on her chest. Liam springs into action, grabbing her and lifting her over his shoulder, then wordlessly carrying her into the living room.

Cara makes a chirping sound and snuffles once from behind me. I turn around to look at her and her fluffy tail is making wide swishes like a cat's, her ears are pulled back, and she's low on her tummy.

She's not wrong, she thinks at me, making a high pitched keening kind of noise as I reach forward and absently pet her soft fur. She flips onto her back and looks me dead in the eyes, her ears standing straight at attention now. *You could have died.*

~*~

Cael seems to be knocked out cold as Liam and Tristan take him into Liam's room to change his clothes and get him cleaned up. But after ten minutes or so I can hear his beautiful accent and my heart becomes less heavy.

It takes a good twenty-five minutes for Vicky's cut to heal though but she wakes up after twenty, just as I'm done changing her into some of Lisa's pyjama pants. I took off her tattered shirt and Cara's ruined sweater, and with the help of Lisa, placed her on the bigger couch to change her pants.

Of course when she wakes up the first thing she does is complain about having no shirt on and being in her bra.

"Oh shut up," says Cara from her place on the other couch, now fully back from being in fox form. She's wearing an old shirt and some sweatpants of Samael's.

For once, Vicky listens, but does so with a scowl.

"Okay," says Liam, as he sits on the couch across from us, ten minutes later. Cael sits down not long after, his eyes heavy.

"The Battle is in less than two months and now we're even more fucked than we were before without that necklace. I don't know who gave it to you but they sure as hell didn't stick around to give us any more help. We're back to Plan A. We are going to have to teach you how to defend yourself against us as well as we possibly can."

"I can help," says Tristan, his smile earnest. "I didn't know what I was before, but now that I do, I'm not afraid of what I can do. I'm not fast like Lisa but I *am* strong. And I can read a mind or two, though I'm not sure how that particular talent can help."

Liam nods. "Khiara can use all the help she can get."

~*~

Three days later, after having a particularly non-average but not *overly* exciting Saturday at Cara's house learning how to fight against a member of the Fae, my body aches. My ribs are probably bruised from trying to tackle Cara to the ground, seeing as she's a lot stronger than she appears to be. How she kept this whole side of her hidden from me is still amazes me. Her whole body burns with this overwhelming heat at the drop of a hat and she can make flames appear out of thin air in the palms of her hands. She hasn't been able to turn into a fox again, but I suspect she has to be under extreme duress and it's not exactly like I want to subject her to that on purpose.

She's taught me how to identify the different types of Faen people, Nymphs, Elves, and Pixies.

Pulling out the list she gave me to study, I look over her neat handwriting.

Elves: Tall, slightly pointed ears, arrows imbued with their elemental magic, can control the elements directly but not with their hands like Nymphs (They can't create it, only draw on it)

Pixies: About the size of the average hand, very pointed ears, exude a small hum when they fly with their tiny wings. They can breathe out dust that does all manner of different things.

Nymphs: About as tall as humans, very high amounts of sexual allure (I'm so sexy), whatever element they correspond to, they can directly use it in their hands (shape it, etc), they can turn into foxes (fuck yeah!).

Elements:
Earth: Brown hair, tanned skin.
Wind: Bright blonde hair, dark skin.
Fire: Red hair, fair skin.
Water: Dirty blonde hair, fair skin.
Spirit: Black hair, tanned skin (slightly lighter than Earth)

All have healing capabilities, but in different ways. THAT'S IT! BRING COOKIES NEXT TIME!

As I lay in my bed at night and think of all that has happened in such a short amount of time, I wonder how I will ever tell my parents about all of this. The thought consumes me until I finally decide that I just can't sleep and on a whim elect to take a cab to Cael's; he told me to stop by anytime, and he even told me where his spare key is. I send him a quick text to let him know that I plan on coming over, and I make my way downstairs.

Dad is sleeping on the couch, having had too much to eat, and I kiss him on the head as I make my way to the door.

"Sorry boy," I say to Pug as I walk to the front door. He grumbles unhappily, but doesn't throw a fit so I know he's not going to wake up my parents who are actually both home tonight. When I got home today from Cara's, they greeted me with dinner and hugs, which was nice. Maybe they'll be home more often.

When I get to Cael's I knock first and when he doesn't come to the door I retrieve the spare key from under the welcome mat and go on in. He isn't in the living room or the kitchen, though the lights are still on, so I decide to just go to his room to see if he's in there.

When I walk into his room the first thing I notice are the words, *I will never regret*, written in English on the wall. But the words aren't painted on like all of the other ones are, not in that fantastic golden script. Instead, they've been written hastily, using liquid paper, as if he couldn't possibly waste any time by getting out the paint from underneath his kitchen sink, where I know he keeps it, because I saw it once when he was looking for dish soap.

"Oh Cael," I breathe, as my gaze lands on his sleeping form. I haven't seen him for three days, though we've spoken on the phone, and his stress is palpable. He's sleeping on top of the sheets in only his boxers but I can see that he is shivering because his window is wide open.

I begin to walk towards him to cover him up, when suddenly my chest catches fire and I break into a fit of coughs that are incredibly painful. I feel like my nose is running not for the first time in the past couple of days and I swipe at it absently with the back of my gloved hand. I don't bother looking but it comes away wet.

Cael stirs, making little sleepy groans that agonisingly contrast the sound of my coughs as he moves to turn onto his side, but suddenly sits up when he realizes the source of his waking isn't from whatever dream he was having.

"God," he says as his eyes focus on me. He stands up and appears before me like magic, but that could be just my suddenly fuzzy head playing tricks on me. I wouldn't know; he's an angel, and Lisa sure can move fast for somebody who's only half.

I can't stop coughing and between coughs when I try to pull in air, all I can manage to do is wheeze. I feel my body begin to sway. I move to wipe at my nose again and realize that my once white glove is now red.

"That's…strange," I rasp between coughs. "This…was just white…"

And then I'm suddenly in the bathroom, sitting down on the floor by the tub. How did I get here?

"Khiara, sweetheart, you're going to be okay."

I try to ask him what he's talking about, but it just comes out as, "Whaa?" and I cough some more. Wipe at my nose some more. Where did my gloves go? Why are my hands red? I close my eyes. Try to concentrate. Something warm and soothing caresses my face and I nuzzle into its touch.

"I need to get you cleaned up," whispers somebody, though I'm not sure who it is or where I am anymore. "Can I," they hesitate. "Can I have permission to strip you to at least your underclothes? There's blood on everything."

That one word, blood, pulls me mostly back into myself and my eyes open. "Cael," my voice is nothing but a hoarse whisper. "Hi." Something around him shimmers into and out of existence for a moment and I squint, trying to figure out what it could have been.

"Hi," he whispers. Tears are streaming down his face and I don't know why. I reach out a shaky hand to wipe them away and realize that he was right. There is blood all over me. "Oh," I say, "I didn't even realize what was happening…"

"It's okay," he says gently, but it's not okay at all. The air around him shimmers again and I have to close my eyes for a second once more. "But I need to get you cleaned up."

"I don't want to be alone." My voice sounds like equal parts fear and pain. I open my eyes again and he looks so worried and I can't help but think that it's not fair. I was on my way to comfort him but I'm just the source of more pain.

"I won't leave then," he says in answer. "But you need to get into the bath. You don't have to get naked but you need to get out of those clothes so I can wash them."

I stand up with his help and slowly undress until I'm in my bra and underwear. I feel almost naked even though he'd see just as much skin if I were in a bikini. Cael helps me get into the tub and when I'm sitting he hands me a wash cloth.

"I'm not sure if you want to do this part by yourself. I was willing to do it when I thought I might have no other option, but I mean, since you're conscious…"

"I was never unconscious," I remind him.

"You may as well have been," he says. "It was terrifying. It was like…what would Cara say? She'd say something witty like, 'The lights are on but nobody's home.' I thought…I thought I was going to lose you." His voice breaks and so does my heart – right into a million pieces. He's gone through so much and it kills me.

I cough and wince. "I'm falling apart, Cael."

He sighs. "It sense in a sick way now that I think about it. When you were born, you were sick and dying despite being the purest soul on Earth, right?"

I nod, not sure where he's going with this.

"And when Morrigan brought you back to life, she cursed you. We know this part. But what if there's another catch?"

"Like?"

"Think about it," he says. "You've been feeling increasingly worse recently, and the Battle is supposed to be in a little less than two months. She probably planned this but never said anything because there's always a loophole and…"

Anger blossoms in my chest and I bring my knees close to me and wrap my arms around them, resting my head atop my knees. "Well that's just fucking great, isn't it? We've exhausted all of the loopholes already and that didn't turn out very well. In the end, I'm still alone. No Guardian. And now I'm going to die alone."

He flinches and instantly I feel like the biggest asshole in the world. "Cael," I say, but he's already pushing past it, shaking his head and putting his hands up as if in surrender.

"No, you're right. I wasn't supposed to get involved on a personal level. This was supposed to play out completely different. I was supposed to help you but mostly from afar, never from where you could see me, and when the battle drew near I'd have placed all of the proper tools for you to realize your role. There was supposed to be the epiphany and the awakening of your soul but I *fucked* up. And now you're going in practically blind, I know that. I think about it every second of every day."

"Cael," I say again, because I have no words that could possibly fix his sadness. He always keeps it locked away, just out of reach, and I realize now that if he'd never literally Fallen for me he would still be in Heaven. Why have I never realized the full importance of that until now? *How selfish am I?*

His expression is pained. "Please," he says, running his hand through his messy hair. "Don't think like that," he whispers, hearing my thoughts as though I'd voiced them.

"Your wall," I say as gently as I can. "I saw..."

He stands up then, lightning quick so my eyes can't track his movement, "I don't regret it. I don't. I won't *ever*. What happened to my sister has nothing –" he stops talking mid-sentence and walks towards the door. "I'll be back; I just have to get you some clean clothes, alright?"

I can't do anything else but nod my head and sink deeper into the warm water. Once he's gone, I start to lather myself with the soap and eventually muster up the strength to unplug the tub so I can take a proper shower. I stand up slowly hoping this isn't a big mistake, turn on the shower, and then close the curtain. A second later I hear a soft knock on the door.

"Your clothes are in the wash," says Cael. "I'll be in the living room if you need me. Clean clothes and towels are on top of the toilet."

I don't have the energy to say anything. *Okay*, I think. *Thank you.*

I emerge from the bathroom in a pair of oversized sweat pants and one of my own shirts that he was nice enough to get for me, probably from my room; I'd left my window open a crack and I assume he is more than capable of moving around unnoticed.

"Hi," I say, as I sit down on the couch next to Cael. He smiles at me, that sad smile that I've grown to love.

He says, "Hey. Was just about to check up on you. I never asked why you came so late at night…never got a chance to."

I try to explain myself, but the words are hard to explain so I settle on, "You dropped me off without saying anything and I hadn't heard from you all day so I just…I was worried. I *am* worried. And I just…I don't know, I felt like something was really wrong. My gut told me."

He smiles a little, "I guess we're still connected in some way. God works in mysterious ways, you know. I guess we haven't exhausted all the loopholes yet."

We sit in silence for a while and then he asks if I'd like some coffee.

"Do you have anything food related?" I ask, hopeful.

Cael chuckles, "Yes, I have food. No, I don't have any baked goods for you. Vicky ate the last of my double-chocolate cake and I forgot to make more. Would a sandwich be okay?"

I nod, and we both go into the kitchen. While he's rifling through the fridge for some sandwich meat, I move to start the coffee. I'm just pressing start when he swears and something clatters to the floor. I whip around at the sound and see him cradling his hand, blood pouring down onto the counter.

"Oh God, Cael, are you okay?" I ask as I run to get him a paper towel to clean the blood.

"It's fine, don't bother," he says flatly.

"Why? You're *bleeding*, we should get that cleaned up!"

"Khiara, leave it. It's okay. I just have to clean up the blood. Don't worry about the cut."

"What?" I ask, but then realization dawns on me. "Oh," I whisper, "right. Does it hurt?" I rip off some paper towel.

"It doesn't matter if it hurts," he replies tiredly, running his hand under cold water. I can see it slowly stitching together on its own, something that has the potential to seem so magical just seeming so sad. It must have been a very deep cut for it to not have been fully healed within seconds though, because it takes a little longer than I thought it would.

"Of course it does," I say, mopping up the blood with the paper towel.

"No, not really. I'm not normal. Normal rules don't apply to me. Look," he shows me his now fully healed hand, "it's all sealed up.

You've seen worse than this; you've seen Vicky heal from a huge chest wound, I mean are you really surprised?"

"Well no," I say. "It's just instinct. I forgot."

"It's easy to forget," he says wearily. "For everybody else. But not for me."

"I…" I try to think of something useful to say but come up blank. "I'm sorry," I say for lack of anything beneficial.

"Don't be," he replies, throwing away the spoiled bread and meat.

"But I am," I say. "I truly –"

Pain flashes in his eyes and he turns towards me and cuts me off. "Don't you *understand?* I want to be human. I want to feel things the way you feel them. If I get cut I want to feel true pain instead of slight discomfort because I know I'll simply heal. When you kiss me, I want…" He doesn't finish his sentence and instead walks into his bedroom, and I trail after him. We sit down on his bed.

"Cael." I feel as though my heart is beating so fast that it might thud straight out of my chest. I can feel myself blushing, but I don't stop myself from finishing his sentence. "You want to experience it the way I do, as a human."

He nods and hangs his head, looking ashamed. I take his face in my hands and tilt his head back up, so I can look into his eyes. "Tell me something Camael," the use of his angelic name sends a visible shiver through his entire body, "when I do this," my lips touch his, feathery soft and quick, "do you not feel like your heart is about to beat right out of your chest?"

A tear escapes his right eye and I kiss it away before it falls down his cheek, saying, "When I did that, did it not let you feel that you're not alone?"

He smiles and it touches his eyes just slightly. I kiss his lips again, this time much more passionate. "You want to experience it the way I do?"

He closes his eyes and I whisper, "But you do. I don't care if you're not human."

Cael looks at me and his eyes are full of tears and an amount of adoration I feel I don't deserve. "I love you," he whispers back.

Wrapping my arms around him and pulling him close to me, I reply, "I love you too. Just because you're practically indestructible doesn't make your body feel things any less like I do." I pull back and cup his face in my hands again. "Unless of course I'm judging your bodily reactions completely wrong…" I glance down towards his thin boxers, and quickly look back up, a small smile tugging up the corners of my lips. We haven't touched this territory yet in our short relationship and I don't know where my boldness comes from.

His face is on fire but so is mine. He looks everywhere but at me. "I'm not hungry anymore," I say, biting my lip nervously. "Let's just go to bed."

"I don't know if I could go back to sleep," he says hesitantly, unsure of what exactly I mean.

I decide to clear it up for him. I grab the waistband of his boxers and pull him closer to me. "I didn't say we had to go to sleep," I say, "just to bed."

And he's kissing me. So deeply, you'd think he's drowning, and there is a level of desperation in this kiss that calls all of my emotions to the forefront. I bite his lip and he groans; and then somehow we're in his room and I'm on my back, our bodies pressed tight together and I can feel every part of him.

I've never felt this way about anybody before, and though I know we're moving fast, our relationship isn't like anything that's ever even existed. His love for me is ages old and I've only known him in person for a short while, but my soul has always felt his presence and his love. A part of my heart has always belonged to him.

I don't care if I wasn't assigned a soul mate; my soul has chosen its *own*.

"God," his voice is husky and so, so wonderful. "You don't understand how amazing it is to kiss you."

I'm drowning in the taste of his fiery kisses and every moan that escapes my mouth elicits one of his own. I never knew I had this much passion; I didn't think it was possible. And we're burning bright, not like logs that have caught fire on top of hot, scorching embers because even that isn't enough to describe what we have.

No, we're like the embers themselves.

Our love burns long after the fire is gone, as I close my eyes and cuddle up to him, right up against his back.

"We'll figure everything out," I whisper.

"I know," he replies sleepily. "I just wish we didn't have to."

"Fate will do what she will," I say, repeating a phrase my mother used to tell me when I was a child and things didn't go my way.

He turns around to face me, and our legs tangle together, then in the dark he smiles, cupping my face in one of his hands while using his other arm as a pillow. "Yes. She will."

"Cael," I say.

"Mm?"

"What am I going to do without my necklace? I don't even know who gave it to me, but it was supposed to keep me safe and it did such…amazing things."

"We'll get it back," he promises. "And don't worry who it was from. Whoever it was obviously knew how much you needed it."

"Cael?"

"Aye, sweetheart?"

"I love you."

"I love you more."

Twenty-Four

Going back to school somehow feels almost wrong considering we only have a couple of weeks back until winter break begins. *Oh yeah*, also because I've begun intense training after work by Liam, Vicky, Lisa (who is also training Tristan, considering he only found out his heritage recently) and Cara, who is getting some training from everybody else as well. Cael is not training me, because most of the training I need involves being repeatedly injured, and he can't handle hurting me.

We're really a motley crew if ever there was one. *How cliché!*

It's now Wednesday.

Damien never bothered showing up to classes this week, having stolen my necklace, and Vicky has dropped all of her I-hate-you, queen bee pretences since she blew her cover to Damien. She has been waiting for Cara and I after school every day. She dropped out of school since being an emancipated minor in the eyes of the State means she can kind of do what she wants.

Apparently, she rather hates everybody in this school, including her number one minion, Janie, who isn't taking it very well at all. Before Vicky came to school, Janie was the top girl and though she spoke to most of the kids in our grade in passing she kept to herself and Chris mostly until she met Cara. But as soon as Vicky stepped in and acted like she hated me, she just kind of fell into her role as minion very well – it helped though that she had that stupid grudge on me.

Right now she looks lost.

Cara and I are sitting with Janie and Chris at the lunch table, and she hasn't said a mean word to me the whole time. Come to think of it she hasn't really said anything nasty to me for the past three days.

"You seem um," starts Cara.

"Tense," I supply for her. She nods her head in agreement.

"Yeah, tense."

Janie looks up from her uneaten pulled pork sandwich and shoots me a half-hearted glare. "You'd be upset if your best friend here left you high and dry out of nowhere, *abandoning* you. Victoria was my best friend...I thought."

I frown. "How much time did you actually spend with her outside of school?"

She shrugs delicately. "Not much. But we texted. And went shopping a couple of times. Never had very many friends back home thanks to my dad and when I moved here nobody really spoke to me besides you guys."

"I think," Cara says slowly, "that *maaaybe* you overestimated her friendship level. Chilling a couple of times and texting for half a year does not a best friendship make. Your best friend has to actually care about you, regardless of your differences."

Janie sighs and runs her hands through her blonde hair, pulling it up into a high pony-tail. "I guess I should've known that." She turns to Cara. "Well I guess I have you," and then she turns to Chris, "and you. Also everybody else in prayer group, though they don't exactly come around me or Chris outside of church."

Then she turns to me. "And...well I don't *always* hate you. It's pretty damned hard, actually, because you're sweeter than sweet tea sometimes and it gets hard some days, to conjure up the exact amount of disdain I have for you," she drawls. There's the ghost of a smile on her face. While I'm pretty sure we will never be friends, this is a good start towards something of a truce.

I roll my eyes. "Thanks for trying to be nice," I say, but I smile at her when I say it so she knows that I actually appreciate her effort.

"Well I guess you're welcome," she replies, picking up her sandwich and taking a ladylike bite from it. How she manages to make eating a messy pulled pork sandwich look delicate, I have no idea. I eat like a pig!

"So," says Cara a little too innocently, turning to me with a smirk on her lips and a mischievous glint to her blue eyes. "How're things with the boy-toy? You've been together for a little while now. Have you guys done the dance with no pants yet? Because there's a bet going on between a couple of us and I want to win."

"You have a boyfriend?" asks Janie, suddenly perking up. "Who is he?"

Cara grins. "Yeah. You've probably seen him around town. He works at a café at the mall. He's Irish…he was with us at the mall that one time…"

"Shut up, Ohmigod!" shrieks Janie. "*He* is *your* boyfriend? I thought you just worked there, but hot damn, girl, he's your boss *and* your guy. He's hella cute! You know in that way where he's not a beefy jock or anything but he's got that brooding musician feel. I mean no offense or anything but he could have *anyone*, though I guess there's a certain charm you've got, as… messy as your sense of style is. I mean he's not my type, but good for you. I thought for sure that day at the theatre was the last date y'all would have."

"Uh, thank you?"

She sighs dramatically. "You're damn right you should thank me. You don't know when you're being complimented."

"It's not often you even give me the time of day," I point out, and she shrugs like it couldn't possibly matter.

Chris smiles a bit. "So Janers, does this mean you officially don't lead the Khiara Banning hate club anymore?"

She appraises me for a second and shrugs again. "I wasn't captain or nothin' if that's what you mean. That was Victoria. I just used her to fuel my hate fire. I was more like vice president. I guess now I should default to president but after a good four years of pointless hatred over a dress, I guess I have to let it go sometime."

Janie reaches a dainty hand out and snatches my pudding cup off of my tray, smiling a bit. "You never eat vanilla pudding anyway," she says as way of explanation.

"So that bet," she says. "I want in. I'm going with no because you don't look like the type of girl to put out."

Startled, I smile a bit at that. "I'm not going to give away answers," I reply. "If there's a bet, I'm going to keep you all guessing."

Cara sighs exasperatedly, flinging her arms in the air. "You're never any fun!"

~*~

Vicky's fist slams into my gut with the force of a freight train. "You need to fight harder!"

I begin to crumple to the ground, stunned, before finding my footing and sending a kick straight towards her temple which she easily blocks.

Dropping my foot, she smiles, and I can't help but think that she looks like a little girl, with her hair in pigtails, wearing that yellow sundress from that day at the library, and a bright pink denim jacket, though it's snowing out and I have no idea how she could possibly be so immune to the cold.

Vicky snickers. "Not bad. I wasn't expecting that. Now try again, *harder*. I'm not going to go soft on you just because you're breakable. If you want to be able to fight, you're going to have to endure pain. This is all you have since you lost your necklace to fuck-face and you're one hundred percent, certifiably human."

She smiles apologetically, as if being human is an insult. "Find your opponent's weaknesses and exploit them. We all have an Achilles heel. *Find mine*. See this is why we don't have your boyfriend here when I'm training you. You're *his* weakness."

"We've only been at this for the better part of two weeks!" I manage to gasp out. "You can hardly expect me to be a pro by now."

Vicky rolls her eyes and lets out an exasperated sigh. "You've been training with everybody," she enunciates like *ev-uh-ree-body* for emphasis, "for two weeks. *Intensively*. I'm sure you have muscles on top of muscles that you never knew you had. Look, we don't have a lot of time. You need to learn to fight." Her expression softens a tad. "You're not that scared little girl you were when we first met, kid. You couldn't fight back against the big bad kidnappers. But now you can – with our help."

I frown, thinking hard about the memory. "Is that why you dyed your hair again? To remind me of who you are?"

She smirks, reaches out and musses my hair. "Yep. When we met, I had blonde streaks. I thought I'd try to jog your memory. Did you ever look at the notes I gave you?"

Surprised, I shake my head. "No, sorry."

"They were all about angels, though not accurate information by any means. The particular angels were Verchiel, Douma, and Camael. Didn't think to include Leliel because I wasn't sure he'd want to get involved. I'm surprised you didn't even glance at them."

"Sorry," a bead of sweat falls down my spine, causing me to shiver, and I'm surprised when I feel the need to strip off my jacket from the intense heat caused by training. "Damien –"

"Douma," she interrupts me.

"Right, Douma. He also brought me some notes that Cara took for me so I just used those and never thought to look at the ones you gave me. And actually, he also brought me some cookies. I threw them out though." I feel it's important to tell her I didn't eat them.

Vicky smirks. "Oh, the cookies were fine; I made them. I just told him they were poisoned…well not poisoned, exactly. They were just supposed to be laced with enough meds to put you to sleep."

Balking, I reach over to smack her on the arm, but she dances out of my way, her streaked hair bobbing with the movement. The streaks are already fading and I find myself wondering why.

"You've gotta be faster than that, girlie!" crows Vicky, sticking out her tongue at me. "Now come on, find my Achilles heel. I am giving you full permission to fuck my shit up."

She pauses her dancing and shoots me a loaded look, "Start with what you know about me, which isn't much. But it's enough."

Two days later, Vicky and I are sparring in our usual spot behind Liam's house. The ground is covered in thick snow and the flurries falling lazily just add to the white blanket.

She sends a kick straight for my left leg, and it hits me – not her kick – that if I'm Cael's weakness, then hers must be…

"Your kids," I shout breathlessly. "Your weakness is your children."

She stops and stares at me, her face a complete mask of indifference, but she nods once.

I take this as encouragement. "Then your husband is too, right?"

She punches my right arm so hard I'm scared it's actually broken and I won't be able to use it ever again.

"You were supposed to use that moment to injure me, Khiara."

Frowning and cradling my arm, I try to understand. "You told me to find your weakness. But you never told me to hurt you with it."

"You can't really hurt me, kid. Only two people in the entire world can hurt me. Douma and myself. I just wanted you to distract me."

"I'm sorry." I'm not sure what else to say, but it seems to be the right thing because she nods once again.

"Just try again next time." She begins to walk back to the cottage, but shouts over her shoulder, "Thanks for playing!"

~*~

"Don't be scared," says Cael, his voice thick with sleep. This is the worst nightmare yet. I've been getting these dreams more and more, dreams of being trapped in a hall of mirrors with this woman's voice asking me to choose, telling me that death is inevitable. Sometimes there is a man made of shadows and he feels evil. But other times Cael is there, bloody and dishevelled.

I have no idea what my subconscious is trying to tell me.

"Shhh," he soothes. "*Camael eepeh behlehaheness Ohleh*," He whispers tiredly, in that musical language of his.

"What did you say?" I ask, and he blinks at me for a second before smiling sheepishly.

He pulls me close to him, pillowing my head on his arm. "Sorry, love. You caught me when I was half-asleep. I said that I will keep you safe. I will protect you." He kisses the top of my head. "We should be getting up now anyway."

I shake my head and groan. "My parents aren't home, and they're not getting back for hours. Plus, they like you well enough."

Cael laughs a little, nuzzling my neck. "That's because they think I'm a legally emancipated nineteen-year-old who owns his own business, drives responsibly, and never makes out with their daughter," he punctuates his by kissing me, leaving me slightly breathless.

"Only chaste kisses, then," I tease when I recover, pecking him on the lips and pulling away, sticking out my tongue at him.

He pouts playfully and says, "What they don't know won't hurt them," and he leans forward to kiss me – but then he frowns for real, his blue eyes taking on that sad look that always breaks my heart. "Only…it will, in the end, if you get hurt, won't it?"

"Don't think like that," I say, kissing the spot between his mouth and chin, where he has a freckle I've only just noticed. "We will figure something out. My training's going well. I can kick Tristan's ass now and I'm half way there to being able to kick Cara's. Soon maybe I'll be able to kick *yours*."

Trying to lighten the mood doesn't work. He just stares at me. "The problem is that you don't have to fight me to beat me. I could never hurt you. You'd have already won the minute we began sparring."

I make an irritated noise in the back of my throat. "We're going to have to spar eventually, Cael. I've fought with Tristan *and* Vicky, two *angels*, learned their *weaknesses*, and…well I know that I'm yours, but you have to overcome it. I'm not some delicate flower you need to preserve; well compared to everybody else, I guess I must seem that way, especially to you. But I don't want to be seen that way. Yes, my body is breakable but I want to fight. I need your help. The closer we get to the Battle and the more I try to prepare myself, the more I feel as if I'm on the verge of…something big."

"Your soul is slowly awakening…" he whispers, and then louder, "your soul is *awakening!*"

"Is it? I mean we don't exactly have a reference point for what that awakening actually is…"

"You were supposed to grow into your role as the harbinger of the Great Battle as you grew up. Your heavenly guardian would protect you from harm as you realized your importance and when the time came, the knowledge of the war between the sides and how to fight *should* have been imbued into your very being. We don't even know what it is exactly that you're supposed to know. We just know the bare minimum of the prophesy that states that you have the potential to set the repentant on the side of Light free. And we're trying our hardest to prepare you."

"How do we know it'll awaken on time?" I ask.

Cael looks towards my window where the red curtain is drawn, letting light into the room and sighs. "We don't."

"We're home!" says Dad, walking into the living room where I'm currently sprawled out on the couch. Lisa is sitting on top of me, and has frozen mid punch to my thigh.

"Uh," she says, hopping off of me. "She was taking up the whole couch?" she says in way of explanation. If I could properly see her face, I'd probably be laughing.

"Such a violent child, you are Lisa Foster!" Mom jokes while chuckling. "Well you two are in luck. We got Chinese for dinner." She gestures to the packages Dad's holding. "We'll have to heat it up mind you since we got it on the way home from the museum."

Mom looks around while Dad walks into the kitchen with the food. "Where's Cael? And for that matter where's Tristan and Cara?"

"K-i-s-s-i-n-g somewhere," sings Lisa.

I get up from taking up the whole couch. "Not all three of them," I point out.

"Never know!" she says, winking at me before launching herself down on top of me. "Hah! Sitting on you!" she cries triumphantly.

I complain, "You're too strong for such a small girl."

The microwave beeps from the kitchen.

"Don't blame *me*, blame my heritage!" Lisa bursts into a fit of giggles, laughing even harder when she snorts. It's endearing, and makes me chuckle.

I smile fondly at her. She reminds me of a younger, more hyper Cara. "Okay, okay. We really need to get to studying your French. Now that Dad is home he can help us."

"You'll help Lisa with her verbs, right Jaques?" shouts Mom, her dark eyes filled with laughter.

Dad shouts back something noncommittal and the microwave beeps again, then "Dinner's about heated up," he says.

We all gather in the kitchen to serve ourselves when there's a brusque knock at the door followed by two rings of the doorbell when Mom isn't fast enough getting to the door.

"I'm coming," she mumbles, shaking her head of dark brown hair. "It's probably Cara," she muses, then stops short of opening the door. "No, she'd have walked in..."

It rings again, frantically, and Mom turns to me with a look I will never forget. Her nose flares, as if sniffing the air, and she scowls. "Khiara," she says, looking around the room for Dad and seeming satisfied when he's nowhere in sight. "I need you and Lisa to go up to your room."

"Uh, what exactly is the matter, Mom?" I say, trying not to look like I'm panicking.

"Listen," she says frantically, "I'm not going to waste any time pretending I know exactly what is going on, but if you don't go to your room with Lisa right now, you are grounded for…a long time. Find your father and take him with you."

I turn to look at Lisa, and her eyes are as wide as saucers. "Come on," she says. "We should listen to her. She's not joking around."

My mother sighs, and then walks over to me, cupping my face in her soft hands. Her scent fills my nose, comforting. "Khiara please just listen to me." She turns to Lisa, "Carry her if you have to."

Lisa blinks obviously confused, but complies, picking me up fireman style and walking to the stairs where she meets my father, and wastes no time pushing him towards my room.

"Merde," mutters Dad.

I search his face and come up with nothing to explain my parents' strange behaviour. "Papa?" it comes out as a whimper.

"Khiara," he says. "We haven't been entirely honest with you about how we came to be your parents."

Twenty-Five

"I am so sorry," says Dad. He is sitting on the end of my bed, his expression stricken. "We should have just told you the real story."

Lisa laughs nervously as she plops me down onto the bed. "Sorry," she says. "Forgot I was holding you."

"Everything we told you was true. But we left out…some details."

"Are you human?" I ask, and Dad laughs like I've just asked him if the sky is green.

He smiles. "Yes, I am. And as far as your mother knows, she is too. But," he breathes a sigh and flops onto his back. "There are things that we both just…know."

"Oh," breathes Lisa, her head bobbing up and down with understanding. "You're both Seers."

Dad makes a noise of agreement, and then says, "Oui. We can sense all things...qui s'avez la magique. When I found you, it was because I knew to take a walk. Something inside of me knew that I would find something important, and there you were. I sensed your presence, because it is like no other. That is what we didn't tell you."

A growl of frustration bubbles up my throat before I can stop it. "Can my life get *any more convoluted?* Because I am seriously getting *really* annoyed at all of the curveballs being thrown my way. My best friend can turn into a giant fox and produce fire out of thin air, my boyfriend is a Fallen angel and ex Guardian, and my other friends are either Nephilim or more of the Fallen! I would like to take a moment of silence for my fucking sanity."

Dad sits up then, looks at me with a quizzical expression and says, "C'est la verité?"

I nod. "Yeah, you heard me right. I'm telling the truth."

"Mon Dieu," he whispers. "This is," he nods to himself, "yes, it feels right, I suppose I knew the company you keep was different, but I never sensed a threat so I ignored it."

There's a knock on my door then, and Lisa walks over to it. "Mrs. Banning?"

Dad gets up and says, "Let her in, it's her…and others."

~*~

Samael is lying on my bed.

Lisa is on the phone, sobbing.

Cael's sister is lying *on my bed.*

Sam's *biological mother* is unconscious *on my bed.*

Why are my thoughts so jumbled?

Yes, oh, I think I'm going insane.

"Listen," says a short, muscular man of approximately the same age as my father, who is standing in the doorway between my room and the hallway. His thick hair is grey at the temples and his skin is dark. "My name is…my name is Jachniel but you may call me Jack." His accent makes everything he says sound kind of staccato.

"I have travelled very far to get here," he eyes my dad, as if sizing him up, and then nods to himself, deciding that he's worthy of his presence. "It seems that I will be stuck with the body of an old man until salvation," he turns his gaze on me. "It has been a very long five hundred years."

"I left you a necklace," he says, peering into my eyes. "I suppose I had hoped you would not lose it so soon."

"It was stolen," I say, feeling defensive. "By Douma."

Jack cringes. "Yes, well, it is the same thing. You do not have it anymore. I suspected one of Lucifer's servants would try to steal it. Samael told me as much would happen. She is the more pessimistic of the two of us, though she was always the most optimistic twin."

"What exactly happened?" I ask, looking between Jack and my mother, who is standing next to him.

"They were attacked," she says, "and sought shelter here. I sensed something was off and didn't want to subject you to it before I knew myself. I can't believe the mess you're in…well I can," she sighs, "I just don't want to."

Samael stirs and the whole room goes silent; nobody breathes. "Christ," she says, "Lisa stop crying, you're killing my head!"

She blinks at the room for a second before realizing the situation. "Oh," she says. "Yes, um…"

Lisa launches herself at her mother in lightning speed. "Mom!"

"Hey there, kiddo," she says, enveloping her in a hug. Samael is Cael's spitting image with blonde hair, though she appears older than him by at least a decade.

"I'm not dead," she says. "But I would have been if not for the wonderful man over there." She points towards Jack, who shrugs like it's no big deal.

"You should thank him. He saved my life," she says, and then turns to me, a radiant smile on her face. "Ah, finally we meet. I suspect you'll meet my brother soon. It's not every day that one of the Fallen is appointed as a Guardian, let alone over the soul they Fell for in the first place."

I gulp. She doesn't know…

Samael frowns, reading my facial expression. "Oh," she says, and then looks at the spot where my necklace should be like Jack did. "What happened? I've been *gone* for quite some time. I enchanted the necklace as a gift to help protect you while your soul awakens but I didn't know that Cam was no longer your Guardian…he interfered when it wasn't time, didn't he?"

"They're a couple now," says Lisa, beaming. "They kiss like, all the time. It's nauseatingly adorable."

My face? It's on fire.

Whatever response I was expecting from her isn't the one she gives. Samael bursts into laughter, the sound like tinkling bells. "I can't believe it," she says. "That's impossible!"

She looks me over then, laughing even harder. "You haven't even awakened yet, have you? Oh my God, this is brilliant. We're all potentially screwed, but this is brilliant!"

Lisa rolls her eyes, used to her mother's attitude. "We've been training her, Mom. Me, Dad, Verchiel, her Faen friend Cara and her boyfriend Tristan – he's Nephilim too. It's been going well."

Samael is still laughing, though. "I can't," she says, "this is fucking brilliant! Salvation is in the form of a teenaged human girl who knows next to nothing about what she's getting in to and her magical posse of misfit toys. I couldn't have written a better plot line for a book than that!"

"Brilliant," says Mom, a smirk on her face.

Suddenly my cellphone rings and everybody's attention is drawn to me. I gulp. It's Cael's ringtone.

"Hi," he says when I answer. "I just finished work. How's studying with Lisa?"

"Cael," I say slowly, "you need to come over."

"What's wrong?" his voice holds nothing but concern. "Did something happen? Are you alright?"

"Just trust me," I say, looking at Samael. "You're gonna want to be here. While you're at it, get Cara and Tristan to come with you."

Everybody is sitting in the living room, sipping tea as if it was a formal affair, and I'd laugh if it weren't such a confusing situation. I'm able to fill my parents in on everything that's going on, though they're only mildly surprised and take everything in stride.

It also turns out that the people who attacked Samael and Jack were Douma's minions, so to speak. Jack had broken Samael out of their custody three months ago as they were both prisoners. He found a way to escape and they had been on the run ever since, trying to get back here. They arrived the day I received my necklace; Jack passed it along to a friend who was passing through town and owed him a favour and he put it in my locker. He was also the person who texted me that one time. They'd been in hiding ever since, trying to lie low before making contact with anybody.

Disturbingly, he was not the reason my locker had been opened the other times. Everybody suspects that it was Douma.

Liam arrives around twenty minutes before Cael, Vicky in tow holding a very sleepy Sam, and the reunion between the family is heart-warming.

Vicky stands back as Lisa, a very groggy Sam, Liam and Samael embrace each other, no doubt thinking of her own children, but there's a small smile on her face as she watches them.

"Morrigan…" whispers Dad, as the reunion goes on. "*Morgan…*Mon Dieu! It makes sense now. The nurse that named you? She must have been that Goddess. I suppose she didn't actually wish you harm or we would never have let you near her."

"Funny way of showing it," I say. "Cursing me and whatnot."

Jack shrugs and makes a vague gesture with both his hands. "The lesser Gods and Goddesses are strange creatures."

Samael, who has her son curled on her lap like a puppy, rolls her eyes. "*As* is Man-Deh. *As are we all.* Right Sam?"

Sam nods his little head. "Mmhmm. Everyone's strange, but that's okay," he says, "but I like Khiara. She's not as strange as others. And she's pretty."

The doorbell rings then, and Cara shoves her way inside. "So where's the party at?" she says loudly, chewing gum like it's her job.

When nobody answers, she takes in the state of the room and frowns. "Oh…so like, Cael's gonna pass the fuck out when he sees this shit," she states.

"I'm gonna what?" asks Cael from behind her, laughter in his voice from some conversation they probably had in the car. He pushes past her into the house, surveys the scene, and drops right to his knees. Instantly his hands find his hair.

It suddenly begins to hail and Tristan swears from just outside the door. "Guys, it is freezing out th–" he walks in and looks at Cael, who is just staring his sister, his face a mask of many different emotions.

"Little brother," says Samael. "My, what an interesting mess you've caused by interfering. But I believe it is the way it was always meant to be. I suspect your meddling is the reason I am alive today."

"Fate will do what she will," my mother says, nodding her head.

"And love can transcend," says Samael, looking between Cael and me. "And boy, is this a love for the story books."

Cael just continues to stare, stunned. In the back of my mind, our connection is buzzing, but it feels faint. I realize it's because there's almost nothing running through his mind.

"What's the matter Uncle Cam?" asks Sam. "You missed Mommy, didn't you? Jack saved her. You don't have to be alonesome anymore."

And Cael is crying. Not the subtle, quiet kind. These are the kind of tears you'd only want to cry in private, where your nose is running, you make those awful distorted faces and when you try to speak, it comes out as nothing more than a whimper and drool. These are the sobs of somebody who has been through *too much*.

I walk over to him, kneel down so that I'm on his level and wrap my arms around him, and he just leans into me, burying his face in my neck. His sobs pierce my soul, and I find myself crying with him, because his pain needs to be shared.

In that moment, I don't believe I have ever found him more beautiful, because in the middle of a room full of people, he bares his soul for all to see.

And *nobody* dares judge him.

Twenty-Six

When Cael is done crying, he grabs my face and passionately kisses me, making my head spin, and then kisses my nose, forehead, both cheeks.

"Will you guys get a room already?" says Lisa.

"We're in a room," mumbles Cael against my lips, which he's worked his way back to, and then to me, "Thank you for not telling me on the phone. This was the absolute best thing to walk into though I almost had a *fucking* heart attack." His voice is husky.

Samael laughs from across the room. "Good thing we can't die from those."

Cael kisses my forehead again, stands up and is hugging his sister, almost in one fluid movement.

"I thought you were dead," he says. "I wanted to believe you were alive, but I gave up. *Ehohpeh-han, Samael.*"

Samael pulls away from the hug, places her hand on her brother's head and says, "No sorrow now, only happiness. *Ehtehharzodee.*"

"Peace," says Sam, rubbing his eyes. All of the angels – and Lisa – in the room nod. Tristan scratches his head like he's trying to figure the language out, as if somewhere inside of himself he recognizes it.

"It is a sacred thing," Jack says. He stands up and straightens out his pants, brushing off crumbs that I suspect weren't actually there. "I think my work here is done. I have reunited loved ones and think I should take my leave."

"Nonsense," says Liam. "You'll stay with us. You saved Samael and you didn't have to do that. You could have escaped by yourself but you didn't."

Cael nods. "Please, stay with Leliel. His home can offer protection. And anything I can do for you, name it and I will try. I owe you for saving my twin's life."

Jack smiles, making him look grandfatherly. "We are all family, especially so for the repentant Fallen. If we do not stick together, I am afraid salvation would not be an option."

Mom clears her throat then, and everybody looks at her. "Sooo," she says, "who wants tea?"

A couple of days later, I'm walking to my locker from English class when a hand on my shoulder startles me into dropping all of my books, making the Coke I was balancing precariously on top of them spill.

"Sorry kid," says Vicky with a very not-sorry smirk on her lips, which she's decided to colour purple today to match her little jacket. "It just so happens that Douma and two of his idiot underlings are holed up in a warehouse a few hours from town. You, me, and Cara are going on a little reconnaissance mission to get your necklace back."

I feel my eyes widen. "What?"

"Tinkerbell is in the car," she says. "Get your shit in your locker and meet us in the parking lot. I don't particularly care if you get in trouble with the school for skipping class; we need to get that back."

She begins to walk away and turns back and appraises me. "Nice outfit," she says. "We're purple shirt twins." She winks at me and then skips off.

~*~

"I *cannot* believe we are actually doing this," says Cara for the fifth time as we wait for Vicky outside Liam's house. It turns out that she'd been babysitting Sam for Samael (who's told us to refer to her as Samantha in public for pretences) and Liam.

A sigh escapes me. "I can." Cara shakes her head, her red locks bouncing at the movement. She seems so absolutely terrified that she's actually come all the way back around to fine; a total one hundred and eighty degrees.

The trunk slams shut and five minutes later Vicky is sitting in the driver's seat of Cara's car, laughing as it skids on ice.

"We're going to die," says Cara, almost conversationally. "We well and truly are going to freaking die." Her voice is casual but her eyes hold true fear.

After twenty or so minutes of driving and bickering over what radio station to choose, Vicky finally relays her plan to us. The forest passes by, tree after tree on either side of the car, and at once I am struck by the beauty of this part of Maine.

"Alright," says Vicky. "Listen up children, because I won't be repeating myself. There are three people we need to get through, and that's only if Douma is even around. I know he still has your necklace because a friend tipped me off."

Cara snorts. "You're so cryptic…"

Vicky pointedly ignores the remark. "He is trying to find a way to use its power, but it's attuned to you, Khiara, which is why we need it back. Samael can't just whip up another one; you only *ever* get one." She glances at me in the back seat from the rear-view mirror.

"I am going to cause a distraction near the entrance. I know there will be at least one person guarding the place. I'll signal you in some way to let you know it's safe to follow. From there we need to douse out the necklace's power. You should be able to feel it, Khiara, but if you can't, I'm a pretty good scout."

Cara shakes her head. "This isn't going to work. It's not well thought out at all. We're screwed."

Vicky shrugs like she couldn't care less. "We'll just have to see."

I cough into my hand feeling suddenly run down and am startled when Cara wordlessly hands me a tissue.

"Thanks," I say, coughing into it. A small spatter of blood stains the white of the tissue.

"You're bleeding," she says, her eyes cast down so as not to meet my own.

She shrugs, "I've been carrying first aid supplies in my purse for some time now. Just in case something happens…you're getting weaker. That's why I agreed to get the necklace, because it will protect you better. I know you can fight pretty great now but…well, I dunno. Best friends don't let best friends die."

I reach over and hold her hand, and just like that, we're silent for the entire two-hour car trip.

~*~

Cara and I are huddled behind some dumpsters and recycling bins in an alley by the entrance to the abandoned warehouse where Douma and his minions are staying. Periodically we peek out from behind them to get a better look at Vicky. For the most part, she's just been talking to the guard and I've kind of grown bored. Cara however has been staring for quite some time.

"Oh…my…God…" Cara whispers suddenly, tugging on my sleeve to get my attention. "We have to endure *this* just to get your stinking necklace back?"

I look up from my phone on which I'm playing some boring "match the fruit" game to see what she's talking about and have to stifle a disgusted gasp. "Is she *really* doing what I think she's doing?"

Vicky is doing the unthinkable. The guard has his pants to the ground and she's…

Cara makes a face and fakes a gagging motion, and then a very obscene gesture. "You mean sucking his –"

I cut her off quickly, "*Obviously* that's what I mean!" I look away, ashamed to have even witnessed that.

I turn to Cara, who's still staring, her eyes wide and her mouth in a disgusted grimace. "*Why* are you still watching?" I whisper-shout.

Cara shakes her head and shrugs at the same time. "That's dirtier than that one time I almost did it behind the dumpster next to your house like last year with Brady Johannesan," she whispers.

I'm *not* even going to ask about that. I silently thank God that she's with Tristan now. Thunder booms in the distance and I take that as a response and smile a bit.

She's still staring. "You know when there's something so disgusting you can't help but watch? This is it."

I groan, "No, I don't. Can you please stop looking?"

"I feel like something is gonna happen – she said she'd give us a signal…"

I'm beginning to say, "I'm pretty sure we *know* what's going to happen," when Vicky pulls out a knife from her pocket, gives a sharp snarl of what can only be described as insane laughter, stabs the guy right in the chest, and then looks right in our direction and waves us over.

"I guess killing him mid-B.J. *was* the signal," I mutter.

"You guys coming or what?" she yells like a kid waiting for their parents so they can get on a roller coaster.

We quickly follow her into the warehouse which is dark, though a quick snap of Cara's fingers produces a nice red flame to help us see better, illuminating the old building. Who needs a flash light when you have a Fire Nymph? A good look around tells us that this used to be a clothing factory; the first floor is filled with sewing machines.

The deeper we walk into the place, the more it smells like…well I don't know a good way to put this, so I'll just say it: *actual* human excrement.

I feel absolutely nauseated as we climb the stairs at the back of the large room. We find that there are small rooms on the higher levels that branch out off of the landings between each floor – there are three floors and two small landings between. We are on the first landing.

"Okay," whispers Vicky. "We're gonna do some Scooby Doo shit right now. Are you ready gang? There are three of us and there are three floors and I figure you can hold your own as long as you keep your cool. Please don't get killed, we have a lot riding on this."

She reaches under her skirt and into her leggings and produces a knife. "This'll do some damage. It was strapped to my thigh, in case ya'll are wondering, and it's charmed thanks to Samael."

She chuckles when Cara whispers, "Ew, it must be all sweaty."

"I had to find a way to keep it concealed," explains Vicky, handing the weapon – which is still warm from her body heat – over to me. "Cara, you take the second floor and I'll take the top floor."

She appraises me. "I don't want to make you feel inferior or anything but I think you should stick to the landings and the little rooms. Now only use that knife if you have to, okay kid?" She surprises me by leaning forward and kissing me on the top of my head.

"I could pass for somebody much younger than you," she says, her voice thick with some unnamed emotion. "But I'm old enough to be called ancient." She seems to be implying something important, but I'm not sure I get it.

She turns to Cara and smirks half-heartedly. "I've haven't known you for very long and I want you to know from the bottom of my heart that I think you're not all that annoying."

Cara smiles right back at her. "Yeah, I don't hate you either. You're like the annoying sister I've always wanted." Cara turns to me and says, "You're like my completely opposite fraternal twin."

"Alright gang," whispers Vicky. "Let's split up and search for clues. If you have to kick some asses, I have every faith in you that you can do it. Our primary search is for Douma but if you find the other guy he's with, that'll work too because he can lead us to him. The necklace *is* in here somewhere. I can feel it."

"How come I can't?" I ask.

She shrugs. "You need to be closer to it, I guess. You'll know when you are. Okay, enough dilly dallying. Let's get our asses in gear!"

I make my way to the first little room which branches off of the second floor landing, while Cara goes in the opposite direction where a door leads to the main room of the second floor. Vicky walks up the stairs, quiet as a mouse, on her way to the third floor. I can only hope to be as quiet.

I use my phone's flashlight app to help me see and shiver in the cold; this place isn't heated and I can see my breath. The room is windowless and dusty and holds nothing more than a pitiful desk with two broken legs on the left side and an equally broken chair. I shrug, not sensing anything and walk to the other side of the room, sure that I'll probably not find anything of importance.

It turns out, I'm half right. I don't find anything that seems significant, but I *do* find a pair of rusted handcuffs that if not for the still mostly wet pool of blood, could have fit right in with the old room. I decide not to touch anything but I snap a picture for evidence. I realize that deeming it not completely important seems callous to whoever lost that blood, but I expected to find something like this, and it's not directly connected to our goal of getting my necklace as far as I know.

I make my way to the third floor landing taking care to be as quiet as I can, and pop my head into the room. Of course that's where the scent of human waste is coming from. The stench of vomit mixed with urine and feces permeates the small room, making me gag. Its layout is identical to the one below save the desk and chair, and the fact that a man who is covered in blood is lying in the right hand corner.

"Oh God," I whisper, my already nauseated stomach turning at the sight. "Please don't tell me he's dead."

I inch my way into the room, slowly but surely walking around puddles of the revolting stuff. When I reach the man, I bend down to take his pulse but stop with my fingers inches away from his throat. *Should I really risk getting my finger prints on him?*

I decide to risk it and touch his neck.

No pulse.

"I'm sorry," I whisper to his not-yet-pale body. "I wish I'd have been able to help you." I momentarily wonder if he was human.

"He was one of the repentant," Vicky's says from behind me.

"Did you read my mind?" I ask, unable to tear my gaze away from the man. His glassy brown eyes that gaze into nothing and his skin colour hint at him having Fallen somewhere in East Asia, perhaps, though his appearance is very little to go by; there is so much diversity that I really couldn't tell you for sure, and I'm not sure why it matters so much to me to know.

"No," says Vicky. "I didn't have to."

"Did you know him?" I ask, finally looking away from him.

Vicky nods her head. "Yeah. He was the guy who tipped me off. I guess Douma caught up with him somehow. We won't find him in here. I found fuck all on the third floor besides more rusted machinery."

Suddenly a furious scream erupts from the level below us. Vicky's eyes meet mine.

Cara.

"I will *end* you!" she screeches and the sound of flesh hitting bone echoes throughout the warehouse as Vicky and I make our way to the second floor, not caring about being silent anymore.

When we get there, Cara is clutching her right arm to her chest, and it is dripping blood and her wrist seems to be sticking out at an odd angle, and I'm pretty sure I can see bone if I squint. A boy of about fifteen is holding his hand to his broken and bloody nose, stunned.

"What's the matter," she taunts, steam pouring off of her in waves from the heat of her body. "You thought a broken arm would stop me from hurting you? I will fucking kill you before I let you go near my friends."

"You're feistier than I bargained for," he says, letting go of his nose, which has now healed. "But I can heal. You can't."

Just as he moves to grab Cara, I do something equal parts stupid and amazing. With almost disturbing precision, I pull out my knife, pull my arm back, and then whip the knife right into the guy's back. This gives Vicky enough time to get to him so that she can pin him down and for me to get to Cara so that I can make sure she doesn't pass out from the blood loss.

As Vicky is busy with Douma's minion, I take off my jacket and quickly shed my sweater, then with my knife begin to cut it into strips so that I can wrap it and make a sling. Cara taught me to do this, in case of emergency.

"I'll be okay, you know," says Cara. "I have magic to help speed my healing process. Plus my mom won't ask questions. That'd mean she'd actually have to care about me and we can't have her doing that now can we?"

I frown. "She cares about you Cara, she's just…"

Cara shakes her head, looks down, then smiles to herself miserably. "She cares about me like I'm an ugly dog she got stuck with because of a divorce. I came to that conclusion at Dad's funeral, when she didn't cry and yelled at me for not wanting to leave the cemetery. Remember he had two different coffins because the first was ruined?"

I nod and begin to wrap Cara's arm, working slowly so that I make no mistakes. In the background, the sound of Vicky repeatedly punching and kicking the man makes the hair on my neck stand on end.

"I burned the first one with him in it. He became one with Father Fire. There was no body in the second casket." She sighs and then looks at me, tears running down her face. "My mother *knew* this whole time, about the Fae, or at least she knew there was something different about Dad and me."

She cringes as I accidentally jostle her wrist as I put it into my makeshift sling having finished wrapping it. "She told me last week that she knows what kind of monster I am. My mother *does not* love me Khiara and she didn't even love my dad in the end. My father loved her with every fibre of his being, and maybe she did love him once, and maybe she loved me at one point too…but that's long gone. She's just stuck with me until I'm old enough to leave the house."

"Boo-hoo," unexpectedly booms a voice from the darkness. "Aren't you just a pathetic bunch? I mean one of you is dying, one of you has a mother who hates you and one of you...well, the past is the past I suppose, but it seems you're holding onto your anger from that one time I killed your family. It's stupid really, when I think about it."

Douma walks out of the shadows and in the time it takes Vicky to let up punching the other angel, and for her to realize her mistake, Douma has her by her throat and picks up her body as if it weighs nothing.

"Stupid whore," he spits. "I don't know what I ever saw in you."

He turns to myself and Cara and shouts, "Do you know the lengths I took to make this bitch love me?"

"No, but you're going to tell us," mutters Cara, sarcasm dripping from her words.

He scoffs. "But then she turns around and tells me that she's in love with a stupid human. And so yeah, in a moment of anger I told Father and she Fell because of that and *yeah*, I felt guilty about it."

Douma shrugs, almost nonchalantly. "Eventually I Fell too, for my own reasons, and by then she'd shacked up with the guy and they had two annoying children. Cute as a button because they looked like their mother but annoying beyond compare!"

He smiles. "So I killed them first."

"You bastard!" Vicky's voice has a hysterical edge to it. I get the sense that she never knew exactly how it had happened.

My suspicions are confirmed when Douma laughs and spits right in her face then says, "I stabbed Aahmes first, and then Hasina second. They both called out for you, you know.

"Stop," wheezes Vicky, "*please*."

Douma ignores her. "'*Ama!*' they kept screeching like it would make a difference. They were too human-blooded and their lives faded fast, but Hasina held on longer than her brother. When Aamesseker found them, he was an easy kill – his grief consumed him, and while he was bent over Hasina, who was still breathing, I slit his throat."

Vicky is thrashing now, desperately trying to get out of his hold. By now, the other angel has healed from her attacks and my knife and he lies in waiting for Douma's next order.

"That's how you found them, right?" says Douma, as he throws Vicky down on to the floor, hard.

The revolting sound of her skull hitting the concrete floor reverberates throughout the warehouse. Douma signals the other angel to hold her down and he complies. In that moment, I realize something. Douma isn't watching me and he isn't watching Cara; and my necklace is dangling from the back pocket of his minion's blue jeans. Its power suddenly hits me like a punch in the gut and I wonder why I didn't recognize it sooner.

Before I can totally think my plan through, I make the universal sign of *shh* to Cara (who frowns with all the energy she can muster and then makes the universal slit throat sign for *I will kill you*) and tiptoe towards the angel as quietly as I can. I can feel Cara's eyes on my back, burning my skin.

The angel's back pocket is facing me and I am so, so, *so* close and – *yes*.

I'm able to grab it!

I hastily stuff the necklace in my bra, but as I make it halfway back to Cara, I trip and fall onto the hard floor. I can't stop the yelp that escapes me as my chin gets scraped and just like that, everybody's attention is on me.

"Jonah, kill everybody except *her*," says Douma, pointing to me. "I'd love to stay and chat but I must be going. Deliver Khiara to me when you're done here. I have a body upstairs to clean up and dispose of."

He walks over to me and painfully grabs me by the wrist then drags me over to Cara, who appears to be growing weak from the blood loss.

He grins, showing his teeth. "Say your goodbyes now. Looks like Cara won't make it, I'm afraid. Sad since it's just a broken bone. Poor little Faen-Halfling. You'll return to the Fire. I promise it'll be over soon."

"Yeah, yeah," whispers Cara. "Don't you have a body to get rid of?"

Douma pats her on the head like a puppy. "Quite right," he says, and walks towards the stairs, but then turns back around to look at me.

"I'm going to destroy your necklace," he announces.

"I've got it right here in my pocket." He pats his pocket proudly. "And you're going to help me destroy it."

The necklace is practically singeing my skin with the heat that it's radiating and it takes everything I have not to smile like an idiot.

"No, I won't. I will never help you."

He turns away again and over his shoulder he says, "You will, Ms. Banning. You'll see."

"No," I mutter under my breath as he disappears into the stairwell. "*You'll* see."

I turn away from the empty space he just occupied, to see Jonah still pinning Vicky down with only his foot. Her eyes meet mine and I nod once and smile slightly.

Her eyes light up and so subtly it could be missed she nods her head as well.

"First, I'm going to rip your friend here apart. And then I'll get to you two," says Jonah.

"Go fuck yourself," snarls Vicky, with every ounce of venom she has. Jonah lifts his foot, reaches down, and pulls Vicky to her feet, and then punches her in the stomach, making her curl into herself.

"Do it again, a little harder, I didn't quite feel it," she rasps.

He punches her in the jaw and a revolting cracking noise comes from her teeth being broken and she falls to the floor again. She spits out some blood and a couple of teeth and smiles, "I can do thith all day. They'll jutht grow back. In fact…they're already healing as we thspeak."

This really angers him and he begins wailing on her, turning his complete attention on her. That's when I understand what she's doing; creating a diversion.

"Cara," I whisper, "I need you to-" but she's already pulled out what appears to be a knife from her pocket and she looks like she feels much better than she just did moments ago. She probably healed herself as much as she could manage.

"I've got this covered," she whispers back.

She runs right towards him before I can stop her.

Thrusting the weapon into Jonah's neck Cara yells, "The pen is mightier than the sword, bitch!"

"What the fuck?" says Jonah, before letting go of Vicky and falling to the ground with a scream, and I see that the weapon isn't a knife at all – it really *is* a pen, though it's red hot from Cara's Fire magic, which is spreading all over his body and lighting up his veins like the fourth of July, making him writhe in pain, unable to do anything else.

"I don't think that's what the librarian meant, Cara…" I say as we help Vicky to her feet while she mutters something along the lines of, "Yeah, but at least she stunned him."

"I have issues, what can I say?" says Cara as she laughs nervously and sniffs the air which smells like burning flesh.

When we reach the dumpsters where she stabbed the guard who is still lying there, not healed, Cara asks, "Jonah's not dead is he? I didn't kill him?"

"You can't kill us. You can beat the shit out of us, but kill us? Naw, we only die when it's another angel at the hilt of a sword and it has to be a fatal blow or else we'll heal," Vicky says. "The guard will heal but he's Nephilim so it'll take him longer."

"Ah, yes," I mumble. "Let's get the hell out of here."

But Vicky doesn't move. "No!" she growls. "You guys go without me. I need to get to Douma. I need to make him pay."

"You're not thinking straight," says Cara. "We need to get to the car and get the fuck out of here."

"No!" shouts Vicky. She's visibly shaking and there's blood covering her jaw, matted in her hair, and along her arms.

"Not right now," says a small voice from behind us. I turn and realize that it's… Sam?

Has he been hiding all this time?

"If you want to make him pay, do it during the Battle. But right now we gotsta go."

"What the fuck are you doing here?" says Cara as Vicky says, "What do you know about my pain, *boy*?"

Sam walks up to us and stands before me, lifting his chubby arms up over his head, "Got in from the trunk. I'm tired." I pick him up out of instinct and he wraps his arms around me and cradles his head in the crook of my neck, his curly blonde locks soft against my skin. He shivers a bit and I realize how cold it's become.

"I know a lot, Aunty V," he says. "It's not my fault."

The hard lines of Vicky's face soften up a bit as Sam turns his big green eyed gaze directly towards her. "I'm sorry," he says, his voice quivering. "It's not my fault. I just wanted to come in case you guys needed me."

"I know it's not, kid," she says to him. "Let's get you home. You shouldn't have followed us. It must have taken some strong magic to get into the trunk. You shouldn't be doing stuff like that." Vicky turns to walk away, but then stops walking.

"Tinkerbell," she says tiredly; she's still not fully healed.

"You're talking to me, I assume," Cara shakes her head and rolls her eyes. Sam shivers some more in my arms. I suppress a sudden cough working its way into my throat.

"Take the kid. He's cold and you're warm. Plus, Khiara's been pretty sick recently herself and we kind of need her to not, you know, die."

Normally Cara would have muttered something under her breath about not being a portable heater; I can tell she even thought about saying something. But instead, she wordlessly reaches out for Sam with her good arm.

"Come here, little guy," she says as I hand the sleepy boy over. She makes her way over to the car, cooing sweet nothings to Sam as they walk.

"We have to get to the car. Douma will know what happened in a minute; he's probably already on his way to find us," I say to Vicky.

She looks as if she wants to throttle me but she sighs and jogs towards the car. I've won this round.

And of course, my necklace.

Twenty-Seven

"My word," breathes Grandma Coal as she takes in the state of Cara's wrist, my chin, and the blood all over Vicky. Sam is holding fast to Cara's hand, refusing to let go.

She exhales a sigh and rolls her eyes at us, a forced smirk on her weathered face. "You'd better come in, then" she says, moving out of the doorway. "You'll do some better explaining if you're not cold."

She ushers us in one after the other, giving Vicky an especially quizzical look.

"And who is this?" she asks, after we're all inside, awkwardly standing by the front door.

"Verchiel," says Vicky. "Angel of Affection, though Fallen. I'm called Vicky though, by friends. You can call me whatever you like. I haven't met a member of the Spirit Clann in a very long time. And this is Sam. He's a friend of my family."

Grandma Coal blinks for a second or two and then nods her head. "Right then, nice to meet you two."

"Grandma Coal, I'm sorry we didn't call you before coming. I normally would have, but the situation is…well…" Cara struggles to find the right words, and Sam blinks at her wordlessly, trying to figure out exactly what's going on before letting go of her hand and quickly grabbing mine.

The old woman smiles kindly and wraps her arms around her granddaughter. "Come now, child. You act like I'm upset. What would your father think?"

"He'd probably have some choice words," says Cara wistfully. "And then he'd make some rhubarb pie, even though it's winter and he could never explain to Mom where he bought it."

"I have some," says Grandma Coal. "But first, Vicky, the shower is on the top floor. I assume you can find your way there. I need to heal these two."

"Yeah," Vicky shrugs and heads off in the direction of the bathroom.

"Okay," says Grandma Cole, looking between Cara and myself. "Cara, give me your arm."

Cara complies, but frowns. "Will it still be broken? I tried to heal it but I'm kind of bad at this whole healing thing since it's not my element."

"It won't be broken. But it will be sprained pretty badly, I'm afraid. It should heal within the week though if you keep healing it in small bursts."

She closes her eyes and inhales a deep breath of air. Her black hair, which is grey at the temples, begins to take on a strange vibrant sheen, almost as if it's actually shining, and then as she blows the air out it turns completely white as her magic flows into Cara's arm, stitching together what's been broken.

"Wow," whispers Sam.

Cara's veins seem to turn black while everything heals until the magic flows back into her grandmother, turning her hair black once again, and Cara's veins return to their normal light blue and green. Her wrist is still swollen but the bone isn't sticking out at that disgusting angle anymore.

"Righty then," says Grandma Coal, turning to me once Cara's sighed from the pain being lifted, and looks visibly relieved. "I think I can take care of the nasty scrape in a jiffy."

She puts her warm hands on my chin and takes a big breath, and then does the same thing for me as she did for her granddaughter. This wonderful tickling sensation flows through me, and I realize with a start that it's her magic. It feels almost *playful.*

"Holy crap," I say when she's finished. "That was amazing."

"I tend to be amazing," she replies. "Now, let's see about getting you that rhubarb pie while you wait for your turns in the shower. And," she turns to little Sam, "I think you'd like some hot chocolate, hmm?"

"Yes please," says Sam. "I've never met a Spirit Fae before," he says conversationally.

Grandma Coal laughs at this. "Well I've never met anybody quite like you, Sam. You'll have to excuse me for any rudeness if I happen to ask later, what race it is exactly that you are."

"I don't mind." He says, reaching out to take her outstretched hand. "I think you're nice."

"Well I can be," she says, chuckling.

Two hours later, scrubbed clean and our bellies full – especially Sam – we're sitting in the small living room with cups of tea in our hands after having explained literally everything that has happened to lead us to this point, when my phone rings.

I'd forgotten that I had it since it died on the way here, but Grandma Coal had an extra phone charger.

"Hello?" I answer on the second ring.

I already know who it is, but the sound of his panicked voice is enough to make me feel so, *so* guilty.

"Khiara! Are you hurt? Where did Vicky take you guys?"

"I'm not hurt," it isn't technically a lie, but it tastes dirty in my mouth and he makes an irritated sound at the back of his throat. "Okay," I say. "I *was* hurt. I'm okay now."

"Where are you?" he repeats. "What happened?"

"I'm at Cara's grandmother's place. She's a healer, remember?"

"Up near Portland? That's *hours* away! Oh my God, you didn't," he pauses, "you went to get your necklace didn't you?"

I'm silent.

"Don't try to tell me this was your plan because it reeks of Verchiel," the use of her angelic name makes me realize how worried he'd been.

"You disappeared from school Khiara; your parents are worried sick about you! They showed up at my apartment. So I called my sister, right? And what does she tell me? You've driven off with Cara and Verchiel and apparently *Sam*, to God knows where to do God knows what, and when we all try to reach one of you, your phones are conveniently turned off!"

"I got it, Cael."

"I don't think you do, love. You're going to give me an aneurism and once it heals, ten more."

"No," I say, slightly annoyed now. "I have the necklace. We got it."

Silence is the sometimes the loudest sound when you're waiting for somebody to say something.

"You have it," he whispers. And then louder, "You have it!"

A thump comes from the other side of the phone and I realize it's because Cael dropped the phone, fell, or both and I can hear him swear loudly.

"Sorry," he says breathlessly. "I got so excited that I fell off of the bed and dropped the phone. You really got it?"

"We do," I laugh.

"And we kicked some ass!" shouts Vicky from beside me, loud enough so that Cael can hear her, bumping into my shoulder with hers triumphantly.

Cael sighs, but not unhappily. "Can I talk to Vicky?"

"That depends. Are you gonna yell at her?" I don't want her to get in trouble for this.

He shifts positions and I hear his bed creak. "Khiaraaa."

"Caaael," I counter, making him chuckle.

I can just see him running his hand through his hair and I can hear smile-when he says, "I can't promise you that I'm not going to yell at her at all, but *maybe* not over the phone. Can I talk to her now?"

I pass the phone to Vicky wordlessly and she ruffles my hair.

"Yo," she says, answering the phone. "I hear I'm in potential trouble for saving your girl's ass?"

Vicky's silent while Cael says something, and then she laughs out loud. "I'd like to see you try, lover boy. But seriously, stop worrying. You're not her Guardian anymore. Just her boyfriend. And as such, protecting her is something you have to share with the rest of the people who love her."

A pause as Cael speaks.

Vicky frowns. "Well…yes."

Another pause.

"Now I have been your partner in crime for literally as long as this child has been alive. Is that any way to speak to me? Christ, you may have been appointed as her Guardian, but I have had my fair share of keeping her alive these past seventeen years. Remember when she broke her wrist falling off of her bike and you were halfway across the town?"

"What?" Cara and I say at the same time but Vicky waves it away, leaving Cara and I to stare at each other in confusion.

After five minutes of silence on her part, clearly Vicky has won this argument because she fist pumps, after Cael is done speaking. "You're damned right. See you tomorrow."

She hangs up the phone then and grins at me. "I've been a part of your life for a long time, kid. I was the one who called the ambulance when you broke your wrist that day. Lover boy was supposed to keep a low profile and being that we're not able to become invisible, it was hard for him to keep track of you every hour of every day like he could've in Heaven. It was a good thing I was scoping out the town for him that day."

"Oh!" says Cara, nodding her head enthusiastically. "I remember! You had such an attitude…"

Vicky laughs. "I still have it, thanks. But whenever I encountered you, I had to make sure that I didn't paint myself in a fantastic light. I was supposed to show up in your memory as a random stranger, not some kind lady that you would think back on. And then last year when Douma decided that his best bet for getting to Khiara was enrolling in your damned school, I was still leading him to believe that I was Unrepentant, so of course I had to pretend to hate you."

She shrugs like it's no big deal. "The things you do for friends, am I right?"

Grandma Coal, who I forgot was listening this whole time, chuckles and says, "Indeed. Now, let's get the sleeping arrangements set up, shall we?"

Twenty-Eight

My combat training has officially ended; there is nothing more I can do, besides fight hand-to-hand, seeing as I'm only human. But I'm a pretty good fighter now and can even take out Liam if I try hard enough.

I'm not in a fighting kind of mood right now, though. Mom has made a special dinner and insisted I call everybody to join us for it, so the dining room is currently filled to the brim; we actually had to get extra chairs from the attic.

Now that my training is over we have to think about the Battle. Cara's grandmother has put in calls to many of the Faen, who in turn have put out calls of their own; One hundred Pixies, Nymphs, and Elves in total – as it turns out, there are only about a million left world-wide, and only about a thousand of them want anything to do with human affairs and whatnot – from around the world are on call, waiting to battle. About forty are able to actually make their way to Maine at the drop of a hat and we are expecting them sometime soon. The rest will come as fast as they can, after next week.

I've just come back into the room, having been tasked to get another bottle of juice from the fridge, and I'm standing in the doorway, taking everything in.

"So Lisa," Dad, who is sitting across the table from Lisa, Samael, and Vicky, is saying through a mouthful of mashed potatoes. "How is French class coming along now that you're getting Khiara's help?"

"Great," she says, as bubbly as ever, spearing a single pea with her fork too hard, making it fly off her plate and onto Tristan's. He reacts only by picking it up and popping it into his mouth with a cheeky grin.

Samael rolls her blue eyes at the scene and lovingly places her hand on her daughter's head. "She's been passing with flying colours thanks to your daughter."

Dad beams, as if he's been given the biggest compliment;, which I suppose as a parent he has. "Yes, she's a smart girl. Takes after her old man."

Mom rolls her eyes from next to him. "Okay, sweetheart. You keep telling yourself that."

Dad mock frowns and says, "Ferme ta bouche, Madame!" and then kisses her on the cheek, pulls back, then winks at her, earning him a loving swat on the arm from her.

I walk into the room and place the bottle of grape juice on the table, then take my seat next to Mom and Cael.

"So," I say to Cael, digging into my dinner. "I've been thinking we should go on a date. We've only had the one."

Cael smiles and reaches over to grab some more mashed potatoes. "Aye, I think that's a good idea. What do you want to do?"

I think about it for a minute, stuffing my face with bread, chicken, green beans and potatoes, and then an idea forms in my mind. "I think we should take a drive somewhere. Go wherever the road takes us."

His smile turns into a full out grin. "I like that idea. When do you want to do this? I'm down for whatever day and time you want."

"Tomorrow? I can maybe stay over and we can go from your place?" I can't disguise the excitement in my voice.

Cael nods and takes a large bite of bread. Through his mouthful he says, "Sounds like a plan!" and I can't stop the laugh that bubbles out of me.

"Young love," says Jack from the head of the table. "There's nothing like it, is there?"

From Liam's lap Sam shakes his head and crows, "Nope!"

I have never had a big family; it's always been Mom, Dad, and me, and of course Cara. Dad's family is all in France and they want nothing to do with him and Mom's adoptive parents passed away.

I have an aunt on her side but I've only met her once and she wasn't very nice and her son – my cousin – was a little brat who tried to cut off my ponytail.

These people, Cael, Vicky, Lisa, Liam, Sam, Samael, Tristan, and even Jack, have become part of my family too in such a short period of time. I don't know that I will ever want to meet my blood relatives the ones who gave me up and damned me to be cursed. They aren't my family. They lost that privilege when they gave me up.

But right now, at this crowded dinner table, with Humans, Angels, Nephilim, a Nymph and the child of two Fallen Angels – a member of the Rephaim race – I have never felt more like part of a big, important, and loving family.

~*~

Mirrors. They're everywhere I turn.

I keep walking down this long hallway, but never get to the end…is there an end to this hallway? Everything seems suspended in blackness, this thick black shadowy stuff that encases the entirety of the hall. It feels like how I assume space would look like without the light of the stars. I know that there is a floor, kind of, beneath my feet, only because I haven't fallen into an abyss yet and because the mirrors must be resting on something. I assume that there are walls on either side of me, holding up the mirrors, but I can't see them. It's just me and the mirrors in this strange darkness.

There is no voice this time.

Usually there's a voice telling me to choose something, or I end up in front of this man made of shadows and I am not aware that I'm dreaming. But I know that this is a dream. I don't remember going to bed, though…I remember sitting on the couch watching infomercials with Cael, laughing like we always do. And now I'm here. But logically I have to be dreaming

I just can't get out of it.

Vaguely, I can hear somebody speaking to me, but I don't understand the words. It sounds like a strange humming. I keep walking down the hall, trying to find a way out.

Time doesn't feel like it's passing as it should. I feel like I've been here for days, but logically it's only been minutes, or maybe an hour…I don't exactly know how long dreams last.

And then, suddenly I'm in front of an old, cracked mirror ignoring the hallway that's still stretching out to the left of me, and…wait, is that Cael? Why is he banging on the mirror? Doesn't he know that it's going to shatter? What if...can I talk to him somehow?

The mirror's reflection only shows him standing there in darkness, illuminated as if there is only a small light overhead, banging on the mirror and soundlessly yelling.

"Cael," *I whisper, trying the idea out while reaching out and placing my palm flat against the mirror.*

"Khiara?" *he stops banging and his reflection ripples under my hand like a pool of water for a moment, fading in and out of view.*

"You took the keys, and I didn't know what to do so I just followed you to the car but I couldn't let you drive, obviously...what's going on?" *he questions, his eyes searching my own.*

"What do you mean I 'took the keys'?"

"I mean you took the keys from my pants. They were on the floor. You just got out of the bed, grabbed my pants and-"

I cut him off. "Wait, what? I don't remember going to bed."

He looks conflicted for a moment and says hoarsely, "What do you remember?"

"Watching old Billy Mays infomercials and laughing."

He frowns, and then swears. "Fuck," *he says.* "If I'd have known..."

And then something hits me. "Cael," *I ask, suddenly frantic, because if what I'm thinking is right, I don't know how to feel.* "Why were we in bed?"

"We were sleeping," *is his careful response. His face has become composed – too closed off to read.*

"Your pants were on the floor," *I say it slowly.* "And we were in the bed. You didn't mention me getting dressed. You just said that I took the keys and started walking to the car."

His face is bright red when he realizes what I mean. "Oh God, no. No. We I mean, I, I mean, we uhh...didn't..."

I'm relieved as all hell. I let out a sigh and sit down on the kind of ground. "Take a deep breath. We didn't have sex. That's all I wanted to know."

"Khiara!" *he sounds scandalized that I even brought up the idea.* "I mean we kissed and stuff, but no. No."

"And stuff?" *Now I'm just being cruel.*

"N-nothing we haven't done before!" *he cries, stuffing his hands in his hair.* "We just made out…a lot." *He looks as if he's about to pass out.*

"Why can't you remember? Oh man is that considered sexual assault? I feel like I should know, but I have no experience in this kind of thing, I mean —"

I put him out of his misery. "It isn't sexual assault. Calm down. I just…wanted to remember if we'd…you know. Anyway, how the hell do I get out of this place?"

"The car?" *he asks, quizzically, looking around.*

"Cael," *my heart does a weird flop that makes me think I'm about to vomit it right out.* "How are we talking right now?"

He frowns. "With our mouths?" *And then he realizes what I mean,* "Oh. Not through our minds…whoa, wait, you're not awake?"

"No? I don't think so…I'm in my own…head?"

"Khiara, you're talking to me right now. We're… in the car. You've been making that weird face the whole time…holy shit." *He pauses. Then,* "You've been making that face the whole time!"

"What weird face?" *I ask, because despite the fact that there are mirrors all around me and I can see my reflection just fine in…well, most of them…and I haven't been making any faces that I'd deem as weird. Terrified and confused, maybe, but not weird.* "I feel awake. I'm staring at you through a mirror…I'm in that hallway I always dream about. I can see you as if you were just standing on the other side, I can see your movements and…"

"Okay," *he says.* "We're communicating through our minds…but also through our bodies. Never happened before. I guess it's our connection."

"Guess so," *I mumble, standing back up.*

Cael is beginning to say, "So if you're —" *but suddenly, his image ripples again, and then disappears completely. Suddenly the hallway stretches out before me again, and I'm back where I started.*

"Oh crap," *I whisper.*

"Choose which way to go," *says the voice that I'd almost forgotten was part of this stupid dream.*

Since there is only one way to go, I start walking forward, down the long corridor. I catch glimpses of myself in some of the mirrors that I pass, and I realize with a start that I'm only in one of Cael's shirts and my underwear. I fleetingly wonder why I'm not cold, but then remember that I'm still technically sitting in the car with Cael and right now I'm just seeing things inside my own head.

Still, this is too strange.

The hallway is a lot longer than usual and suddenly I come to the end of one hallway and the beginning of two- one goes right and one goes left. They both look equally as foreboding.

The voice purrs from all around me. "Choose, child."

"And if I don't?" *I ask, suddenly feeling a sense of dread.* "Or what if I choose wrong?"

"Little Dark One," *says the voice.* "You have to choose. And if you chose wrong, I cannot help you. That is all I will say."

"Who are you?" *My voice cracks on the last word.*

Her voice is soft an almost musical when she says, "You know who I am, child."

I go down the left corridor. Something inside of me makes the choice without my brain's permission and suddenly I'm at another corridor exactly like the one I just left. I go right this time. The voice has disappeared.

I go down three more of these strange hallway branches, following my gut each time, until finally I'm back in front of the mirror I was talking to Cael through, and the voice whispers, "Good. Child, death is inevitable. But if you continue down the right path, so is life."

And suddenly, I'm gasping for air, choking on it at the same time I'm desperately trying to fill my lungs with it and I am so, so cold. My lungs feel as if I've been submerged in water for far too long and I'd begun to drown, my body having given up, when suddenly I've been pulled to safety.

"Death is inevitable," are the last words I hear before blacking out.

Twenty-Nine

I wake to the sound of Cael's terrified voice. "Khiara for crying out loud what is going on?"

I get the sense that he's been trying to wake me up for quite some time now because though fear is lacing his voice, so is exasperation.

I open my eyes, slowly but surely, and see that we're still in the car but it's too dark outside, like there was a power failure and all of the streetlights went out. But then my eyes begin to focus on the surroundings outside and I realize that we're not in front of Cael's building.

We're pulled over on a dirt road somewhere in the middle of the woods.

"What the hell?" I ask. "Where are we?"

Cael's covered me up in the sweater he keeps in the backseat of his car, and though the air vents are blowing warm air into the car, I'm still freezing seeing as I'm in nothing but his shirt and my underwear.

"You told me where to go," he says, baffled. "You kept saying 'left, right,' like you knew where you were going…we're only twenty minutes from town."

I stare at him for a second and it comes out harsher than intended when I say, "And you just listened to me? You just followed your practically comatose girlfriend's directions."

Cael furrows his brows and sucks his bottom lip. "You weren't comatose. You looked like you'd come out of whatever it was that…was up before, with the talking with our bodies and minds and the creepy face –"

In an effort to calm him down, I lean over and kiss his cheek. "You're starting to talk like a mixture of me and Cara, you know, all rambling and awkwardness. Not very angelic or old. Also, I said *practically*."

Cael grumbles a bit until I kiss his cheek again and then sighs. "Okay then. So, I'm assuming you don't know why we're here do you?"

I explain what happened inside of my head and he listens with equal parts curiosity and apparent fear. The whole time, he absently runs his hands through his hair every so often, and when he catches himself doing it the third time, he smiles sheepishly at me.

When I'm done my explanation, he simply whispers, "Morrigan."

My nose crinkles and I think back to the voice. "I guess it is her. She called me 'Dark One' but I have no idea what that means exactly."

Cael shrugs. "I guess it's to do with the curse."

"Must be," I breathe, sitting back in my seat and stifling yet another shiver.

But then something distracts me. I catch a movement just outside the window and upon closer inspection, it's just a crow that has stayed behind somehow, and is drifting lazily upon the icy wind, darting through the trees. I follow it with my eyes for a second longer, before suddenly opening the door without my brain's permission.

"What are you doing now?"

"I need to follow that bird." The words sound strange, just tumbling out of my mouth, but there it is. I have to follow it.

Not of my own accord, I end up walking through the snow and down this dirt road, past Cael as he swears and grabs at me to stop me (I know he's afraid to hurt me because he has the strength to simply pick me up and carry me back to the car). It's weird. I'm not in a daze, exactly, but I'm certainly walking down a dark dirt road in my underwear, an oversized shirt and a flimsy sweater around my shoulders, and with my sockless feet in boots that are quickly becoming soaked, so I must be in some sort of odd state.

I find that I'm not really shivering like I was in the car. I can hardly feel the cold, though I acknowledge its existence with every visible puff of my breaths and Cael's, as he tromps through the snow beside me.

We don't talk. He must sense my urgency.

And so we walk, following the crow into the forest eventually, and away from the road. Onward we walk as it begins to snow lightly. We keep walking even when Cael's phone dies, leaving us with only the light of the moon. My gait becomes a sort of strange march eventually and the uniformity of my steps becomes almost comforting in this dark winter wonderland. Eventually Cael falls behind me just a bit, watching my back.

Finally, we reach a large clearing in the forest and I think my journey is done, but my last step falters, making me fall to my knees.

"Khiara!" Cael exclaims, rushing to catch me just a second too late, as I hit the cold ground.

Instantly I feel the tell-tale drip from my nose as if it were a faucet turned on after years of being shut off, one drop, and suddenly a warm gush the ground in front of me has turned red. I move to use the sweater to staunch the bleeding but find that I have no control over my arms.

"Help," I whisper to Cael as he takes my arm but he is helpless as I begin to seize uncontrollably.

~*~

Khiara is in full on seizure mode and all I can do is hold her body down and hope to God that she doesn't choke as she thrashes around, mumbling incoherently. I don't know why I even drove the *damned* car to this *damned* forest – it was like something came over me and I just couldn't get past it. I could have sworn I had my own wits about me, though.

I think.

Khiara practically screams at whatever is going on behind her rapidly moving eyelids and I'm forced to admit to myself that I clearly *didn't* have my wits about me, or else I'd have pulled her into the car the minute she stepped out of it, and brought her home. I wouldn't have even let her walk out of the apartment.

"Morrigan," I whisper, "what are you doing?"

The crow caws in the distance, as if answering me, but my eyes can't focus on where the sound came from.

And then it hits me. The crow.

"Show yourself!" I shout angrily, and before my eyes, a woman begins to materialize.

Her black hair is pulled back by a leather chord, and she wears a loose grey toga-style dress.

"Hello Camael," she purrs, as she crouches before us, placing a hand on Khiara's chest and stopping the seizure in its tracks, leaving her to look as if she were sleeping.

My heart fissures at the sight but she is very much alive, though drained. I have to remember that.

"Hello," I echo silently. I wanted to yell at her, to scream at her, but all of the words that I had feel like they're stuffed too tight in my throat, and they can't seem to bubble up.

"Man-Deh is not pleased with me," she says coolly, cocking her head to the side as she looks Khiara over, as if she were nothing special. "I cannot understand why. That idiotic prophesy of his will still come to fruition regardless of my curse. It is a prophesy. They always come to fruition in one way or another. Hardly ever as planned."

I suddenly find my words. "She's going to die once the Battle arrives. Her health has been deteriorating rapidly. How is that fair? Just because her parents were idiots, you *had* to curse her?"

Morrigan shrugs like my opinion is of no importance to her, which it probably isn't, seeing as lesser Gods and Goddesses see my kind as their less powerful, annoying little cousins. She runs her fingers through Khiara's damp hair and then begins braiding a small plait into her hair in an almost motherly fashion.

"A moment, Camael," she says, holding up a hand for me to be quiet.

When she is finished her braiding, she turns to me and smiles. "Her parents sealed her fate. Death *is* inevitable. That does not mean that she will die *forever*. Her soul is pure, Camael. I am not cruel; you would do well to remember that."

She begins to fade, and before I can ask what exactly she means, she says, "The braid makes her look like a warrior."

~*~

When I wake up I'm in Cael's bed, pulled close to his side. It seems I've been doing a lot of passing out and waking up lately, and I genuinely hope I have reached my quota for a long time.

"Hey," he whispers when he sees that I'm awake. "Morrigan appeared in the clearing and stopped your seizure by putting you to sleep. You've been out cold for four hours now and we've been home for three."

"She was there?" I'm rather dumbfounded.

"Yes," he says solemnly. "And she wasn't a very big help in the information department."

He relays everything that happened with Morrigan, and then falls silent for a second before asking, "What happened when you had that seizure?"

I stiffen, trying to remember the images that flashed before my eyes. "Something important is going to happen in that clearing. I just…don't know what, exactly. But there were people and they were fighting, and then I saw…" I strain my mind to recall exactly what I saw but the images have already begun to float into the deep recesses of my mind where I can't reach.

It's okay, whispers Cael, using our connection. *We'll talk more about this tomorrow.*

"Alright," I murmur, just before I cuddle closer to the warmth of his body and let sleep take over my exhausted soul.

Thirty

Some of the Fae that Grandma Coal personally called in have arrived and I don't think anybody could have prepared me for the sheer amount of awe they inspire when all together. They're camping out in the woods behind Liam's house in tents. The fifteen Elves with their pointed ears though nothing like in the movies, all about seven feet tall, are idly sitting by the fire, holding what looks like arrows and breathing on them reminiscent of how Grandma Coal breathed on Cara and I when she healed us. Cara informs me that they're embedding magic into them. The smallest of them all and about the size of my hand, Pixies, all perch on the shoulders of the Elves. There are twenty-five Pixies in total.

Ten of the eighteen Nymphs have chosen to be in fox form, and they languish in the heat of the fire, and when they become too hot, roll in the snow, barking with appreciation. I've never seen anything like it and I can't help but soak it up.

Three of the eight Nymphs who chose not to be in their fox forms are currently standing with me and Cara at the edge of the forest, giving Cara tips of the trade. There are only two Nymph Halflings – Halfling meaning half Fae and half human – as opposed to the four Elf Halflings; Cara and, ironically a boy from town named Paul Virtue who as it turns out, is Cara's cousin though not by blood, but by element. It makes sense, now that I think about how awkward he was being when I caught him with her in the car – they'd just been talking about a gathering they were supposed to attend out in Portland.

Of the two, Cara is the most advanced as it turns out, mostly because she was able to shift into a fox at all, an accomplishment which is rather rare for a Halfling, and also because she can do other magic that isn't part of her element. For some reason, she's more Fae than human and her powers just keep getting stronger the more she uses them, since before she had to use them in secret most of the time. But Paul, it seems, can hardly produce enough fire to light a match.

"I don't know if I'll be much help," he says, "but I'll do my best when the time comes."

Trying to sound like I know what I'm talking about, I pat him awkwardly on the shoulder. "Don't worry about it. Any help is appreciated…for whatever is going to happen."

"You don't know?" asks a woman with dark brown skin and bright blonde dreadlocks, a Wind Nymph named Melania whose accent marks her as a sister Mainer. She looks to be about thirty years of age but insists she is actually fifty by saying, "The Wind has kept me young."

"Wellll," Cara draws the word out, "no. It's a long story, none of it very good," she bites her lip shyly and I smile. She's always playing damage control when I open my dumb mouth and say something idiotic.

"How's about we hear all about it when dinner arrives," says a voluptuous middle aged woman named Patty, with a thick Australian accent. Her tanned skin and brown hair mark her as an Earth Nymph.

"Vicky and Tristan should be back with the food soon," says Cara. "If they don't kill each other first. It's just pizza and fries for most of us, but there are veggies and berries for anybody who doesn't want that. They agreed on Millie's Pies for desert, since that's about the only place you can actually find edible goods outside of Cael's shop – that would be Khiara's boyfriend – who is probably the best baker in this whole town. Millie's the oldest person in this town, actually. She turns eighty in four months!"

"Wow," says Melania. "Well then, I guess we'll talk when the food gets here."

"Guess so," I say quietly. So many eyes are on me, it feels so strange. "Guess so."

Over a large bonfire, people's stories are slowly told, and information is divulged as the snow falls above us never making it past the flames. Patty talks about her plane ride over from Australia, and how she grew up adopted by a human couple, never having known her birth parents due to their deaths at the hands of superstitious religious bigots. She and Melania met when she first visited the States just eight years ago.

Cael talks of his Fall and how he became my guardian, Vicky talks about her involvement, though nothing too personal about herself, and of course Cara talks enough for both her and Tristan because he's too shy to speak up. Jack stays quiet as well.

Interestingly, it turns out that most of the Pixies of the world live in various countries around Europe and only a few in the Americas. They can become invisible to the human eye at the drop of a hat, which explains why there are hardly any reported sightings.

Liam and Samael – who has asked me to call her Samantha at all times now, since I refer to the other angels by their human names and she felt a little left out – don't talk much, but Lisa chats about all sorts of random things, and what being Nephilim is like; Paul had asked, timidly raising his hand like we were in school.

Sam is quiet for most of the night, happy to sit on my lap and listen to everybody, sometimes fiddling with my necklace, but around eight he begins to yawn, and by ten o'clock he's all but passed out in my arms.

Samantha moves to bring him to bed but Sam says, "I want Aunt Ki-Ki to do it."

"Alright honey. I'll be in to give you your kiss soon." Samantha smiles and sits back down. She seems almost relieved that her son has taken to me like he has.

Picking up the boy, I excuse myself from the bonfire and make my way to the house. By the time I've opened the back door, he appears much more alert than a tired child should.

"What's up?" I ask, placing Sam down on the doormat so that he can take his shoes and winter clothes off.

"I needa show you something," he says matter of fact. "But you prolly won't like it a lot because you have to keep it a secret of secrets."

Chuckling, I reach out and muss his curls. "I'm good at keeping secrets."

He smiles wide, revealing all of his tiny teeth, save one on the far right that he must have just lost today. "Well then you're gonna think it's cool."

Suddenly he scampers off, too fast for me to catch him, but he quickly returns with the book about the Rephaim that is bound with

Samantha's wings, takes my hand, and leads me to the kitchen island before placing the book down and pushing me towards it.

"Open," he says, seriously. "You'll see."

I smile at him, not sure what he's playing at, but open the book anyway, only to be able to see words on the page where before there had been none. The first part I recognize, but the rest is new;

"The Rephaim race is the purest in existence; it is the offspring of two of the Fallen. They must be guarded, as they are hunted for all they can do. Rephaim are the closest to God and should not theoretically exist, yet they do, and have the potential to change the world."

The words feel as if they are taking all of my attention and forcing it on them a whirlpool at sea, sucking me under.

"Of course they share genetic material with Angels and for all intents and purposes they could be considered angelic in nature; but because their parents are of the Fallen, the Rephaim possess free will. They are like a strong mixture of the angels in Heaven, and the Gods who created them."

"Sam," I say. "I can read it. Shouldn't we tell the others?"

"No," he says. "Everything isn't what it looks like, Aunt Ki-Ki. I know lots. I can help you. I just needed to let you see that Mommy's magic necklace worked in a special way. I am half Mommy and the book is made out of her wings, so you can see it 'cause her magic answers to the wings. Or…the other way around. I'm not so good at explaining yet."

"That's okay Sam. Thank you for showing me." I ruffle his curls and cup his cheek, bend down, and kiss it. He goes back and forth between being a regular five-year-old and a strange and confusing magical being.

He grins again, having heard my thoughts, no doubt. "I'm really tired now." He kisses my cheek in return.

"Well then let's put you to bed, little guy."

Sam's room is that of a dinosaur lover; there are decals on the walls and a T-Rex stuffed animal sits on his bed next to a beat up old teddy bear with a blue bow around its neck. He jumps on his bed and into the covers, cocooning himself without my help but laughing when I pull the covers back so his head sticks out.

"Rexy is mine and Mr. Bluebell used to be Lisa's," he says, nodding his head towards the toys.

"Do you like dinosaurs? I got Rexy when I was a baby, and I used to carry him everywhere, but Lisa says I'm too old to do that no more so I keep him on my bed *all day* now 'cause I'm big." He looks so proud of himself.

I kiss his forehead. "I *love* dinosaurs. Does Rexy like good night kisses too?"

"He loves them!" Sam squeals, thrusting Rex towards me so I can kiss the soft green toy.

"Good night, sweetheart," I whisper as I turn off the light by his bed, and walk towards the door.

"Gunnight," whispers Sam, before quickly falling asleep, clutching Rexy tightly to his chest.

Just before I close the door, his dream floats into my mind for just a second, a still-life picture of me lying asleep in a hospital bed, hooked up to way too many machines, with Rexy under the sheets next to me.

The scene fades as fast as it appeared when I close the door, and it hits me that this must be my fate in the near future.

When I return to the campfire, most of the Nymphs have decided they would be more comfortable in fox form, snuggled up by the warmth of the fire, and all of the elves and pixies save for two of each, have retired to their tents (or in the case of some of the others who prefer every day comforts, retired to the motel that is just outside of town).

Cara and Tristan seem to have already left and Samantha, Liam, Jack, and Lisa look like they're ready to join Sam in dreamland and as I reach the campfire, they bid me a warm good night, with lots of hugs, and a huge kiss on the forehead from Samantha as a thank you for putting Sam to bed.

As they begin walking away though, Liam turns back for just a second and meets my eyes with a serious look, nodding his chin in the direction where Cael and Vicky are standing, talking a good ten feet away from the fire.

He turns back to his wife and daughter, telling them to go ahead of him, that he'll be right there. Samantha hesitates for only a moment before nodding and walking to the house.

Liam gestures for me to come forward and I meet him where he's standing just by the wood pile behind the house.

"Khiara," he says. "Something's wrong. I don't know what…but something has changed. I want you to go home tonight. I'm not saying this as a friend of your boyfriend's and I am not saying this as a "Liam". I am asking you right now as *Leliel*, former angel of the Night." His voice is wrought with tension.

"Okay," I say, taking his outstretched hand and shaking it. "I'll go home. Scout's honour," and he walks towards his family, apparently satisfied.

When I reach Cael and Vicky I gently nudge Cael's mind with my own, asking a small question, but he doesn't answer.

"Guys," I say, standing in front of the two. "You two look like you've been hit by a bus. What's up?"

Vicky looks to Cael for a second, but he shakes his head and holds up his hand before she can say anything, and she frowns.

"Nothing," he says. "We're just really tired."

Vicky's face hardens even more than I thought possible, and she stomps her foot on the snow covered forest floor. "Damn it, I won't lie to her, Camael!"

"Verchiel, she doesn't need to worry about it right now," he warns, but she ignores him.

She grabs my arms, probably harder than intended because when I yelp in surprise she instantly loosens her grip but doesn't let go. "Khiara, we're fucked up the ass so hard right now, it's not even funny, and we don't even know how to explain it. Something's wrong. We all, the Fallen, the Faen, *all of us*, we all feel it…"

She lets go of my arms and takes my face in her hands and brings it close to her own. I realize that she's almost crying and she's trembling like a leaf in a heavy wind storm. "Why can't you *feel* it?" she whispers, her voice cracking slightly.

"I don't know," I say, frightened. "I didn't ask for any of this! I don't know what I'm doing!"

"It's okay," says Cael from behind me, placing his hand on my left shoulder. "It's okay."

Vicky lets go of my face and shouts to the sky, "It is *not* okay!"

She stomps over to Cael, pushing me aside gently. Cael's looks could probably kill her if she cared about them. "The Battle is coming whether we want it to or not! It's early!"

"We don't know that for sure," he retorts, but I can feel that he's lying to himself, because through our connection I can feel his pain, his worry, and the sheer amount of panic that is running through his mind.

"Cael," I say, but he doesn't respond to the name as if it's foreign to him.

"*Camael*, look at me," I say slowly, and his eyes dart to mine in panic. "I don't understand what is going on."

"I need to take you home," he whispers. "Let's go to the car."

He turns to Vicky and says, "You catching a ride with us?" and she simply nods, still shaking.

We say a quick good night to the remaining Fae, who all seem rather anxious themselves, and I send a quick text to Cara, asking her to call me around midnight which is in an hour.

By the time we're on the road, nobody has said anything and the silence is killing me. "Guys," I say. "You need to tell me what the hell is going on exactly. The Battle isn't supposed to be for a little while but you said it's soon…how soon is it?"

Vicky clears her throat from the back, and Cael says in a measured voice, "We think, perhaps, tomorrow. But it could be any time before or after."

"Liam said I should go home," I whisper, and Cael does something truly terrifying.

He asks, "Who?"

"Leliel," says Vicky. "She's using his human name."

We're reverting, whispers Cael to my mind. *We're reverting to our angelic selves.*

Suddenly it is clear to me why Liam told me to go home. It may be the last time I ever see my parents again. Somehow, something inside of me tells me that they knew when I left the house the other day, that it was the last time they'd see me. They'd hugged me extra close before I left.

They knew.

"I can't go home," I whisper, feeling strange. "I want to go home with you."

"Khiara," Vicky says reproachfully. "Are you sure?"

"*Camael eepeh behlehaheness Ohleh,*" he says to me, taking my hand for just a second and squeezing it. I recognize it.

He's telling me that he will keep me safe.

But Vicky whispers from the back, "*Ehohpehhan Ah.*"

I don't quite know the exact translation, but her voice tells me that she's saying sorry.

"It's not your fault," I say to her, turning around to face her, but she bows her head regardless.

"Verchiel eepeh behlehaheness Ohleh," she promises, before Cael pulls up in front of his house. We're left to sit in the car in silence as my time slowly runs out and the Battle looms closer than ever.

Thirty-One

My phone rings at exactly midnight.

Cael and Vicky passed out as soon as we got inside, Vicky on the couch and Cael in his bed, refusing to let go of me. So here I am, my phone blasting Cara's ringtone and vibrating on the night stand, desperately trying to get to it before it wakes Cael up.

When I'm finally able to wrestle away from the sheets – and Cael's arms – I grab the phone off the night stand and whisper, "Cara *please* tell me you know about the weird shit going on."

"I don't just know," she whispers back. "I'm fucking living it. Patty called me, I gave her my number, and she told me to meet her at this clearing just outside of town, but I dunno, man. I'm kind of nervous to go. They say the Battle is soon and we have to prepare, whatever that means…and Tristan is all screwy, saying he has to come with me. We're in the car…I should probably get off the phone before I kill us."

"Wait a clearing?" I ask. Why does that feel so familiar?

She replies, "Yeah, I don't know. I'm on this long dirt road right now. I'll call with updates later." And with that, she hangs up.

I move to place my phone back on the night table, as Cael stirs in his sleep, mumbling something in Angelic before waking up and looking at me as if he's not sure I'm real. He reaches over, slowly, almost tentatively and cups my face in one hand.

"Sweetheart, get some sleep while you can," he whispers, his voice thick with sleep. "I love you."

"Love you too," I say, kissing his cheek and settling down in the bed. "I'll try to get some sleep. Promise."

Four hours later, I awake in the car, Cael next to me in the back, and Vicky driving. "It's time," he says simply as I blink blearily at him with my still sleep-heavy eyes and take in a surprisingly wheezy breath.

"My head hurts," I hear myself whisper.

Cael nods and brushes aside some hair that's fallen in my face. "You had a bad nose bleed before, it probably caused the headache."

"Oh," I've been getting them more and more, but yesterday I hadn't had one, and I began to forget that they were even a thing that was happening. I forgot that my body is falling apart.

"Where are we going?" I ask, and Vicky replies, "Not sure. We'll know when we get there. Also, there's a breakfast sandwich in the front seat for you, Romeo insisted we make you one before leaving. It's probably cold now."

She says it like it's somehow my fault that the sandwich is cold, but I know it's from her nerves.

"Thanks," I say, as Cael reaches into the front seat to get the sandwich for me.

My stomach growls, right on time, and as soon as he passes me the bacon and egg sandwich, I stuff it into my mouth without thinking. Cael's eyes crinkle when he smiles at me, and suddenly I'm transported to our first date, when I did the exact same thing.

"Good thing you find this endearing," I say conversationally, through the food.

"You could take a shit and he'd find it endearing," Vicky says. I can see her roll her eyes from the rear-view mirror.

"Gross," I mumble after swallowing.

"He wouldn't find it gross. That's the whole point!" I can see her fighting a small smile.

Ten minutes later though, the car has fallen into an uncomfortable silence. Ten minutes after that, I suddenly recognize the road we turn on.

"We're going to the clearing Cara was talking about…I've…been there before?" I turn to Cael and he nods his head.

He shrugs apologetically. "I'm not surprised the memory is fuzzy. Morrigan knocked you out pretty good."

"It's not fuzzy anymore…I…" I pause, thinking of it, and find that there's a big black hole between the time I passed out and the time I awoke in Cael's bed that morning.

"I can't remember my vision," I admit, and Cael cringes.

"I don't think it was very pleasant," he mumbles, as Vicky stops the car and pulls over beside Cara's, the only other car in sight. Just past the cars, about ten feet into the woods, all of the Fae, Liam, Samantha, Lisa, Sam, Jack, Cara and Tristan are standing expectantly, waiting for us. There are also about fifteen people I don't recognize and I wonder who they are.

"Why are we the only people sane enough to drive here?" complains Vicky, shaking her head.

"Priorities," I reply, shrugging.

"Why'd they bring Sam?" I wonder aloud, and Vicky shrugs this time.

"Probably as some form of protection. The kid could kill a whole small village just by throwing a tantrum."

When we meet up with everyone, we're introduced to the new fifteen; three Nephilim triplets named Brandy, Matilda, and Beth, and twelve of the Fallen, who were able to make it to the area – I recognize Brandy as the guy from the Tilt a' Whirl and he smiles.

One of the Fallen, who tells us to call him Gregory, a boy with dark brown hair and light green eyes who looks about thirteen – but informs us Humans and Faen that he is the oldest being present – jokes that this has a very "Twilight-esque" feel to it, what with the clearing in the woods and the gathering of what he deems with his perpetually cracking voice, "the good guys and a regular human girl."

"It's such an overused trope," agrees Matilda, smiling nervously at me to assess my reaction.

I smile weakly back at her. "Yeah, I know. I had a similar conversation with my boyfriend over here when I was first introduced to this whole new world."

"Calm down there Aladdin," says Cara under her breath, before most of us begin to laugh, full of nervous energy.

Before long though, Gregory holds up is hand, all traces of joking gone from his eyes. Clearly he's the highest in the hierarchy of the angels and I briefly wonder what his angelic name is, because while the rest of the angels are going by their angelic names now, at least for the most part, he's still content to be called Gregory.

"Alright, enough. If you don't feel the shift in the air, you will soon. The Unrepentant have arrived and will keep doing so. You probably think this is the end game but there are fights like this going on all over the world, with the exception of the involvement of the good Faen people here today and those who unfortunately could not make it on time, and I am here to tell you that this is just the beginning. I don't expect you to know this, because I didn't until just today. But Father has given me the knowledge to pass on. The only thing that makes us special is the fact that somehow we were able to come together today in this particular area in support of Khiara as the harbinger who could potentially set us free."

"How could we have known it would happen now? It isn't possible to say. Our Father and his family work in difficult ways. The curse put on Khiara completely changed the course of the prophesy. She hasn't fully awakened. I suspect she won't, having this curse upon her. But we must accept that. I do not know what will happen when we meet with the side of Dark, today. I don't know if this is the day of the Battle or even what the Battle will entail. I just know that this is the beginning and I can only thank you all for coming here today."

Suddenly I feel what he is talking about. That feeling I grew accustomed to over the course of my life, the feeling that I am being watched, the spiders down my spine; it hits me with a vengeance. I feel my body growing weaker by the second and my breathing begins to come out in awkward wheezy breaths that don't feel satisfying. It reminds me of when I had bronchitis as a kid.

Cael stares at me, worried, and asks me a question in Angelic before realizing his mistake. "Are you alright?" he amends, his Irish accent fading into the musical lilt of the Angelic language.

"I'll be okay," I say, smiling at him, and he nods reluctantly before saying something in Angelic to Gregory, making the boyish Angel look grim for a second as he contemplates whatever it is he said.

After a moment he nods his head and replies to Cael in the same language, but I hear my name, and a small burst of panic floods my veins.

Absently I finger a braid in my hair that I've just noticed is even there. How long has it been there? When was the last time I had a decent comb through of my hair? I've been so busy I hadn't noticed the small plaited part of my hair, even when washing it.

Gregory claps his hands to get everybody's attention and then says in English, "Alright. Let's start walking towards the clearing."

Cael takes my hand, though he doesn't say anything, and surprisingly it's Sam who takes my other hand.

"You're gonna stay with me, Aunt Kiki," he explains as we walk through the forest.

From in front of me, Liam turns around and says, "It's not babysitting duty on your part. More on Sam's. He's five, but anybody with ill intentions trying to get close to you will be dead within ten seconds with Sam around."

I'm not sure how I should feel about this. "Leliel," I say, because I know it'll probably resonate more with him – what with the whole weird reverting thing going on. "Don't you think that it's dangerous to expose Sam? You said it yourself, his kind needs to be protected."

He thinks for a second before shaking his head. "You need all the help you can get."

Samael voices an agreement. "He is stronger than almost all of us put together."

Cael nods as well and simply says, "They're right."

When we're about a football length from the clearing, Gregory says something in Angelic, and then for the benefit of people who don't understand the language, repeats himself in English. Oddly, I feel like the longer I hear Angelic though, the more I seem to understand it. It must be the necklace.

"I need you to be ready for the worst. I hope that it doesn't come down to that but it just might."

He adds, "Khiara, you are to stay here with the child – Sam. We want this to be as painless as possible for you. The power from the Battle is drawn from your soul."

"The necklace will help as well," says Samael with some difficulty. Most of the Angels now have lost most of their ability to speak English while still being able to understand it and say a few words.

"I'm ready to kick ass," says Cara. "If it means dying for my best friend, I'm ready to do that."

"I don't want you to die, Cara," I whisper, as she envelopes me into a huge hug. "I don't want anyone to die because of me."

"Oh sweet cheeks," she says, pulling away. "You're the only family besides my grandmother that actually loves me. You are my sister and I will fight to keep you safe. It is my duty. It is the duty of the Faen people. It may not have started out that way, but however my kind got involved, it happened. And I wouldn't have it any other way."

Tristan takes her place and mumbles, "We haven't known each other long. But I am honoured to know you." Behind him, Vicky rolls her eyes even though they've been filled with tears.

Suddenly, Cael is in front of me, and even though he can hardly speak a word of English now, he whispers just one sentence, awkward and stilted but still recognizable. "I…will never…regret...love you."
Tears fall down my cheeks onto his and from his to mine. "I love *you*," I say, kissing him fiercely.

After everybody is done saying their goodbyes to me, they slowly but surely begin to walk off to meet with the Unrepentant, leaving Sam and I alone.

"I can show you what's going on," he says. "I can see in their heads."

He takes my hand and suddenly it's like I'm watching the whole scene as a bystander just a couple of feet away. I see the Nymphs turning into foxes on the sidelines, all but Paul, who has been appointed a lookout with June, a Pixie, and the Elves getting their arrows ready.

The Angels and Nephilim of both sides come together and both leaders, Gregory and Douma, step into the middle of the clearing to talk to each other.

I can't hear what they're saying but after ten minutes of them talking, a loud crack of thunder booms and lightning lights up the quickly darkening sky like the fourth of July fireworks. In one swift movement, both leaders hold out their hands and look up to the sky, before strange blue balls of light fill their hands, and they throw them up into the air. The light balls collide, and more lightning fills the sky.

And just like that, both sides begin to fight. Gregory calls out the Faen people with a soundless yell and they come charging from the forest into battle alongside the Angels and Nephilim who have already started to fight. It looks like we might have the upper hand but I've seen enough.

"Sam," I say urgently after about twenty solid minutes of him having caught me under this weird spell. "I have to stop watching," and he lets go of me for a moment, before whispering, "Sorry, but you needa see," and pulling me back under.

Pixies, little warriors in their own right, flit between the fighters, sprinkling dust on the Faen people that need extra help. The Fallen shoot balls of pure light at each other, white and grey orbs that exude an unearthly glow.

Elves shoot their specialized arrows, imbued with their power. Nymphs go between shooting balls of their magic from their bare hands to shifting into large foxes of red, white, brown, and black.

The only two Nephilim that bothered to show up on the side of the Unrepentant are grossly outnumbered by those on ours. Five on two almost doesn't seem fair.

"Okay, Sam, please," I plead. "I feel nauseated."

Just as he lets me go, I vomit all of my breakfast into the snow, and whisper, "Fuck."

For a second, he says nothing, but then he reaches out and tugs my jacket sleeve. It hits me that I'm just standing here like an idiot, hiding behind some trees with a five-year-old child who could destroy us all just by throwing a tantrum, and who just showed me a play by play with his *mind* and I just vomited instead of acting like the potential saviour I'm supposed to be. The irony would kill me if my body weren't already doing a good job at that.

"I don't like this," he whimpers, tugging on my sleeve. "I have a bad feeling, Kiki."

I smile at his adoption of Cara's nickname for me, but the smile doesn't last long. "It'll be okay," I lie, because I don't know what else to say.

"I feel funny," says Sam. He closes his eyes and squeezes them shut, as if he could get away just by doing that. His little hands move up to his hair and he grasps it in fistfuls.

"I'm sorry, that's probably my fault," I say, remembering the vomit. "We should probably just move away from it."

"It hurts!" he shouts, and suddenly bursts into tears. "I don't want to but I know I gotta."

"Wait, what?" I ask, fearing another play by play.

"I'm sorry," he says, "I'm sorry. I have to."

I crouch down to his level. "Honey? What are you saying?"

Sam's eyes open and he sighs.

"I'm sorry." My necklace pulses as he reaches out and takes it in his hand, and for just a second it shines with a brilliant light, and then just as fast as it appears the light fades. Fat tears are falling down his cheeks now and his curly blonde locks are being tossed to and fro by the wind.

The mournful sound of a crow cawing in the tree above us sends shivers down my spine, because I know without a doubt who that crow really is.

"Sam," I say. "This doesn't have anything to do with that dream you had, does it?" I ask, remembering the image of myself in a hospital bed.

Sam pushes me away from him suddenly, using a force that knocks me right on my butt. "Sam?" I ask, as he begins to back away from me. My head suddenly feels like it's made of lead and my nose begins to drip.

"I have to!" he shouts, running straight for the battlefield. "You needa be awake!"

"Damn it, Sam!" I swipe at my nose with a heavy hand and ease myself up as fast as I can, bursting into an awkward sprint. My stupid human body can't keep up with him though and soon I've lost the boy and I'm about half yard away from the fight, out of breath and wheezing.

June, the pixie who is on lookout duty, lands on my shoulder and says in her lilting voice, "Please go back. It's too dangerous."

"I can't," I say. "He's so small…"

"He could blow this whole clearing up if he wanted to. You need to worry about yourself. Go back!" She flits away, and only looks back once before heading over to where Patty sits, not fifteen feet away from me. She looks far too worn out, half-lying on the ground, being held by Melania who is breathing healing magic into her. They must be taking a much needed break away from the fight. I wonder for just a second why I couldn't hear the sounds of the fight when Sam was with me but as soon as he left me, I could hear them crystal clear.

The sound is now deafening.

"Sam!" I scream, and absently swipe at my nose. I run until somehow I'm right in the middle of the fight. I dodge the kick of somebody who quickly gets taken out by Beth, who shoots me a questioning look and a warning to go back, before running off to fight the next person.

Stupid child, somebody suddenly thinks directly into my mind.

My voice cracks painfully as I yell for Sam again, my panic reaching a new level as I hear a strange humming noise coming from behind me.

"Khiara!" shouts Cael from somewhere in the clearing but it's too late. As I turn my head to try to see where the noise is coming from, a hurtling ball of light hits me right in the stomach and I crumple like a rag doll. How ironic that something so beautiful could be so deadly. As I look around, I become aware that I am not the only one, it would seem, who's been hit by this – whatever it is. But the only ones who seem to have been hit are those on the side of dark…and me.

My mind whispers Sam's name and that crow caws in the distance.

Blood is everywhere.

Death is everywhere.

And I am *awake.*

I am blood and death all wrapped up in one; a pathetic mass of what was once a human being. I was told this would happen, that this would be the end of me. I just wanted to believe that I had a chance. That Cael and I could be together. That Cara and I could laugh together as Tristan does something awkwardly endearing and Vicky gives him hell for it, telling him to be a man. I wanted to get to know Liam, Sam, and Lisa better. I wanted to tell my parents how much they mean to me. I can do none of those things. I see that now; I see *everything.*

The forest is filled with people that were willing to die for the cause. The Fallen, Faen, Nephilim. And they fight against each other for me, some insignificant, cursed, and sickly *human.* I am nobody, and yet, somehow, apparently somebody who is very important. All of a sudden my mind which had just become so clear begins to feel fuzzy, and I can't quite figure out *why.*

I can hear a voice in my head that isn't my own telling me that I'm going to be okay, but I know for a fact that it isn't true. I'm going to die.

"Khiara!" it says, "Please, stay with me!" *Cael.* Somewhere in the back of my mind, I realize that he isn't actually speaking English, but I understand him perfectly.

I want to tell him that I love him but I know that if I try to speak, I'll just be in more pain.

"Please, don't go now! You *can't* die, there's nowhere left for you to go except Limbo. You'll be stuck in between and almost nobody comes back from that. You have to hold on, sweetheart." I hear Vickie's voice but it's muffled by the sound of my own gurgled breathing. I want to tell her that it's no use because I am going to die no matter what.

Cael is shaking me and I can see the tears that he refuses to shed glisten in his eyes, until finally, Vicky slaps him in the face and they make their way down his cheeks.

"Stop it! Can you stop shaking her like a fucking mental patient? News flash, this is bigger than the two of you; it always has been. There is a *war* going on, Camael, and right now, nobody is winning." She wipes at her eyes furiously. "And FYI, you're not the only one losing somebody they love." Her voice breaks on the last part and I wish I could reach out to them, wish I could comfort them.

But I can't.

I close my eyes for a second and try to concentrate on my thoughts. When I open them, I can see their true forms. This is how I finally realize that this is the end for me. *You never see an angel's true form unless you're about to die.*

Camael is beautiful. He is the complete personification of divine love, and he shines in a breathtaking blue light. His sobs are gut-wrenching. Verchiel is not shining as bright but she radiates a warmness that feels contagious and I can't help but smile. Her glory is purple. They are both so beautiful that my eyes close without my permission.

Somebody moves me and my head is cradled in hands that are too gentle.

People keep talking.

I can't distinguish between the voices anymore

"No, no, no. You can't die, no, you can't."

I'm so tired.

"She's not dead, Camael, s*top!*"

I suddenly can't feel the pain anymore.

"No!"
Death is a sweet release.
"She's still breathing! We need to get her to the hospital, now!"
I welcome it.
Invite it in.
And die.

You are waiting for someone to confirm it,
You are waiting for someone to say it plain,
Now we are here and because we are short of time
I will say it; I might even speak its name.

It is moving above me, it is burning my heart out,
I have felt it crash through my flesh,
I have spoken to it in a foreign tongue,
I have stroked its neck in the night like a wish.

Its name is the name you have buried in your blood,
Its shape is a gorgeous cast-off velvet cape,
Its eyes are of your most forbidden lover
And its claws, I tell you its claws are gloved in fire.

You are waiting to hear its name spoken,
You have asked me a thousand times to speak it,
You who have hidden it, cast it off, killed it,
Loved it to death and sung your songs over it.

The red bird you wait for falls with giant wings –
A velvet cape whose royal colour calls us kings
Is the form it takes, uninvited, it descends,
It is the Power and the Glory forever, Amen.

The red bird you wait for – Gwendolyn McEwen

End of Book One

Sydnie Beaupré

www.ingramcontent.com/pod-product-compliance
Lightning Source LLC
Chambersburg PA
CBHW051240250626
47155CB00009B/3107